the Archie® DIGEST LIBRARY

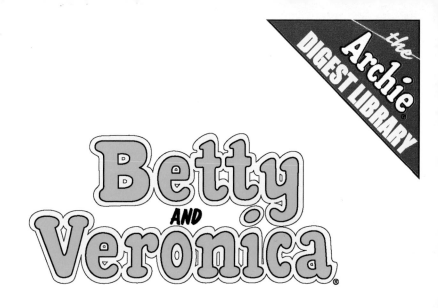

Betty AND Veronica®

– in –

The Unexpected

JOHNSON
SCHOOL
LLC

**visit us at
www.abdopublishing.com**

Exclusive Spotlight library bound edition published in 2007 by Spotlight, a division of ABDO Publishing Group, Edina, Minnesota. Spotlight produces high quality reinforced library bound editions for schools and libraries. Published by agreement with Archie Comic Publications, Inc.

Library of Congress Cataloging-in-Publication Data

Betty and Veronica in The unexpected / edited by Nelson Ribeiro & Victor Gorelick. -- Library bound ed.
    p. cm. -- (The Archie digest library)
    Revision of issue 120 (June 2001) of Betty and Veronica digest magazine.
    ISBN-13: 978-1-59961-270-6
    ISBN-10: 1-59961-270-4
    1. Graphic novels. I. Ribeiro, Nelson. II. Gorelick, Victor. III. Betty and Veronica digest magazine. 120. IV. Title: Unexpected.

PN6728.A72B497 2007
741.5'973--dc22

                                                                2006050265

All Spotlight books are reinforced library binding and manufactured in the United States of America.

Contents

Betty AND Veronica®

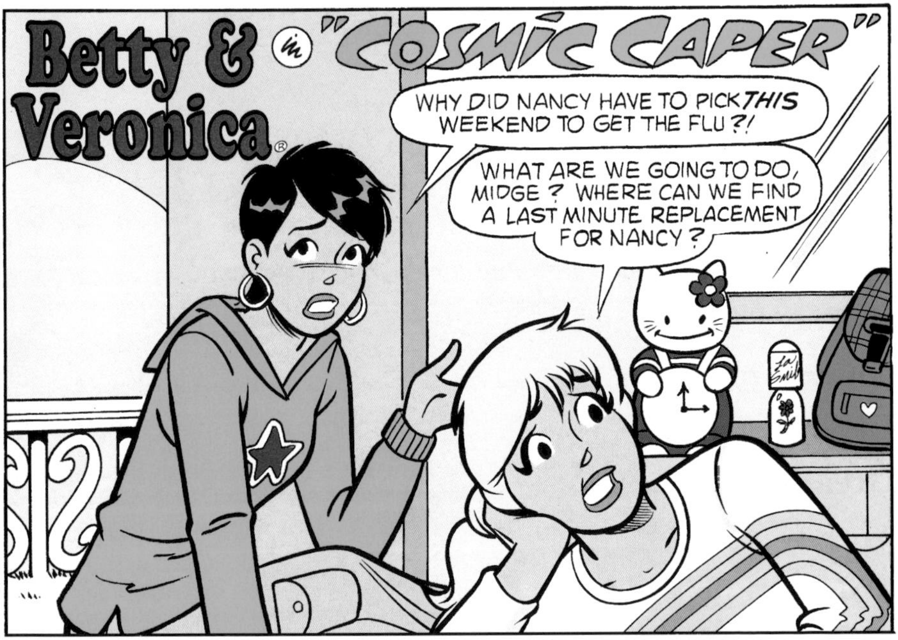

Betty & Veronica® in "COSMIC CAPER"
WHY DID NANCY HAVE TO PICK THIS WEEKEND TO GET THE FLU?!
WHAT ARE WE GOING TO DO, MIDGE? WHERE CAN WE FIND A LAST MINUTE REPLACEMENT FOR NANCY?

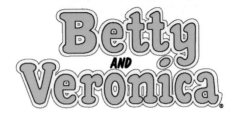

SCRIPT: MIKE PELLOWSKI PENCILS: HOLLY G! INKS: JOHN COSTANZA
COLORS: BARRY GROSSMAN LETTERS: BILL YOSHIDA
EDITORS: NELSON RIBEIRO & VICTOR GORELICK EDITOR-IN-CHIEF: RICHARD GOLDWATER

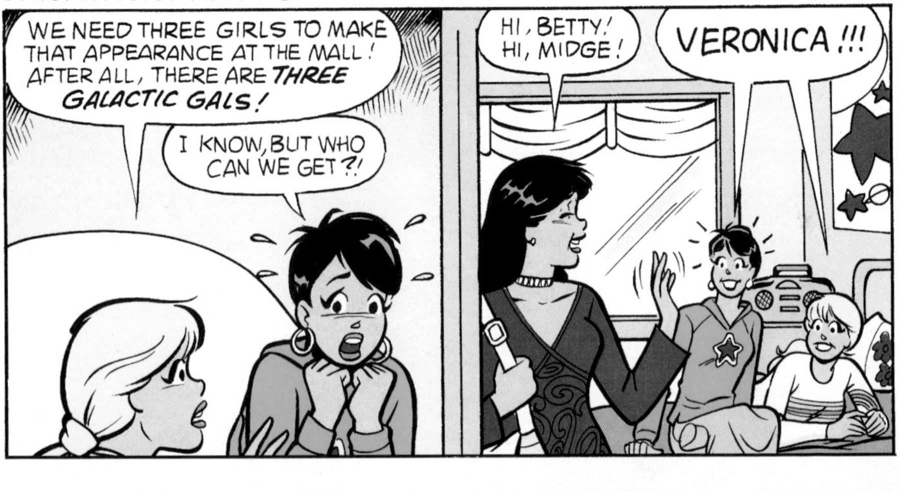

WE NEED THREE GIRLS TO MAKE THAT APPEARANCE AT THE MALL! AFTER ALL, THERE ARE THREE GALACTIC GALS!
I KNOW, BUT WHO CAN WE GET?!
HI, BETTY! HI, MIDGE!
VERONICA!!!

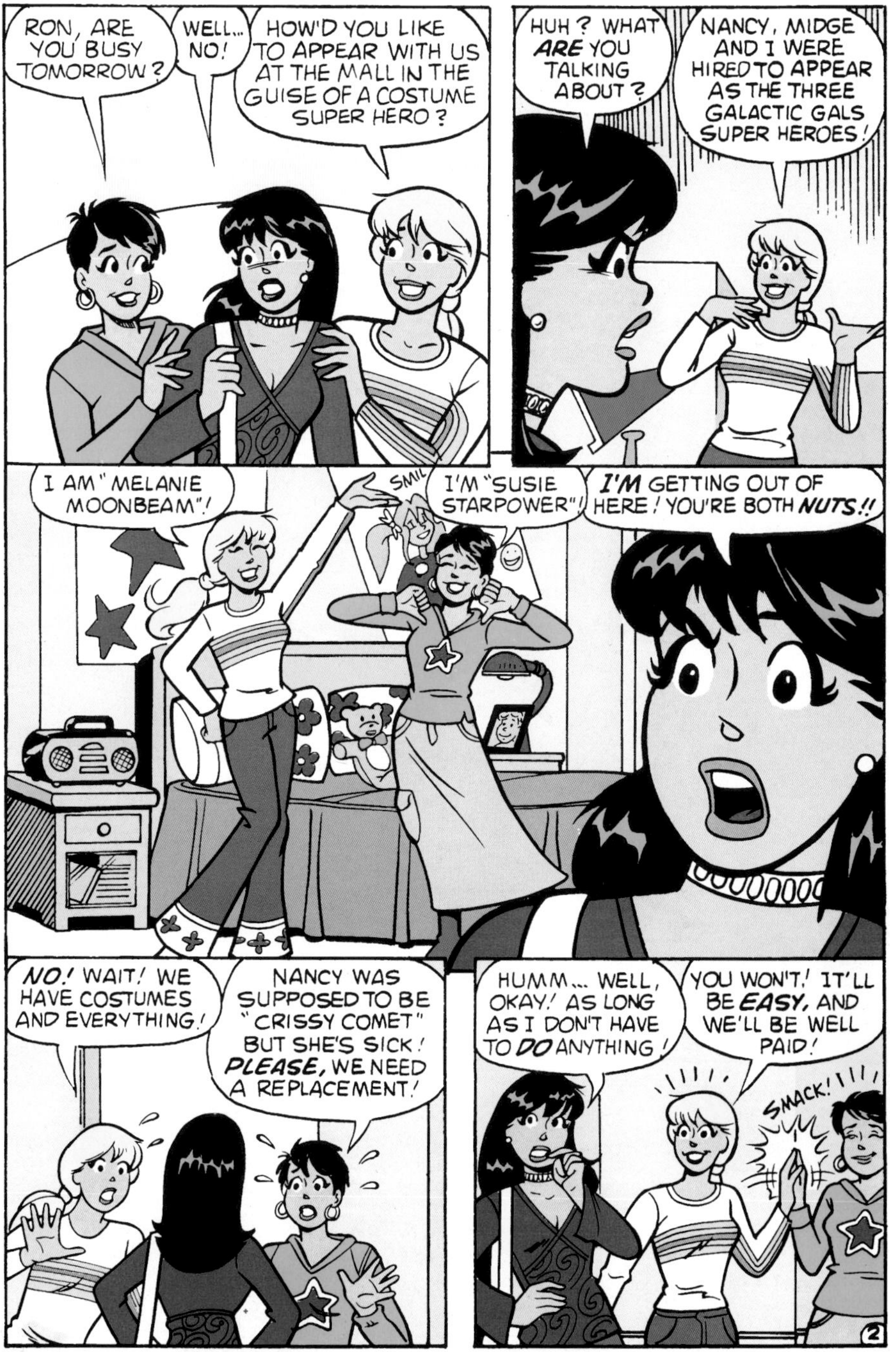
RON, ARE YOU BUSY TOMORROW?
WELL... NO!
HOW'D YOU LIKE TO APPEAR WITH US AT THE MALL IN THE GUISE OF A COSTUME SUPER HERO?
HUH? WHAT ARE YOU TALKING ABOUT?
NANCY, MIDGE AND I WERE HIRED TO APPEAR AS THE THREE GALACTIC GALS SUPER HEROES!
I AM "MELANIE MOONBEAM"!
I'M "SUSIE STARPOWER"!
I'M GETTING OUT OF HERE! YOU'RE BOTH NUTS!!
NO! WAIT! WE HAVE COSTUMES AND EVERYTHING!
NANCY WAS SUPPOSED TO BE "CRISSY COMET" BUT SHE'S SICK! PLEASE, WE NEED A REPLACEMENT!
HUMM... WELL, OKAY! AS LONG AS I DON'T HAVE TO DO ANYTHING!
YOU WON'T! IT'LL BE EASY, AND WE'LL BE WELL PAID!
SMACK!
2

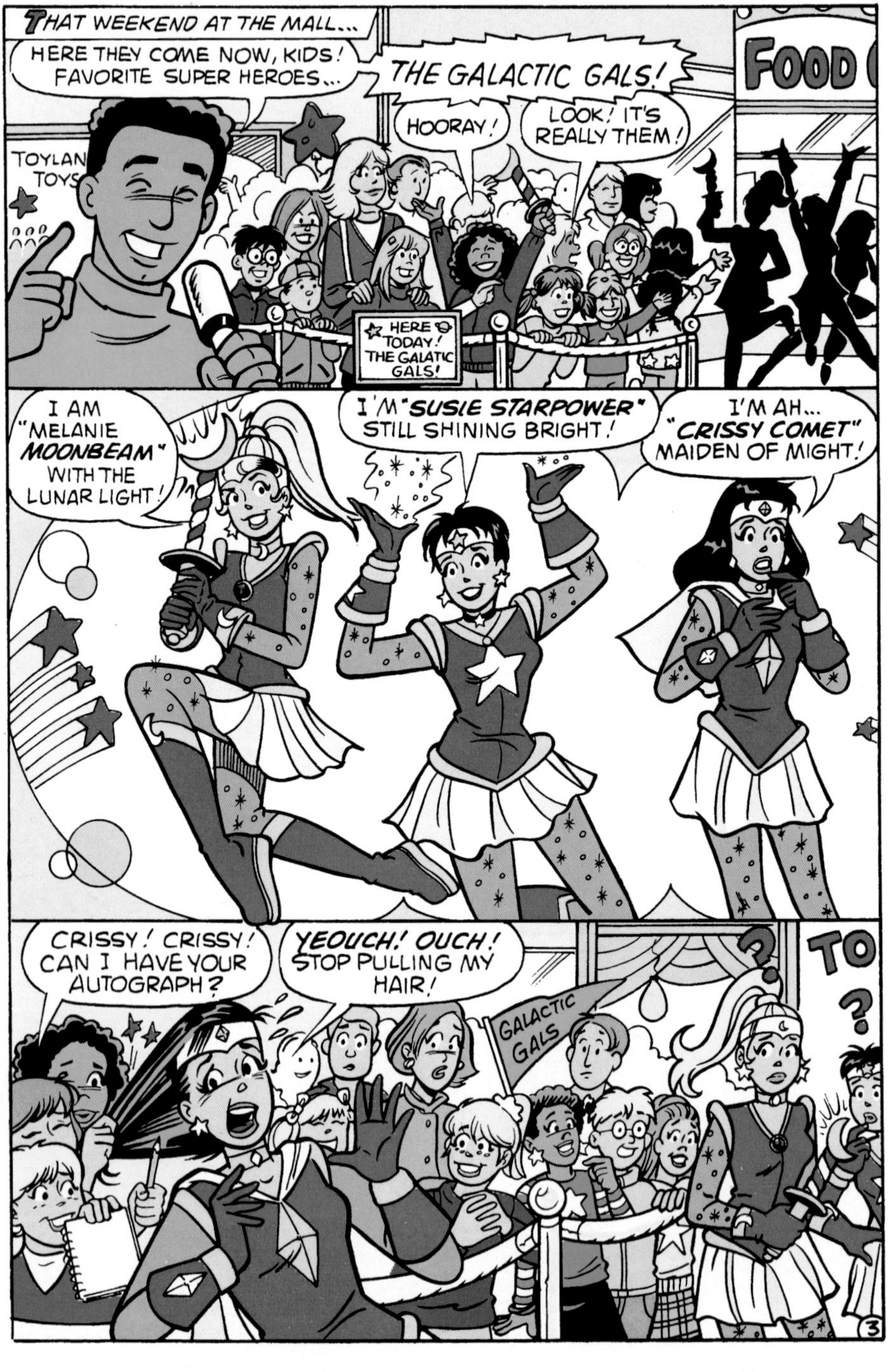
THAT WEEKEND AT THE MALL...
HERE THEY COME NOW, KIDS! FAVORITE SUPER HEROES...
THE GALACTIC GALS!
HOORAY!
LOOK! IT'S REALLY THEM!
FOOD
TOYLAN TOYS
HERE TODAY! THE GALATIC GALS!
I AM "MELANIE MOONBEAM" WITH THE LUNAR LIGHT!
I'M "SUSIE STARPOWER" STILL SHINING BRIGHT!
I'M AH... "CRISSY COMET" MAIDEN OF MIGHT!
CRISSY! CRISSY! CAN I HAVE YOUR AUTOGRAPH?
YEOUCH! OUCH! STOP PULLING MY HAIR!
GALACTIC GALS
TO
?
?
3

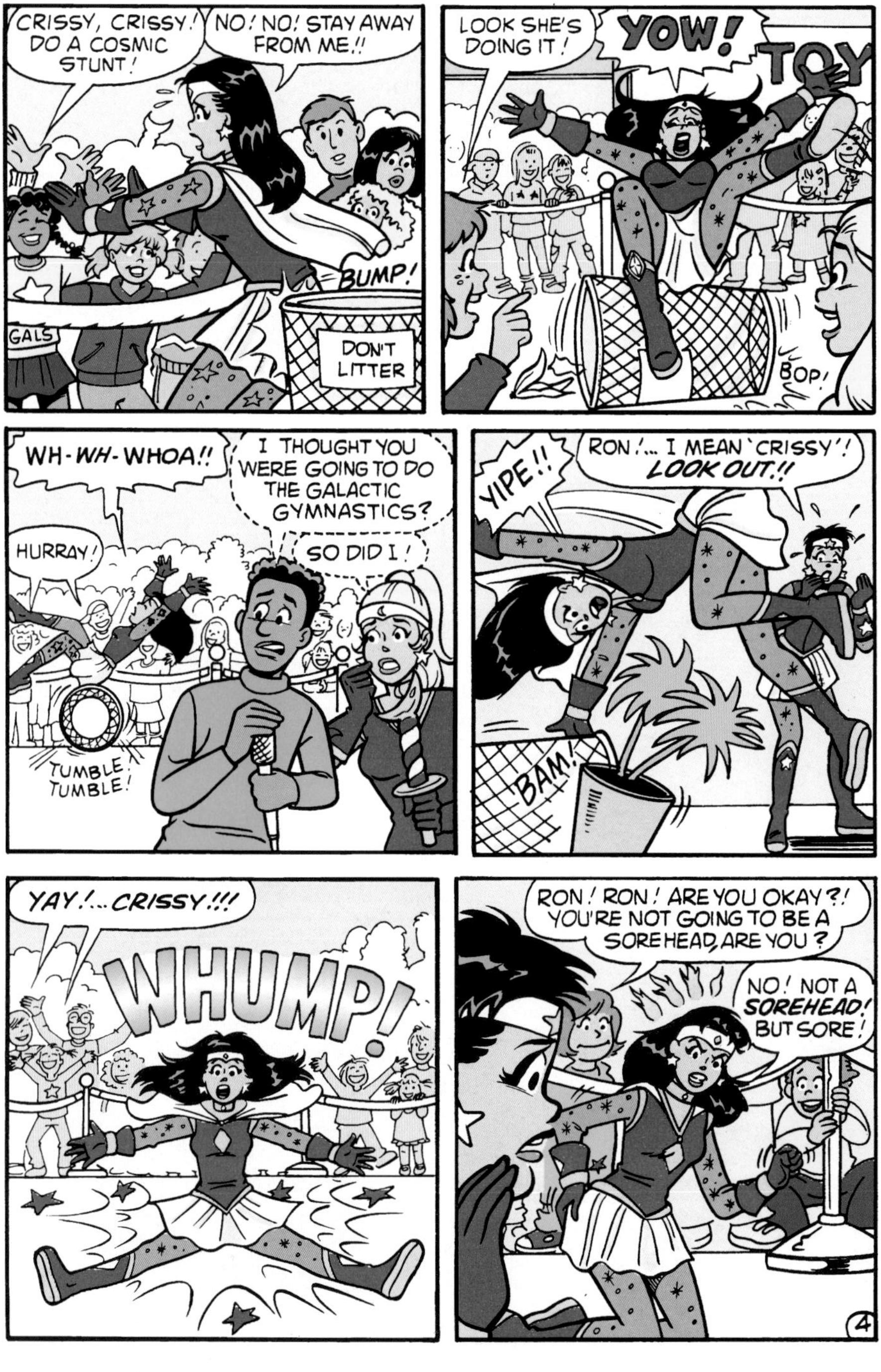
CRISSY, CRISSY! DO A COSMIC STUNT!
NO! NO! STAY AWAY FROM ME.!!
BUMP!
GALS
DON'T LITTER
LOOK SHE'S DOING IT!
YOW!
TOY
BOP!
WH-WH-WHOA!!
I THOUGHT YOU WERE GOING TO DO THE GALACTIC GYMNASTICS?
HURRAY!
SO DID I!
TUMBLE! TUMBLE!
YIPE!!
RON!... I MEAN 'CRISSY'! LOOK OUT!!
BAM!
YAY!... CRISSY!!!
WHUMP!
RON! RON! ARE YOU OKAY?! YOU'RE NOT GOING TO BE A SOREHEAD, ARE YOU?
NO! NOT A SOREHEAD! BUT SORE!
4

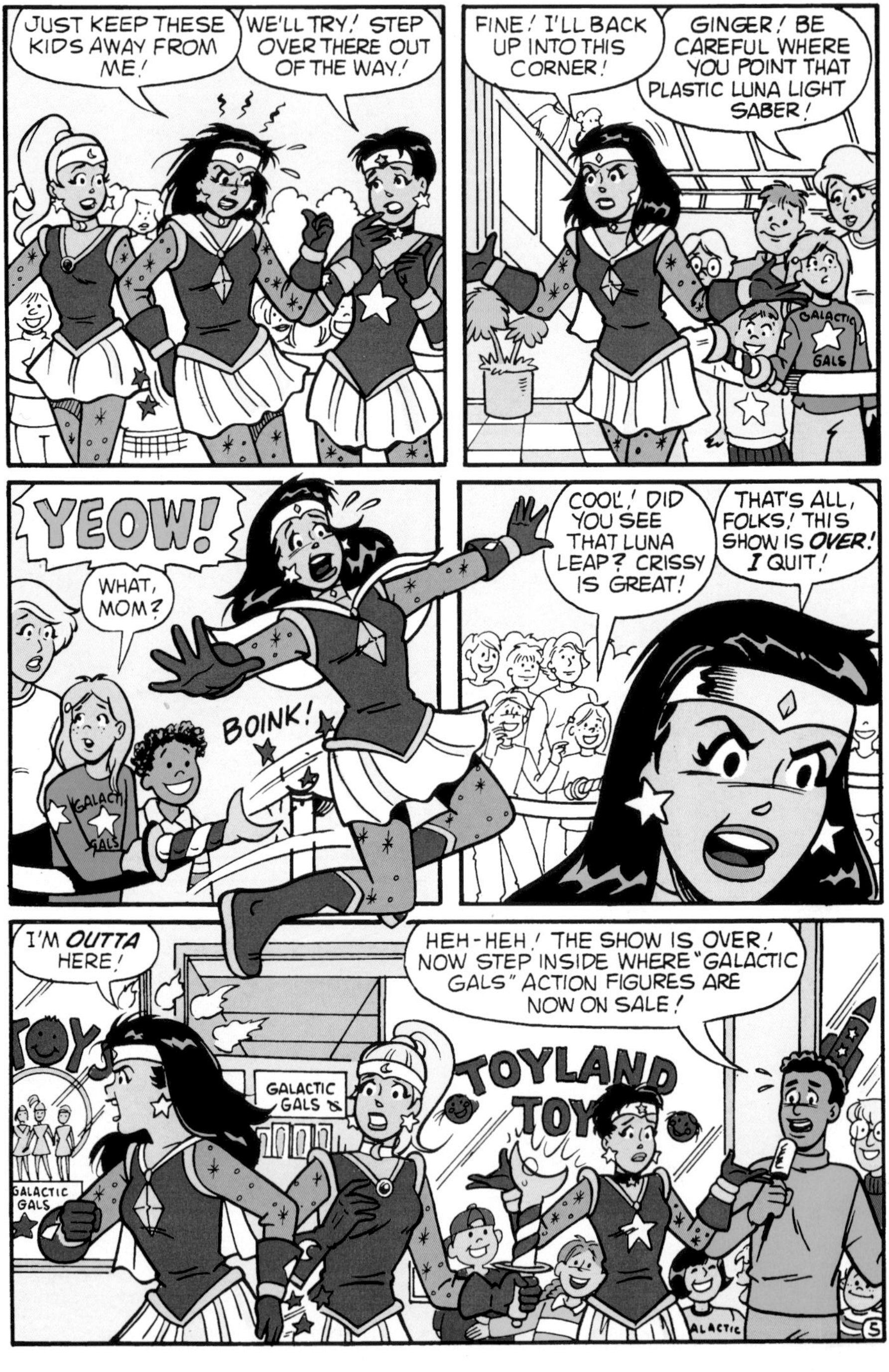
JUST KEEP THESE KIDS AWAY FROM ME!
WE'LL TRY! STEP OVER THERE OUT OF THE WAY!
FINE! I'LL BACK UP INTO THIS CORNER!
GINGER! BE CAREFUL WHERE YOU POINT THAT PLASTIC LUNA LIGHT SABER!
YEOW!
WHAT, MOM?
BOINK!
GALACTIC GALS
COOL! DID YOU SEE THAT LUNA LEAP? CRISSY IS GREAT!
THAT'S ALL, FOLKS! THIS SHOW IS *OVER!* *I* QUIT!
I'M *OUTTA* HERE!
HEH-HEH! THE SHOW IS OVER! NOW STEP INSIDE WHERE "GALACTIC GALS" ACTION FIGURES ARE NOW ON SALE!
GALACTIC GALS
GALACTIC GALS
TOYLAND TOY
5

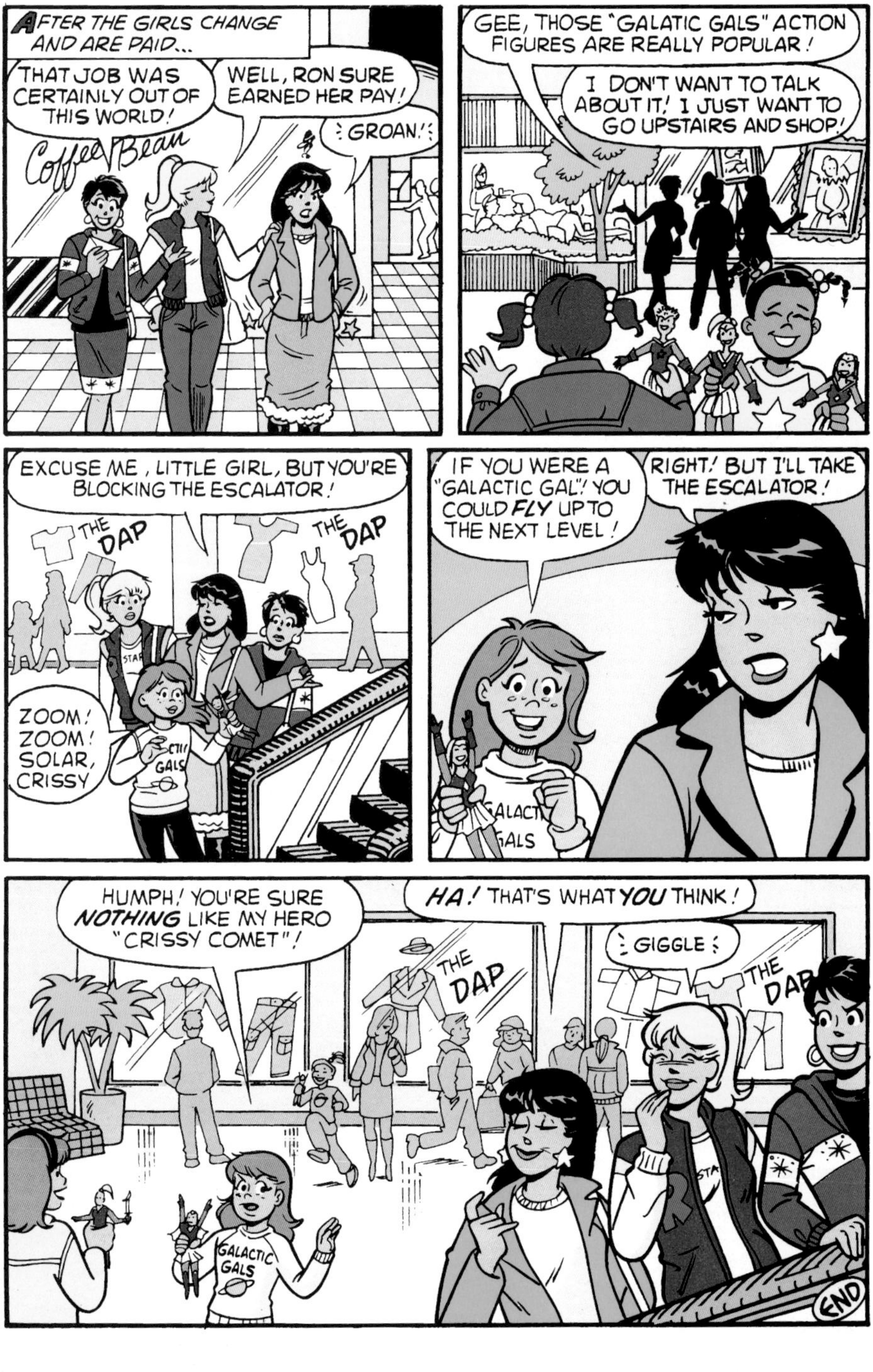
AFTER THE GIRLS CHANGE AND ARE PAID...
THAT JOB WAS CERTAINLY OUT OF THIS WORLD!
WELL, RON SURE EARNED HER PAY!
GROAN!
Coffee Bean
GEE, THOSE "GALATIC GALS" ACTION FIGURES ARE REALLY POPULAR!
I DON'T WANT TO TALK ABOUT IT! I JUST WANT TO GO UPSTAIRS AND SHOP!
EXCUSE ME, LITTLE GIRL, BUT YOU'RE BLOCKING THE ESCALATOR!
THE DAP
THE DAP
ZOOM! ZOOM! SOLAR, CRISSY
IF YOU WERE A "GALACTIC GAL"! YOU COULD FLY UP TO THE NEXT LEVEL!
RIGHT! BUT I'LL TAKE THE ESCALATOR!
HUMPH! YOU'RE SURE NOTHING LIKE MY HERO "CRISSY COMET"!
HA! THAT'S WHAT YOU THINK!
GIGGLE
THE DAP
GALACTIC GALS
END

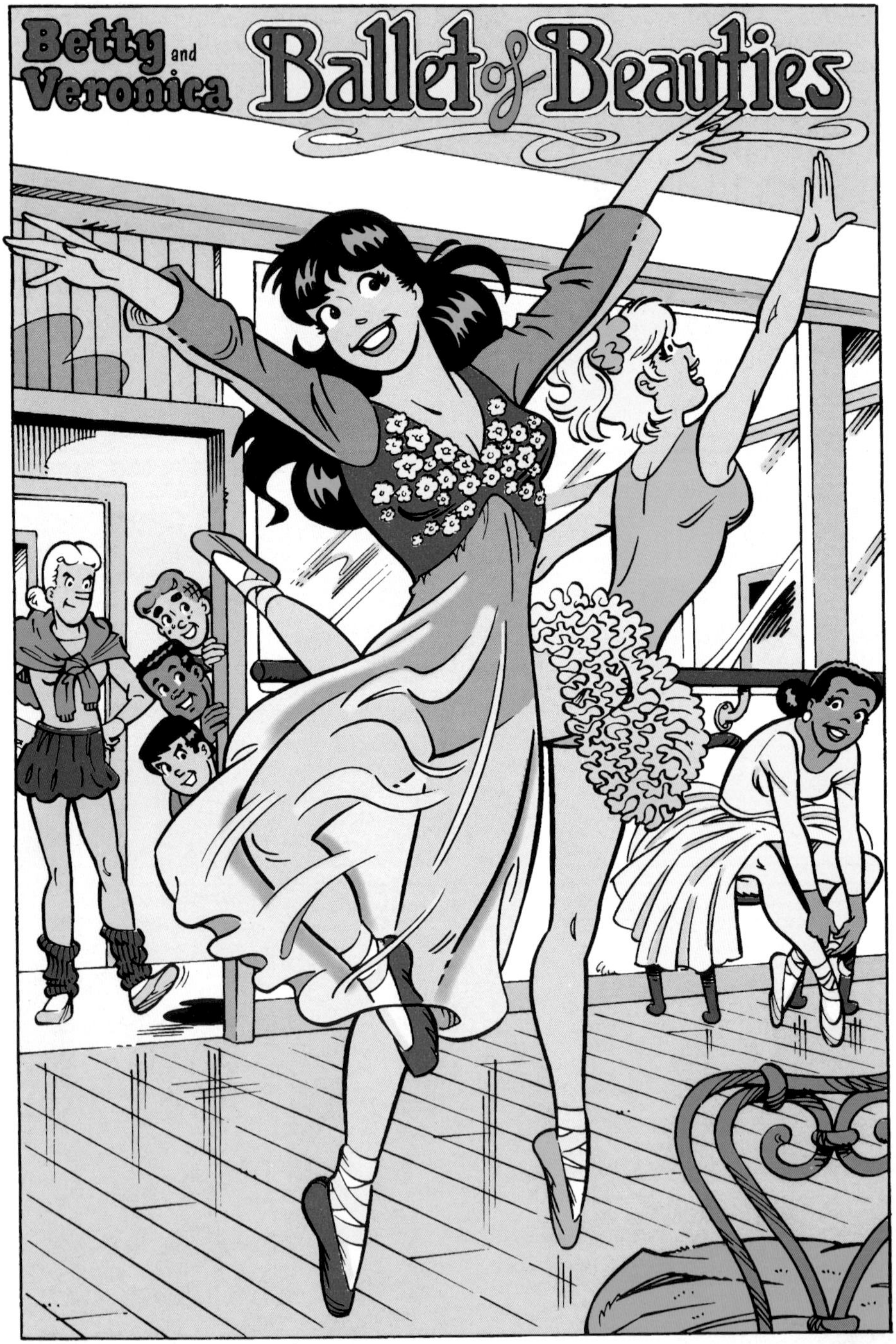
Betty and Veronica
Ballet of Beauties

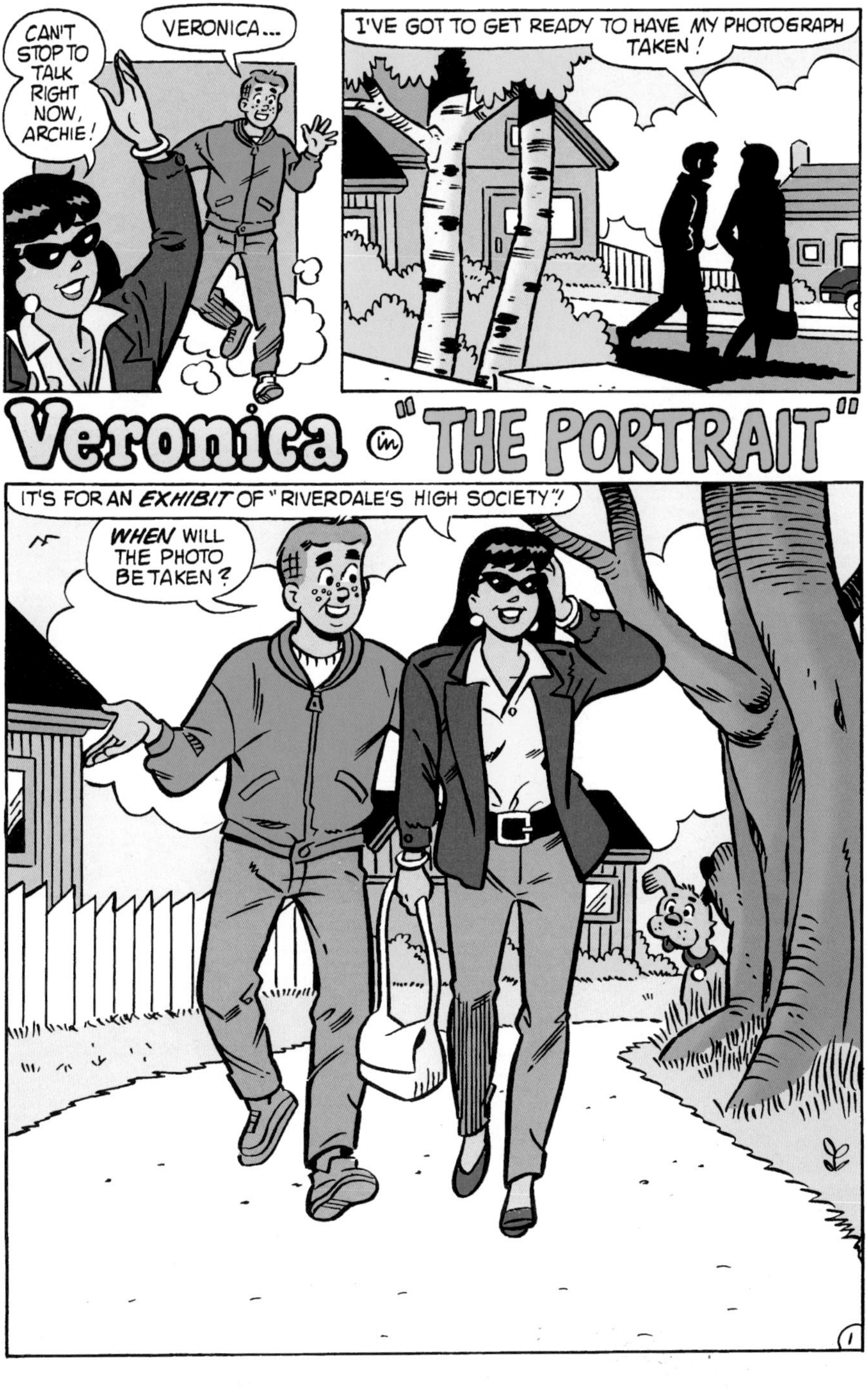
VERONICA...
CAN'T STOP TO TALK RIGHT NOW, ARCHIE!
I'VE GOT TO GET READY TO HAVE MY PHOTOGRAPH TAKEN!
Veronica in "THE PORTRAIT"
IT'S FOR AN EXHIBIT OF "RIVERDALE'S HIGH SOCIETY"!
WHEN WILL THE PHOTO BE TAKEN?
1

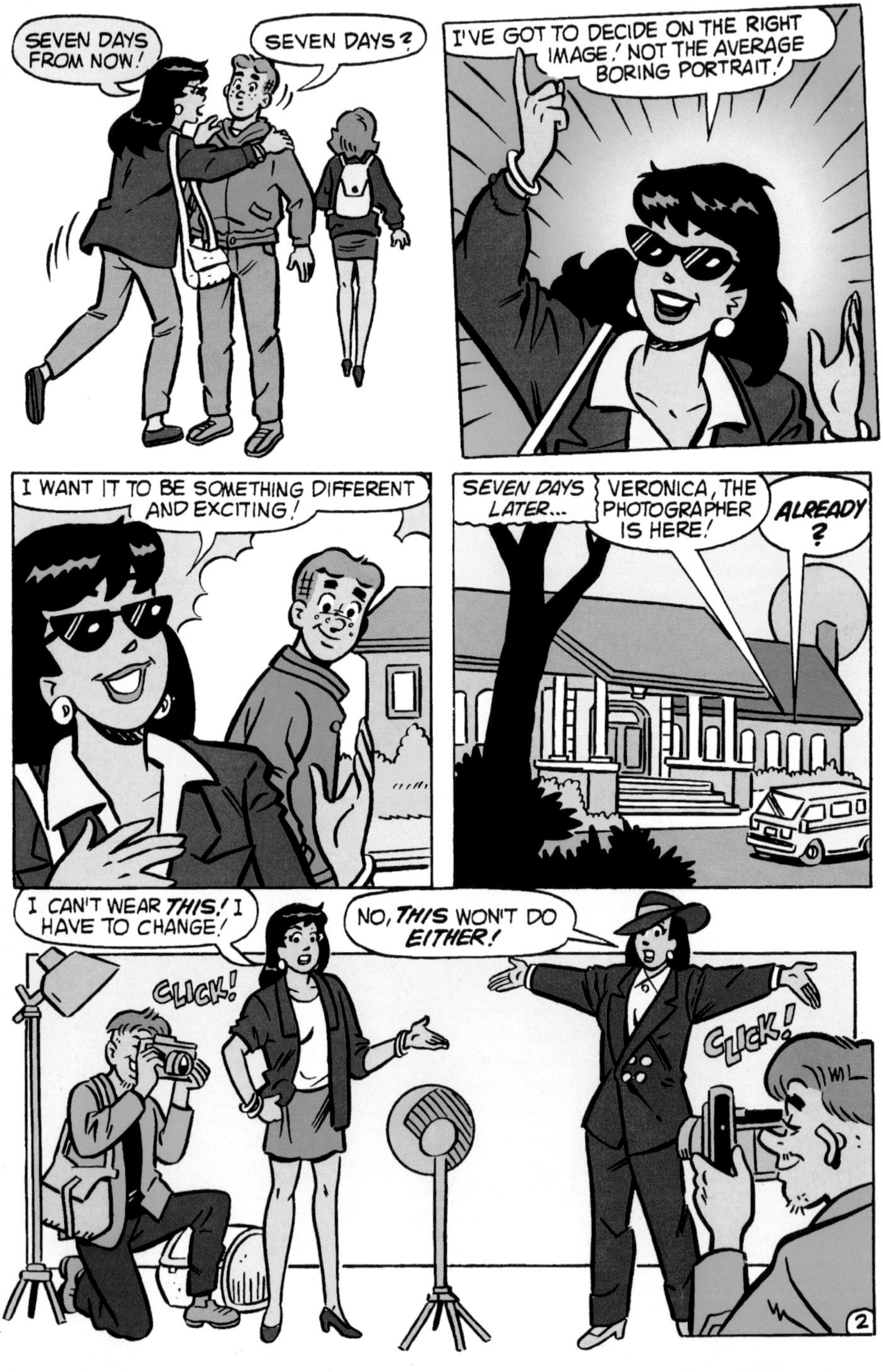
SEVEN DAYS FROM NOW!
SEVEN DAYS?
I'VE GOT TO DECIDE ON THE RIGHT IMAGE! NOT THE AVERAGE BORING PORTRAIT!
I WANT IT TO BE SOMETHING DIFFERENT AND EXCITING!
SEVEN DAYS LATER...
VERONICA, THE PHOTOGRAPHER IS HERE!
ALREADY?
I CAN'T WEAR THIS! I HAVE TO CHANGE!
CLICK!
NO, THIS WON'T DO EITHER!
CLICK!
2

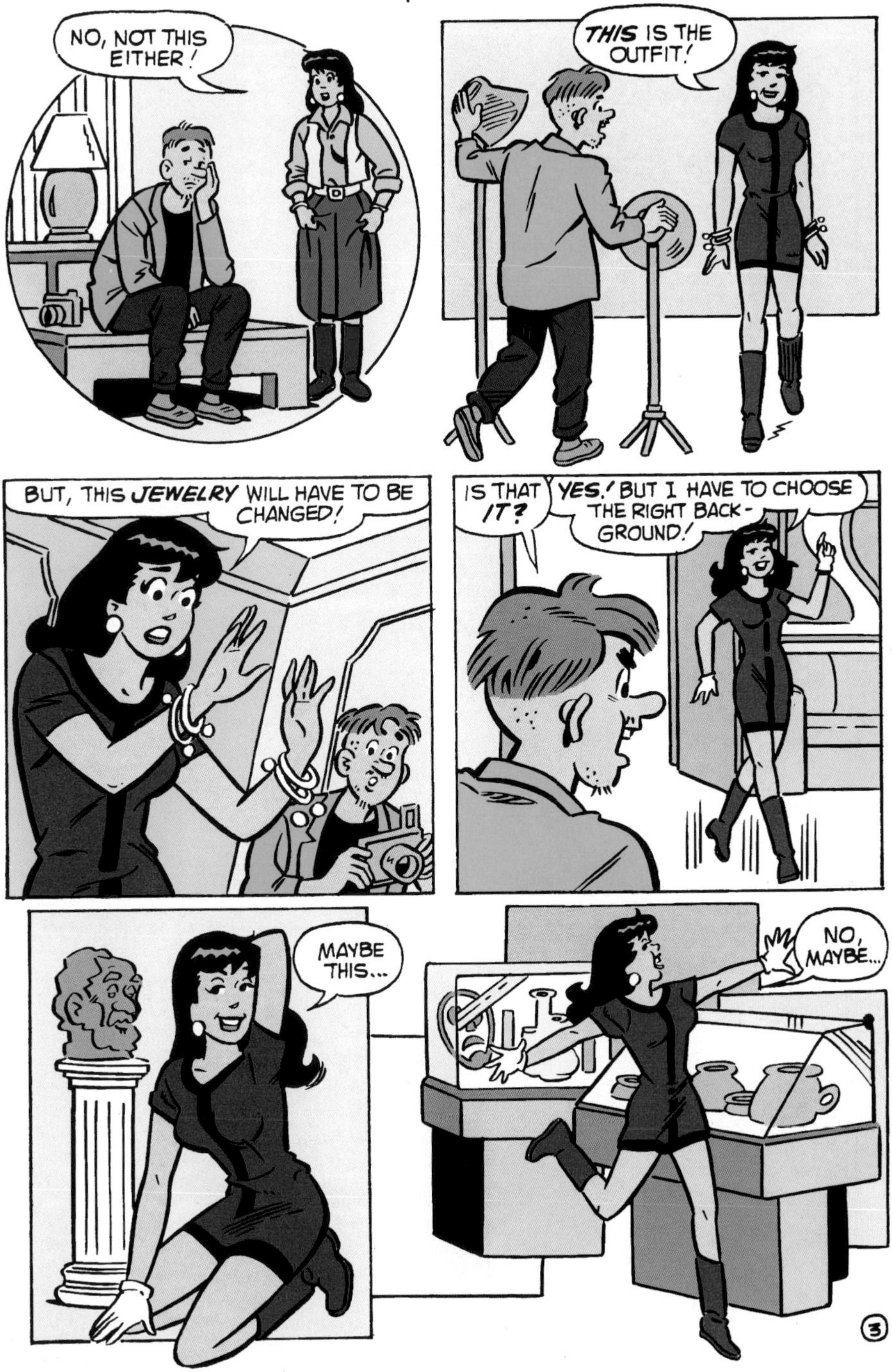
NO, NOT THIS EITHER!
THIS IS THE OUTFIT!
BUT, THIS JEWELRY WILL HAVE TO BE CHANGED!
IS THAT IT?
YES! BUT I HAVE TO CHOOSE THE RIGHT BACK-GROUND!
MAYBE THIS...
NO, MAYBE...
3

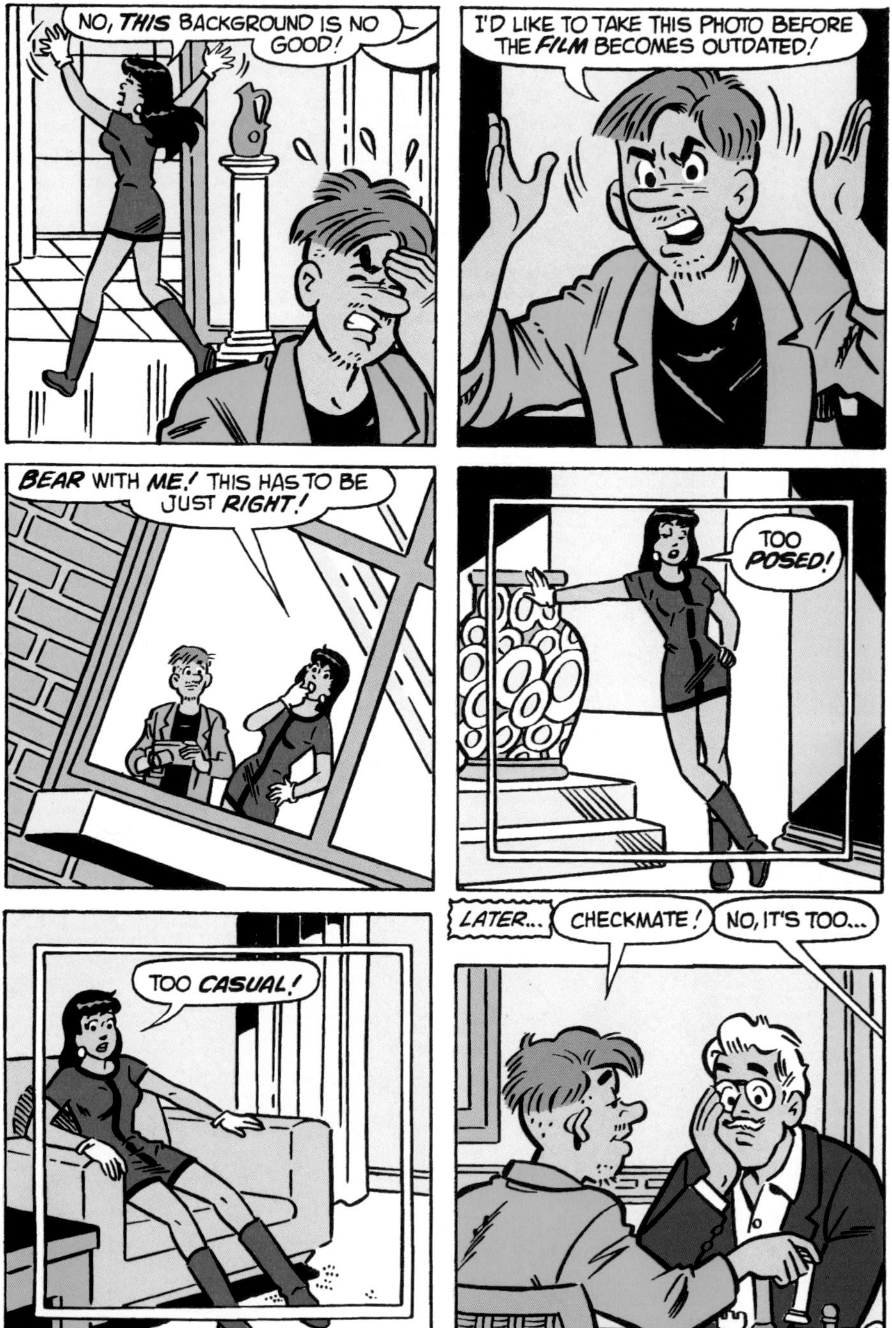
NO, THIS BACKGROUND IS NO GOOD!
I'D LIKE TO TAKE THIS PHOTO BEFORE THE FILM BECOMES OUTDATED!
BEAR WITH ME! THIS HAS TO BE JUST RIGHT!
TOO POSED!
TOO CASUAL!
LATER...
CHECKMATE!
NO, IT'S TOO...
4

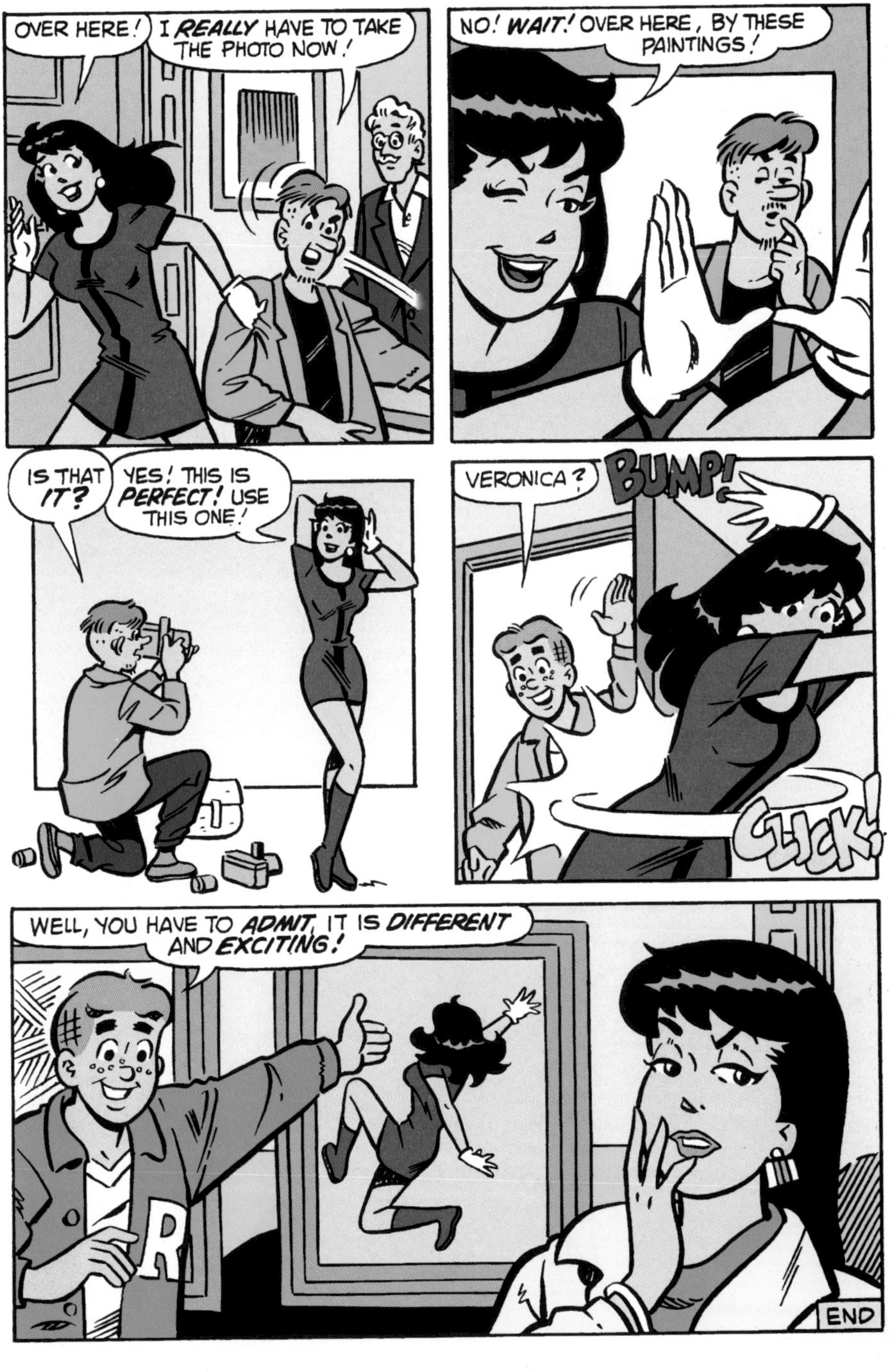
OVER HERE!
I REALLY HAVE TO TAKE THE PHOTO NOW!
NO! WAIT! OVER HERE, BY THESE PAINTINGS!
IS THAT IT?
YES! THIS IS PERFECT! USE THIS ONE!
VERONICA?
BUMP!
CLICK!
WELL, YOU HAVE TO ADMIT, IT IS DIFFERENT AND EXCITING!
END

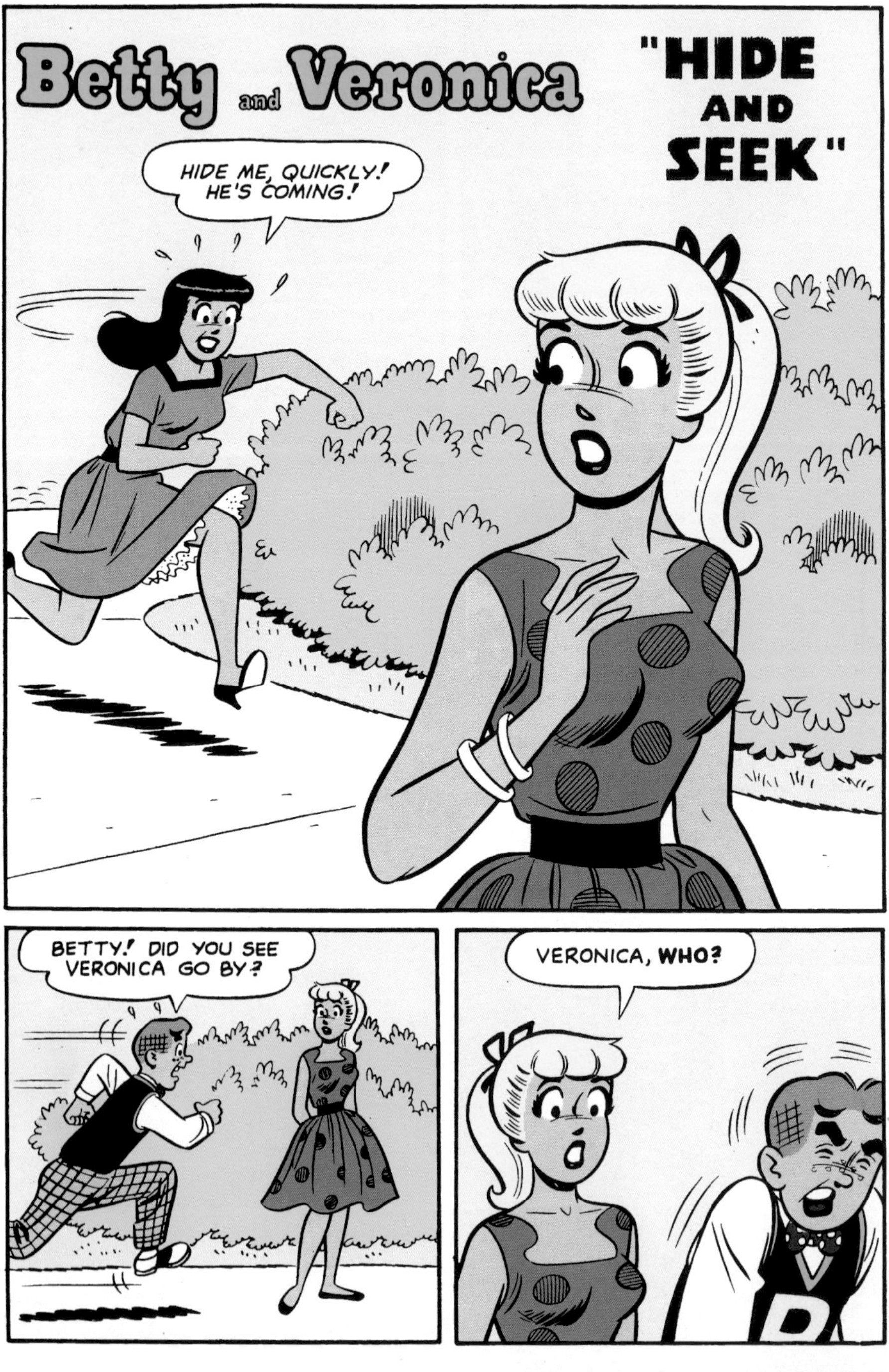
Betty and Veronica
"HIDE AND SEEK"
HIDE ME, QUICKLY! HE'S COMING!
BETTY! DID YOU SEE VERONICA GO BY?
VERONICA, WHO?

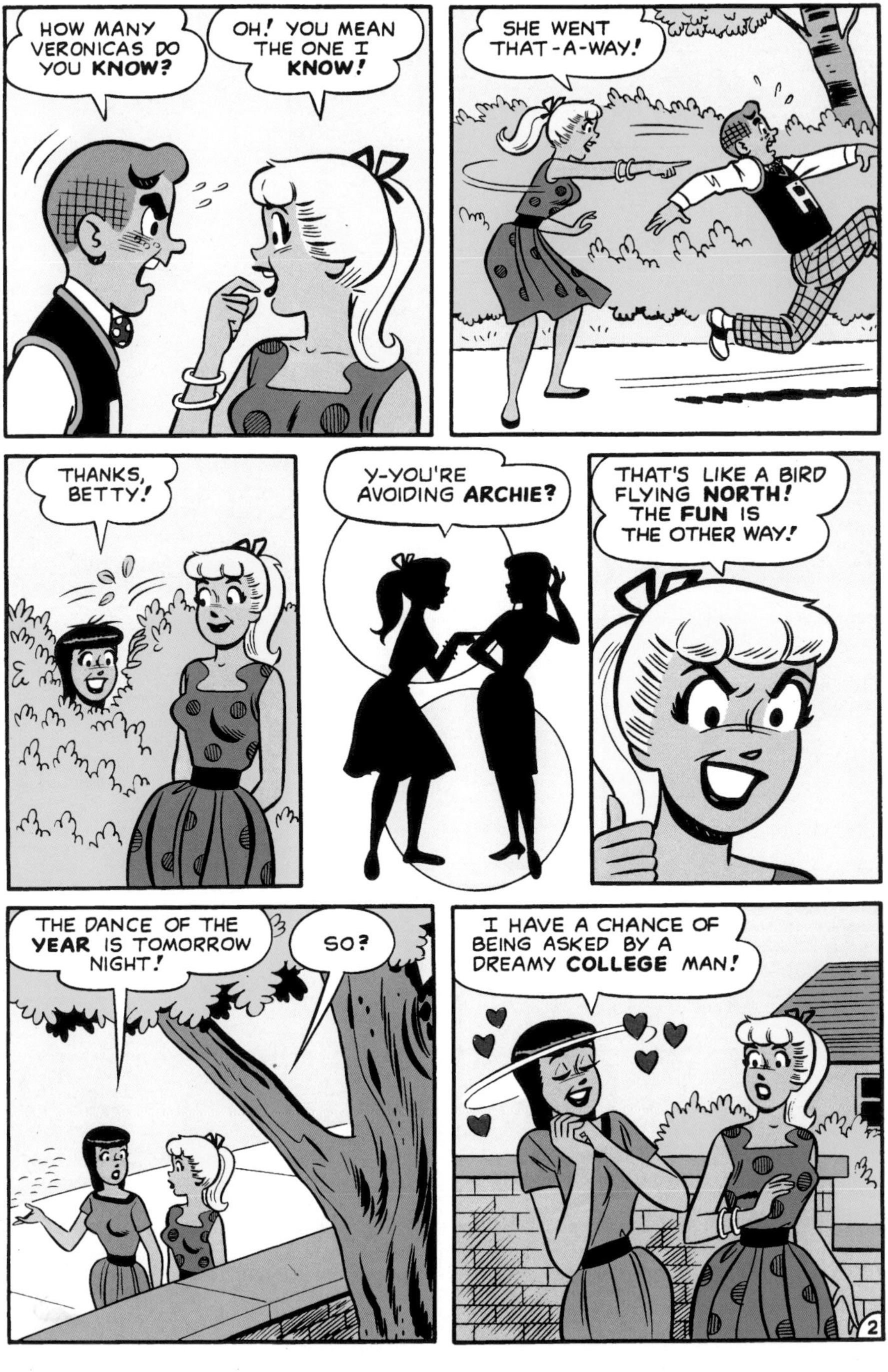
HOW MANY VERONICAS DO YOU KNOW?
OH! YOU MEAN THE ONE I KNOW!
SHE WENT THAT-A-WAY!
THANKS, BETTY!
Y-YOU'RE AVOIDING ARCHIE?
THAT'S LIKE A BIRD FLYING NORTH! THE FUN IS THE OTHER WAY!
THE DANCE OF THE YEAR IS TOMORROW NIGHT!
SO?
I HAVE A CHANCE OF BEING ASKED BY A DREAMY COLLEGE MAN!
2

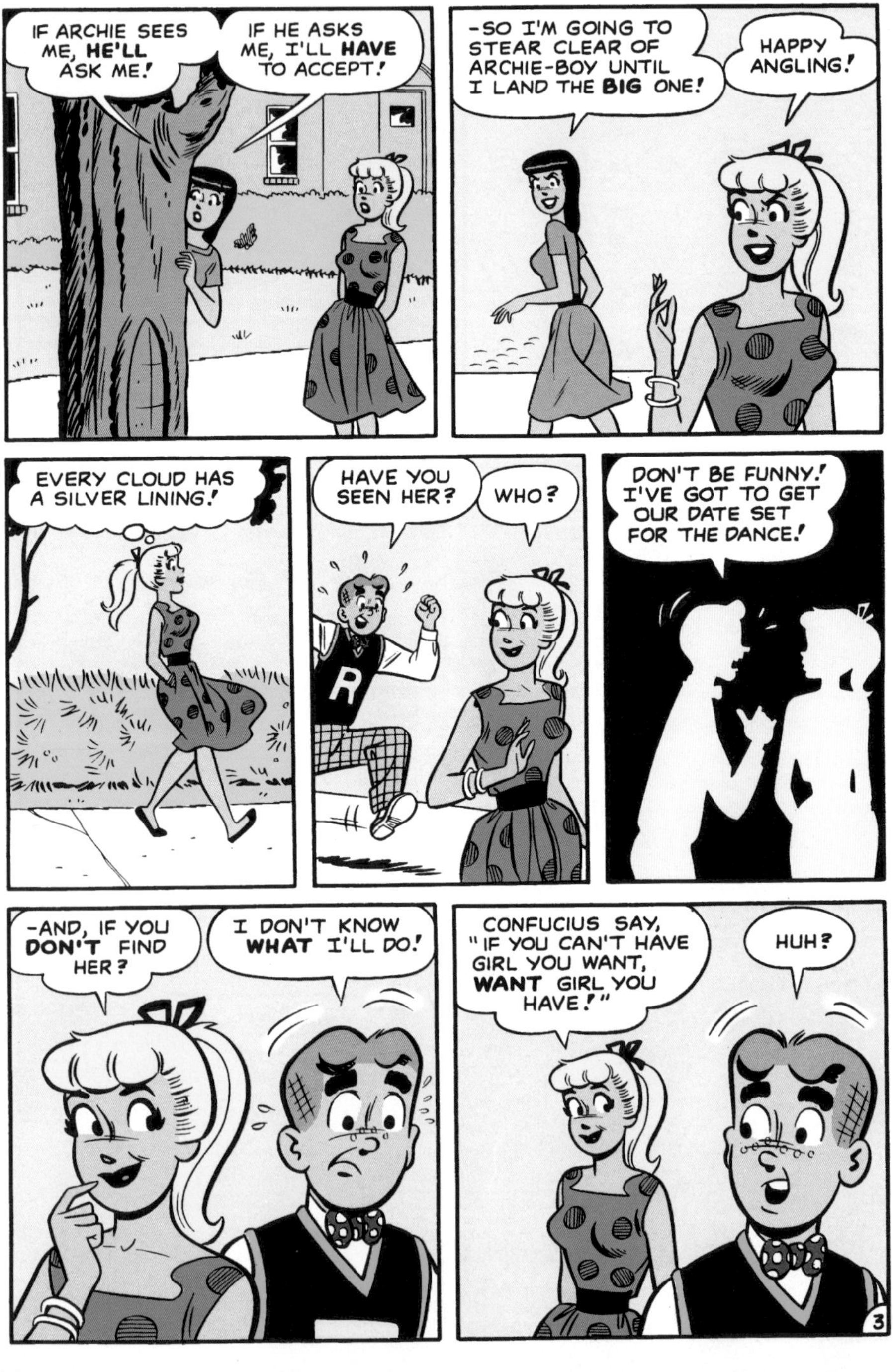
IF ARCHIE SEES ME, HE'LL ASK ME!
IF HE ASKS ME, I'LL HAVE TO ACCEPT!
-SO I'M GOING TO STEAR CLEAR OF ARCHIE-BOY UNTIL I LAND THE BIG ONE!
HAPPY ANGLING!
EVERY CLOUD HAS A SILVER LINING!
HAVE YOU SEEN HER?
WHO?
DON'T BE FUNNY! I'VE GOT TO GET OUR DATE SET FOR THE DANCE!
-AND, IF YOU DON'T FIND HER?
I DON'T KNOW WHAT I'LL DO!
CONFUCIUS SAY, "IF YOU CAN'T HAVE GIRL YOU WANT, WANT GIRL YOU HAVE!"
HUH?
3

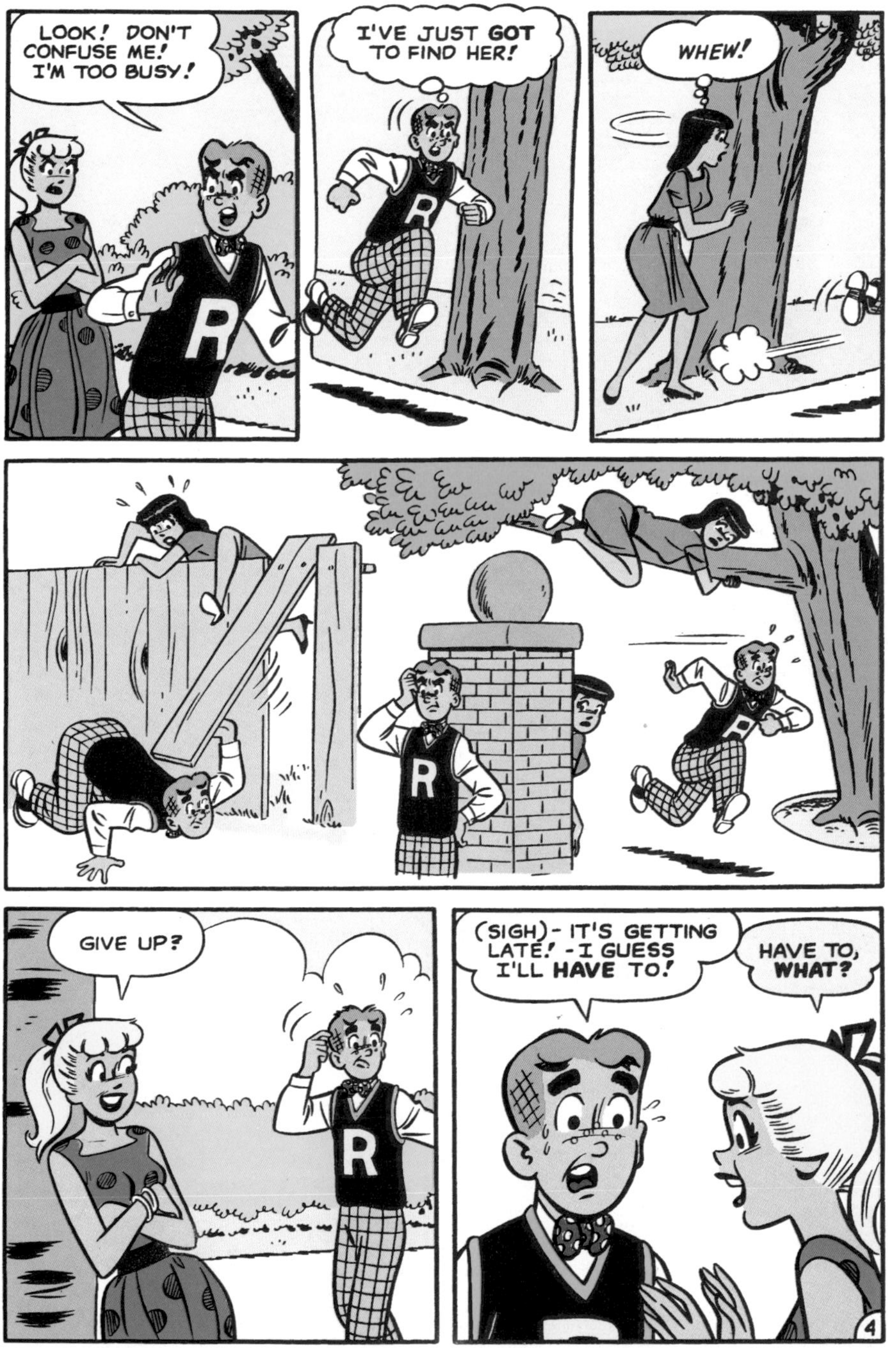
LOOK! DON'T CONFUSE ME! I'M TOO BUSY!
I'VE JUST GOT TO FIND HER!
WHEW!
GIVE UP?
(SIGH)- IT'S GETTING LATE! -I GUESS I'LL HAVE TO!
HAVE TO, WHAT?
4

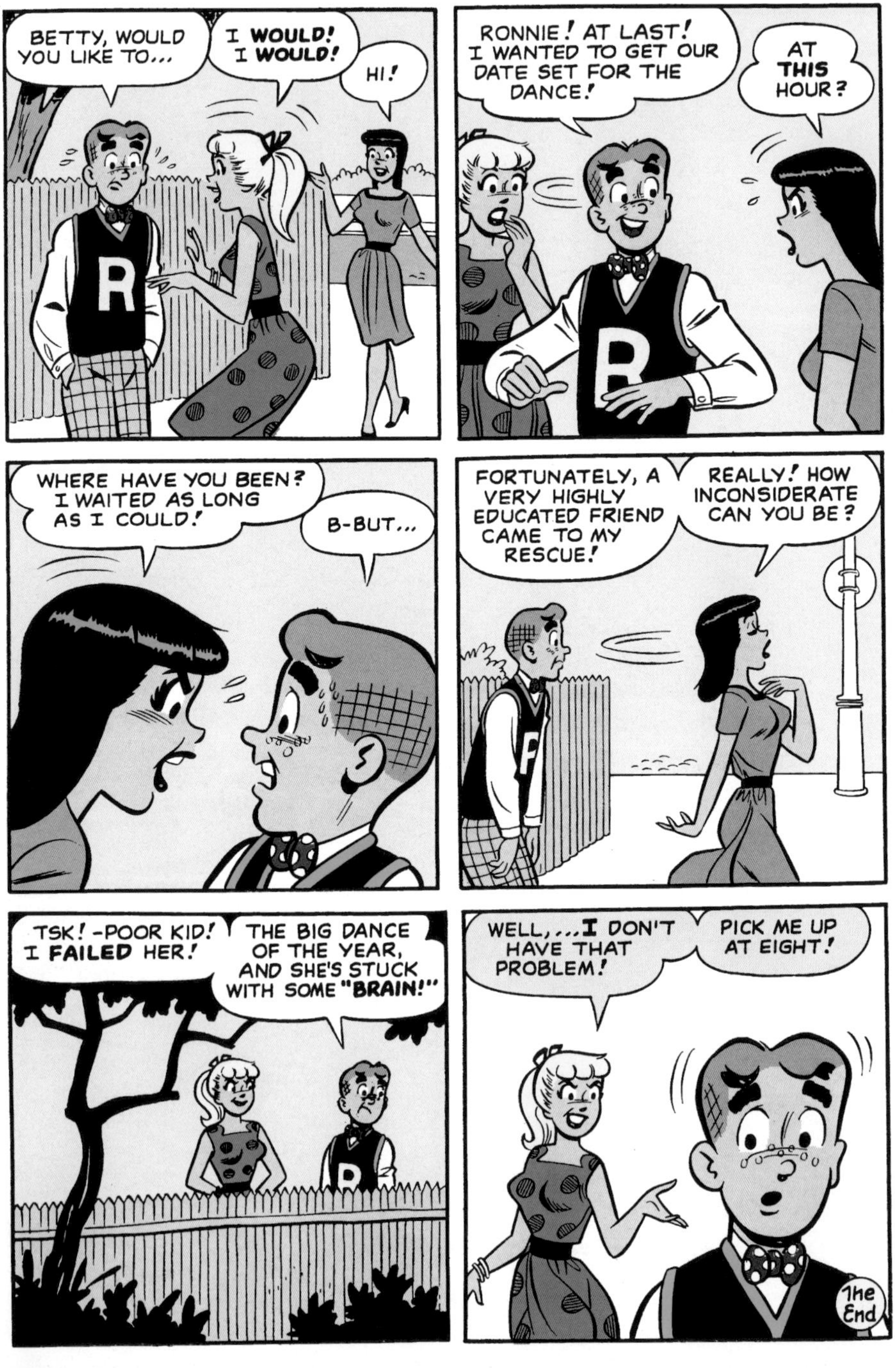
BETTY, WOULD YOU LIKE TO...
I WOULD! I WOULD!
HI!
RONNIE! AT LAST! I WANTED TO GET OUR DATE SET FOR THE DANCE!
AT THIS HOUR?
WHERE HAVE YOU BEEN? I WAITED AS LONG AS I COULD!
B-BUT...
FORTUNATELY, A VERY HIGHLY EDUCATED FRIEND CAME TO MY RESCUE!
REALLY! HOW INCONSIDERATE CAN YOU BE?
TSK! -POOR KID! I FAILED HER!
THE BIG DANCE OF THE YEAR, AND SHE'S STUCK WITH SOME "BRAIN!"
WELL, ...I DON'T HAVE THAT PROBLEM!
PICK ME UP AT EIGHT!
The End

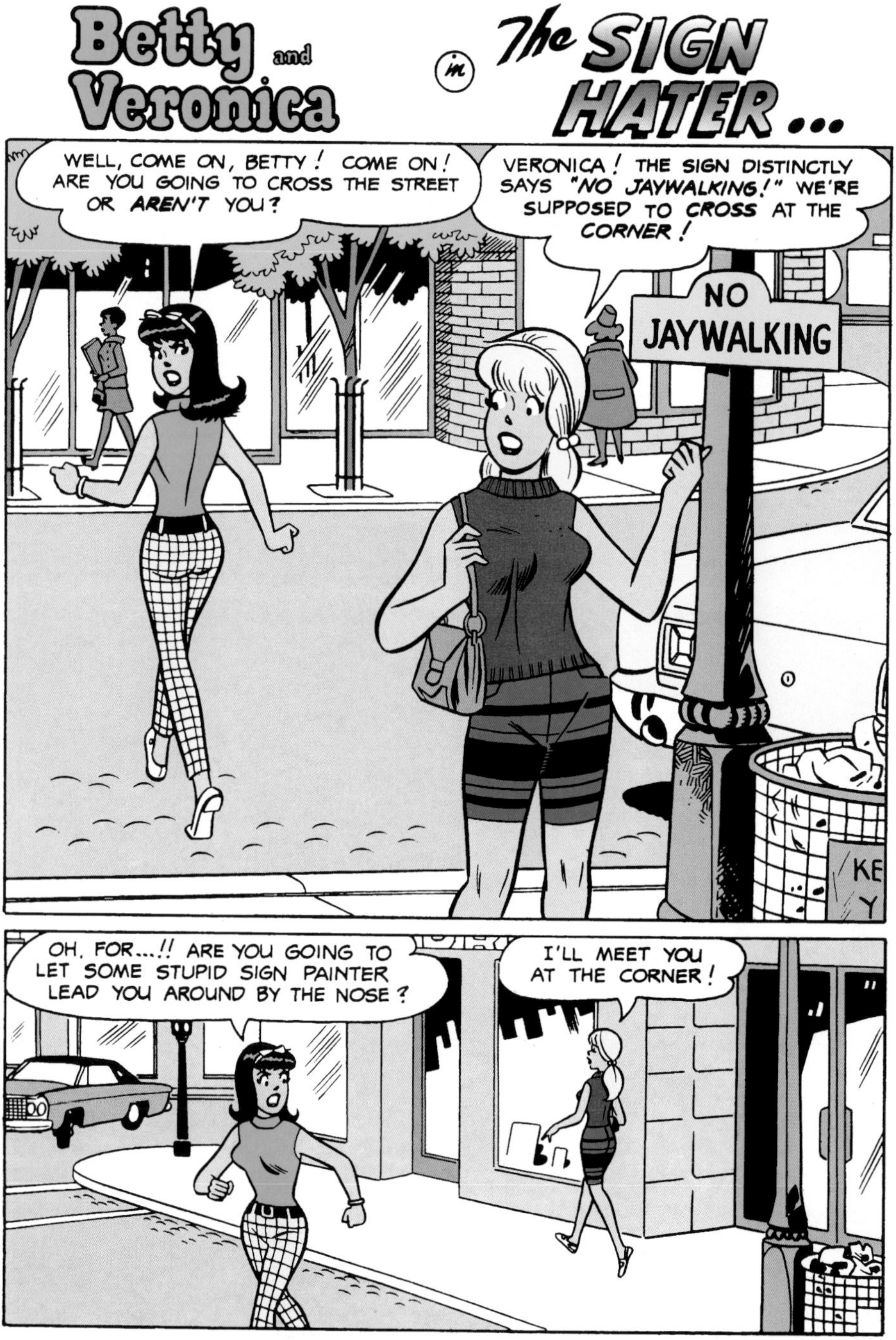
Betty and Veronica in The SIGN HATER...
WELL, COME ON, BETTY! COME ON! ARE YOU GOING TO CROSS THE STREET OR AREN'T YOU?
VERONICA! THE SIGN DISTINCTLY SAYS "NO JAYWALKING!" WE'RE SUPPOSED TO CROSS AT THE CORNER!
NO JAYWALKING
OH, FOR...!! ARE YOU GOING TO LET SOME STUPID SIGN PAINTER LEAD YOU AROUND BY THE NOSE?
I'LL MEET YOU AT THE CORNER!

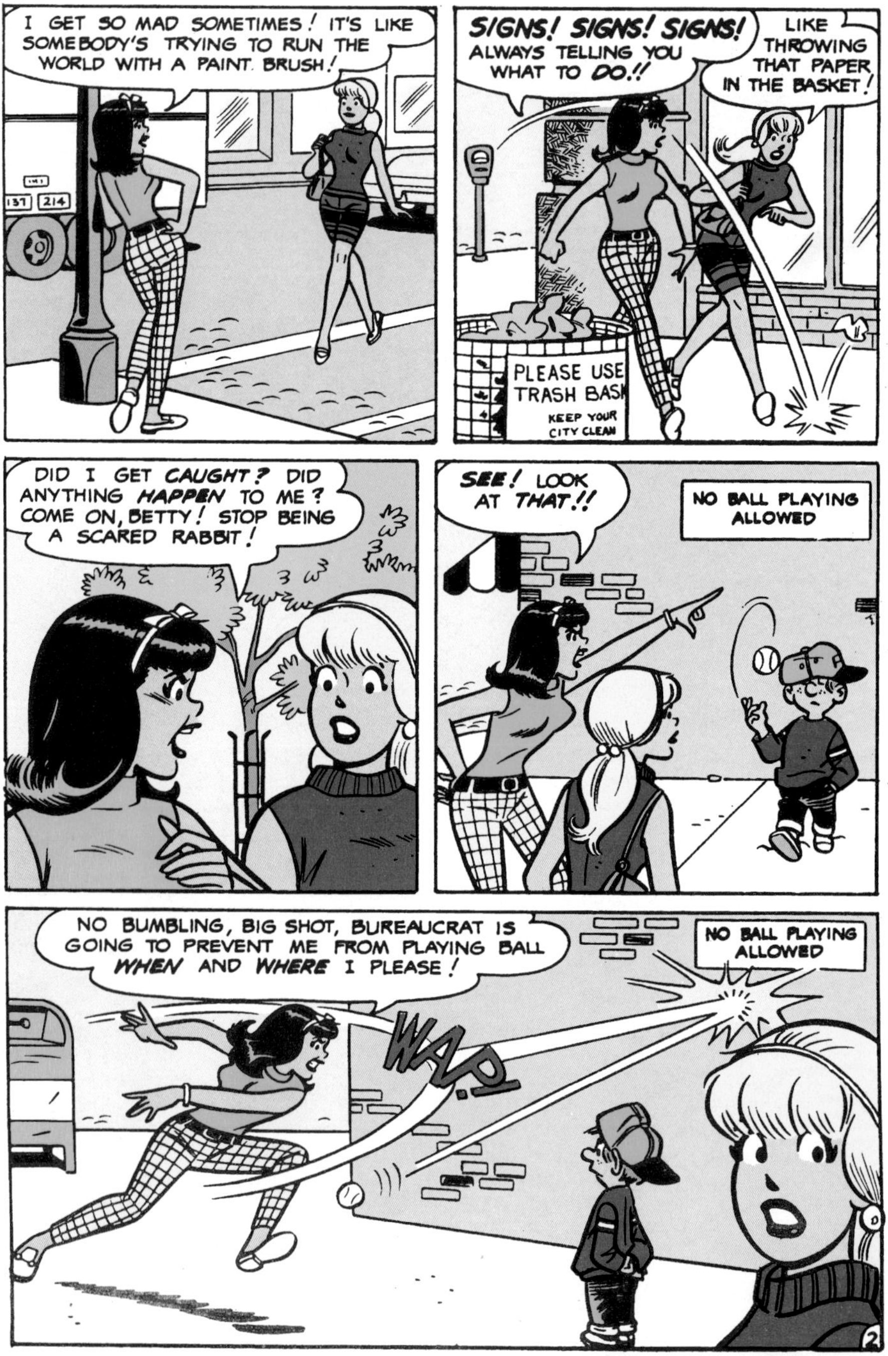
I GET SO MAD SOMETIMES! IT'S LIKE SOMEBODY'S TRYING TO RUN THE WORLD WITH A PAINT BRUSH!
SIGNS! SIGNS! SIGNS! ALWAYS TELLING YOU WHAT TO DO!!
LIKE THROWING THAT PAPER IN THE BASKET!
PLEASE USE TRASH BAS
KEEP YOUR CITY CLEAN
DID I GET CAUGHT? DID ANYTHING HAPPEN TO ME? COME ON, BETTY! STOP BEING A SCARED RABBIT!
SEE! LOOK AT THAT!!
NO BALL PLAYING ALLOWED
NO BUMBLING, BIG SHOT, BUREAUCRAT IS GOING TO PREVENT ME FROM PLAYING BALL WHEN AND WHERE I PLEASE!
NO BALL PLAYING ALLOWED
WAP!
2

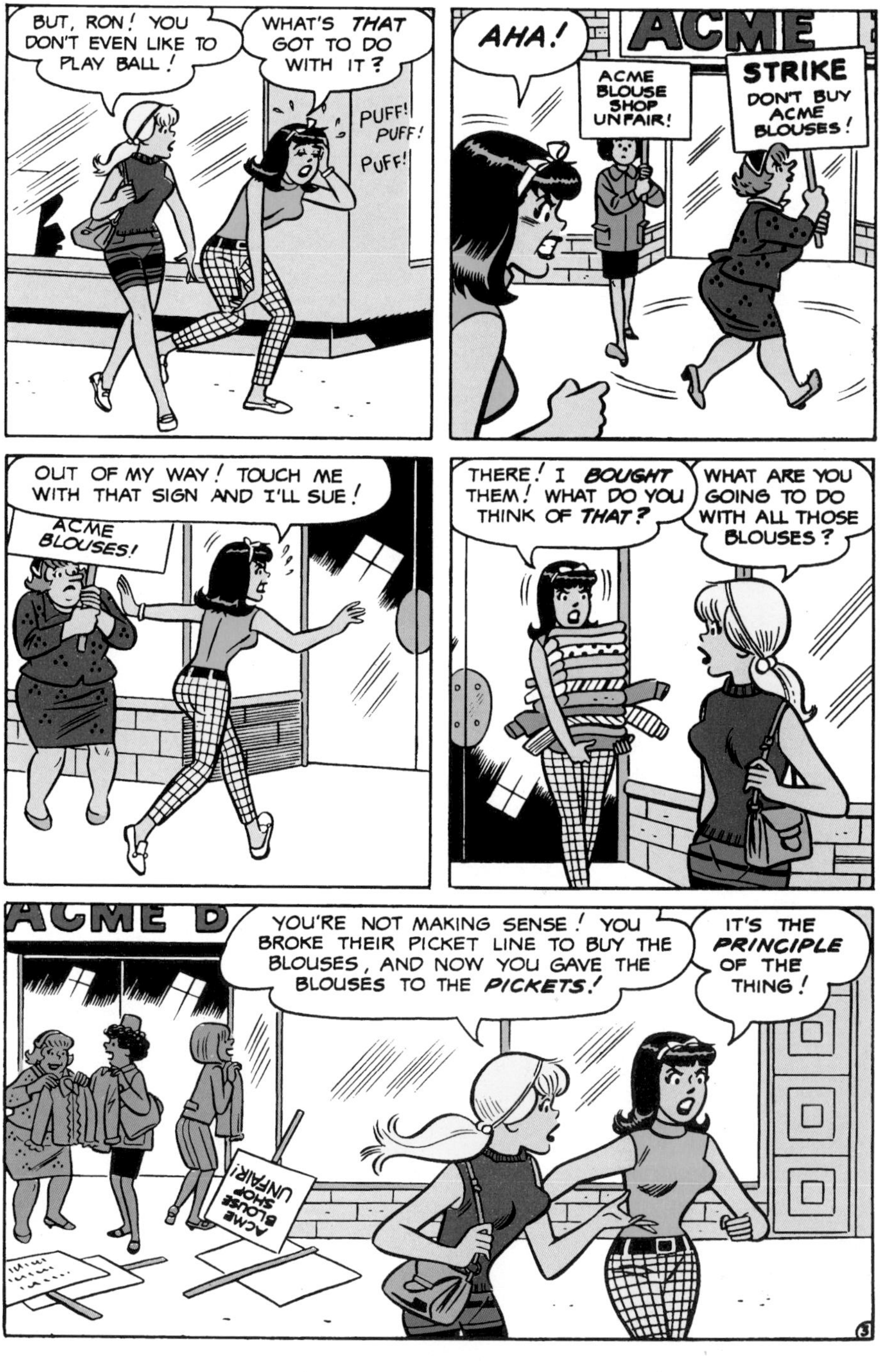
BUT, RON! YOU DON'T EVEN LIKE TO PLAY BALL!
WHAT'S THAT GOT TO DO WITH IT?
PUFF! PUFF! PUFF!
AHA!
ACME
ACME BLOUSE SHOP UNFAIR!
STRIKE DON'T BUY ACME BLOUSES!
OUT OF MY WAY! TOUCH ME WITH THAT SIGN AND I'LL SUE!
ACME BLOUSES!
THERE! I BOUGHT THEM! WHAT DO YOU THINK OF THAT?
WHAT ARE YOU GOING TO DO WITH ALL THOSE BLOUSES?
ACME B
YOU'RE NOT MAKING SENSE! YOU BROKE THEIR PICKET LINE TO BUY THE BLOUSES, AND NOW YOU GAVE THE BLOUSES TO THE PICKETS!
IT'S THE PRINCIPLE OF THE THING!
ACME BLOUSE SHOP UNFAIR!
3

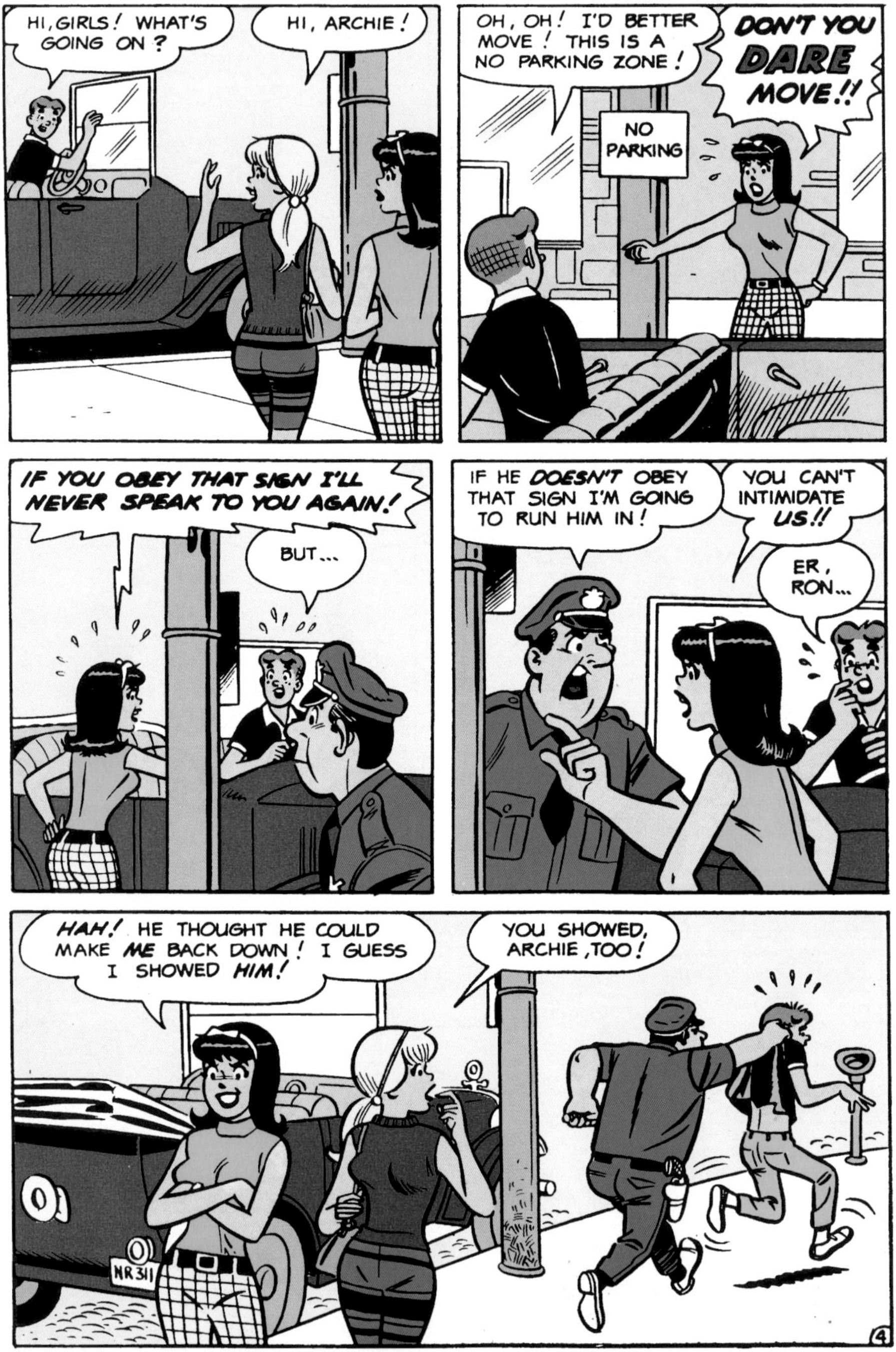
HI, GIRLS! WHAT'S GOING ON?
HI, ARCHIE!
OH, OH! I'D BETTER MOVE! THIS IS A NO PARKING ZONE!
DON'T YOU DARE MOVE!!
NO PARKING
IF YOU OBEY THAT SIGN I'LL NEVER SPEAK TO YOU AGAIN!
BUT...
IF HE DOESN'T OBEY THAT SIGN I'M GOING TO RUN HIM IN!
YOU CAN'T INTIMIDATE US!!
ER, RON...
HAH! HE THOUGHT HE COULD MAKE ME BACK DOWN! I GUESS I SHOWED HIM!
YOU SHOWED, ARCHIE, TOO!
NR 311
4

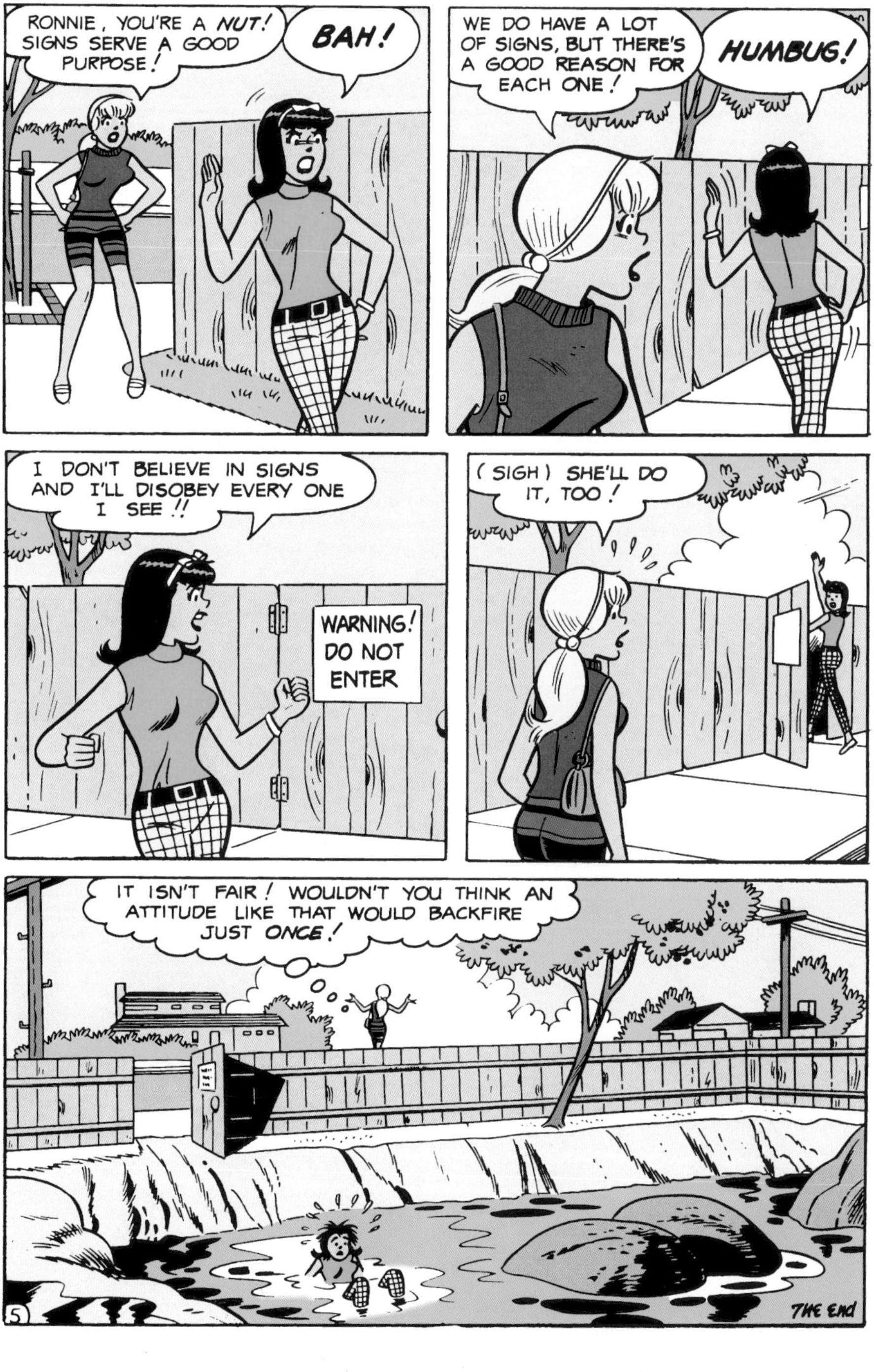
RONNIE, YOU'RE A *NUT!* SIGNS SERVE A GOOD PURPOSE!
BAH!
WE DO HAVE A LOT OF SIGNS, BUT THERE'S A GOOD REASON FOR EACH ONE!
HUMBUG!
I DON'T BELIEVE IN SIGNS AND I'LL DISOBEY EVERY ONE I SEE!!
WARNING! DO NOT ENTER
(SIGH) SHE'LL DO IT, TOO!
IT ISN'T FAIR! WOULDN'T YOU THINK AN ATTITUDE LIKE THAT WOULD BACKFIRE JUST *ONCE!*
5
THE END

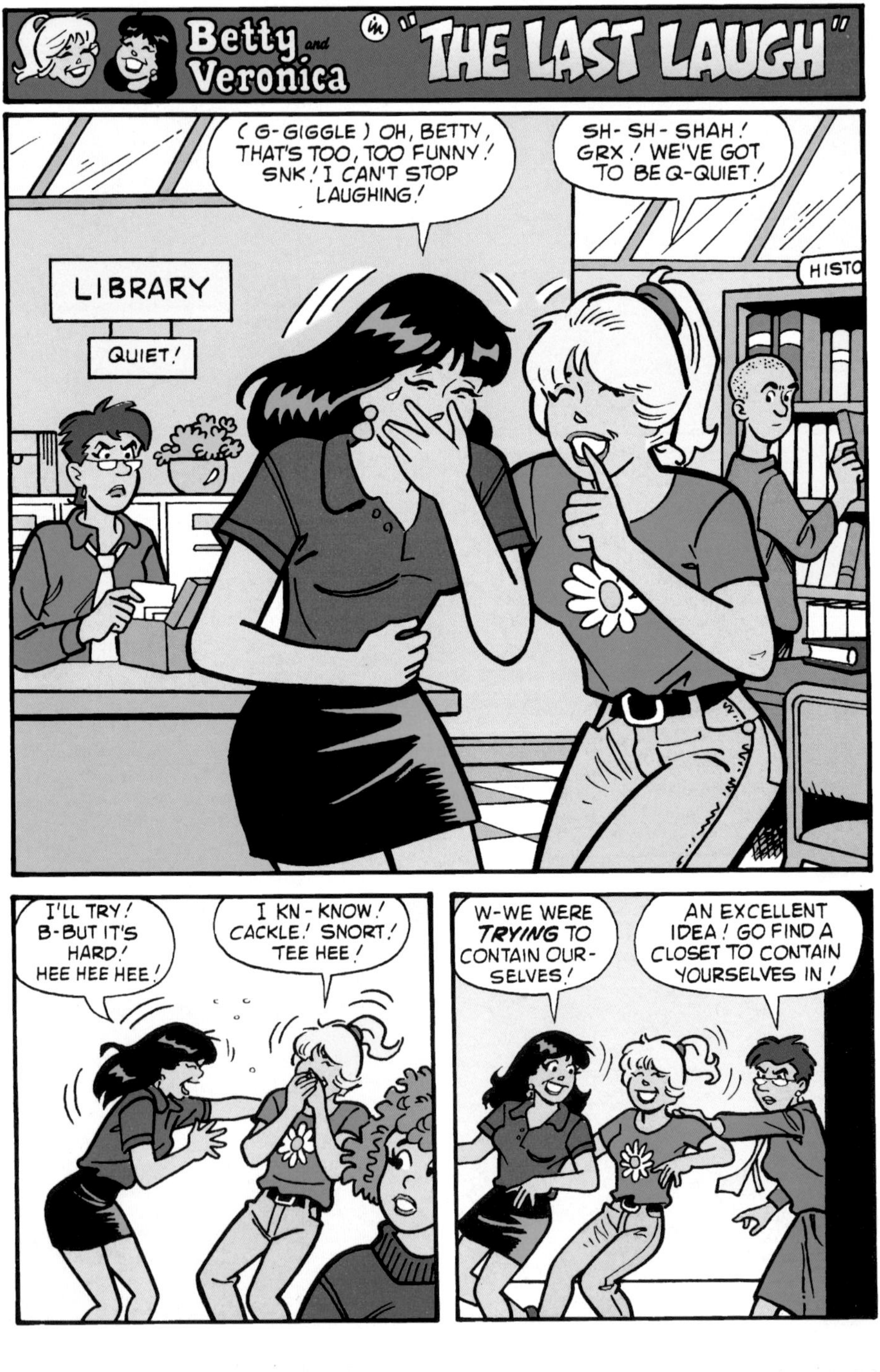
Betty and Veronica in "THE LAST LAUGH"
(G-GIGGLE) OH, BETTY, THAT'S TOO, TOO FUNNY! SNK! I CAN'T STOP LAUGHING!
SH- SH- SHAH! GRX! WE'VE GOT TO BE Q-QUIET!
LIBRARY
QUIET!
HISTO
I'LL TRY! B-BUT IT'S HARD! HEE HEE HEE!
I KN - KNOW! CACKLE! SNORT! TEE HEE!
W-WE WERE *TRYING* TO CONTAIN OUR-SELVES!
AN EXCELLENT IDEA! GO FIND A CLOSET TO CONTAIN YOURSELVES IN!

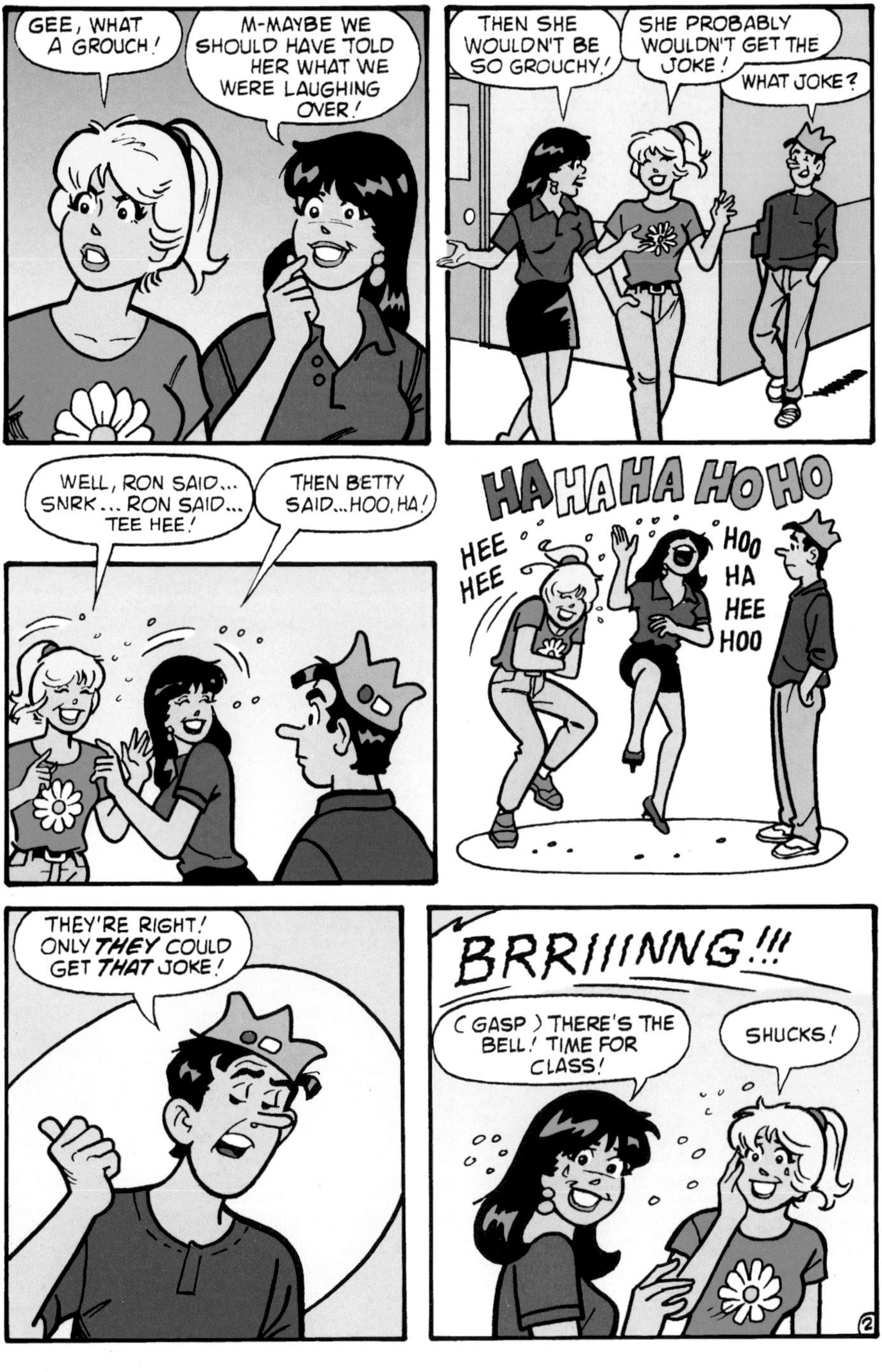
GEE, WHAT A GROUCH!
M-MAYBE WE SHOULD HAVE TOLD HER WHAT WE WERE LAUGHING OVER!
THEN SHE WOULDN'T BE SO GROUCHY!
SHE PROBABLY WOULDN'T GET THE JOKE!
WHAT JOKE?
WELL, RON SAID... SNRK... RON SAID... TEE HEE!
THEN BETTY SAID...HOO, HA!
HAHAHA HOHO
HEE HEE
HOO HA HEE HOO
THEY'RE RIGHT! ONLY THEY COULD GET THAT JOKE!
BRRIIINNG!!!
(GASP) THERE'S THE BELL! TIME FOR CLASS!
SHUCKS!
2

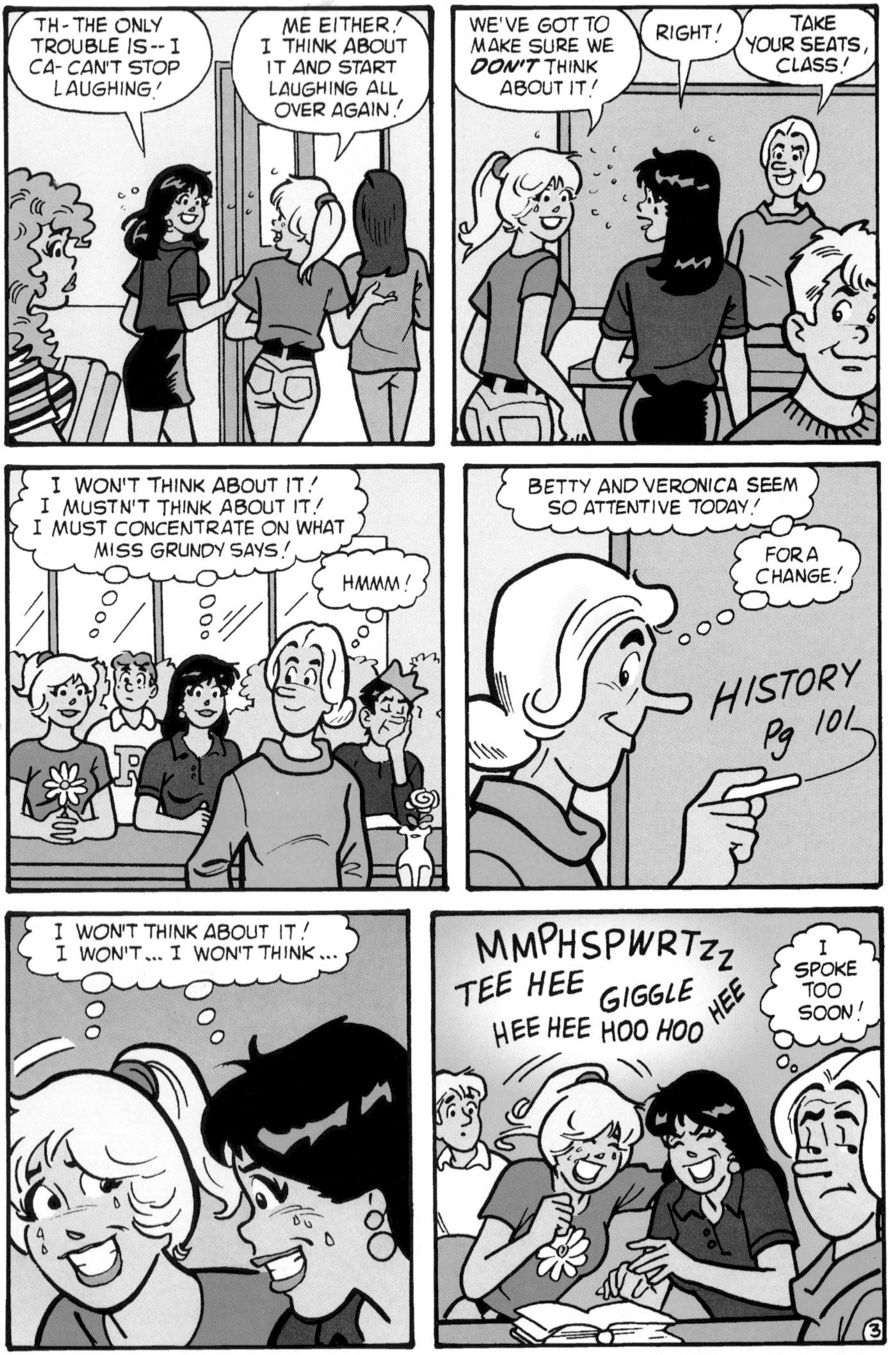
TH-THE ONLY TROUBLE IS-- I CA-CAN'T STOP LAUGHING!
ME EITHER! I THINK ABOUT IT AND START LAUGHING ALL OVER AGAIN!
WE'VE GOT TO MAKE SURE WE DON'T THINK ABOUT IT!
RIGHT!
TAKE YOUR SEATS, CLASS!
I WON'T THINK ABOUT IT! I MUSTN'T THINK ABOUT IT! I MUST CONCENTRATE ON WHAT MISS GRUNDY SAYS!
HMMM!
BETTY AND VERONICA SEEM SO ATTENTIVE TODAY!
FOR A CHANGE!
HISTORY Pg 101
I WON'T THINK ABOUT IT! I WON'T... I WON'T THINK...
MMPHSPWRTzz
TEE HEE
GIGGLE
HEE HEE HOO HOO HEE
I SPOKE TOO SOON!
3

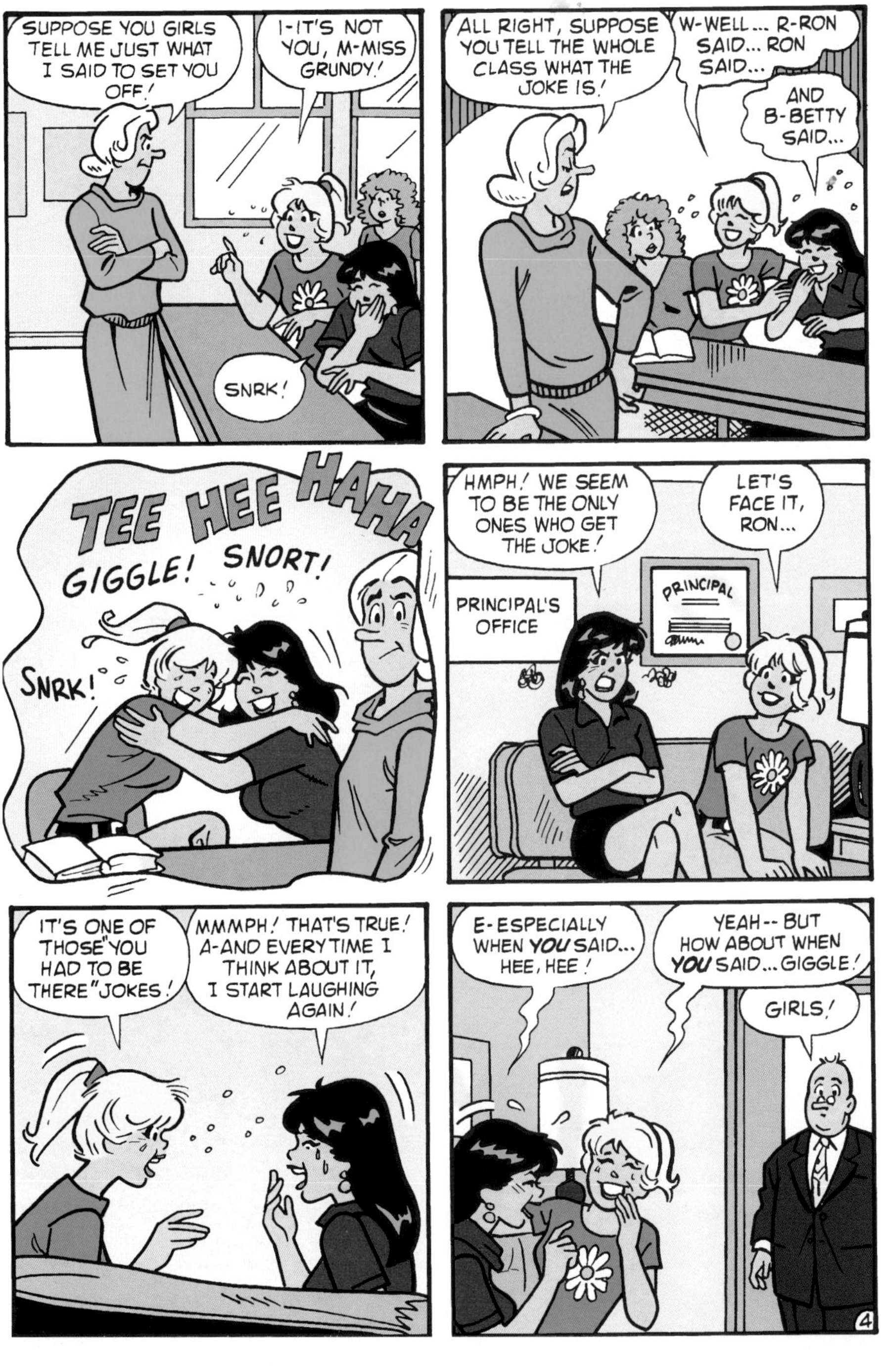
SUPPOSE YOU GIRLS TELL ME JUST WHAT I SAID TO SET YOU OFF!
I-IT'S NOT YOU, M-MISS GRUNDY!
SNRK!
ALL RIGHT, SUPPOSE YOU TELL THE WHOLE CLASS WHAT THE JOKE IS!
W-WELL... R-RON SAID... RON SAID...
AND B-BETTY SAID...
TEE HEE HAHA
GIGGLE! SNORT!
SNRK!
HMPH! WE SEEM TO BE THE ONLY ONES WHO GET THE JOKE!
LET'S FACE IT, RON...
PRINCIPAL'S OFFICE
PRINCIPAL
IT'S ONE OF THOSE "YOU HAD TO BE THERE" JOKES!
MMMPH! THAT'S TRUE! A-AND EVERY TIME I THINK ABOUT IT, I START LAUGHING AGAIN!
E-ESPECIALLY WHEN YOU SAID... HEE, HEE!
YEAH -- BUT HOW ABOUT WHEN YOU SAID... GIGGLE!
GIRLS!
4

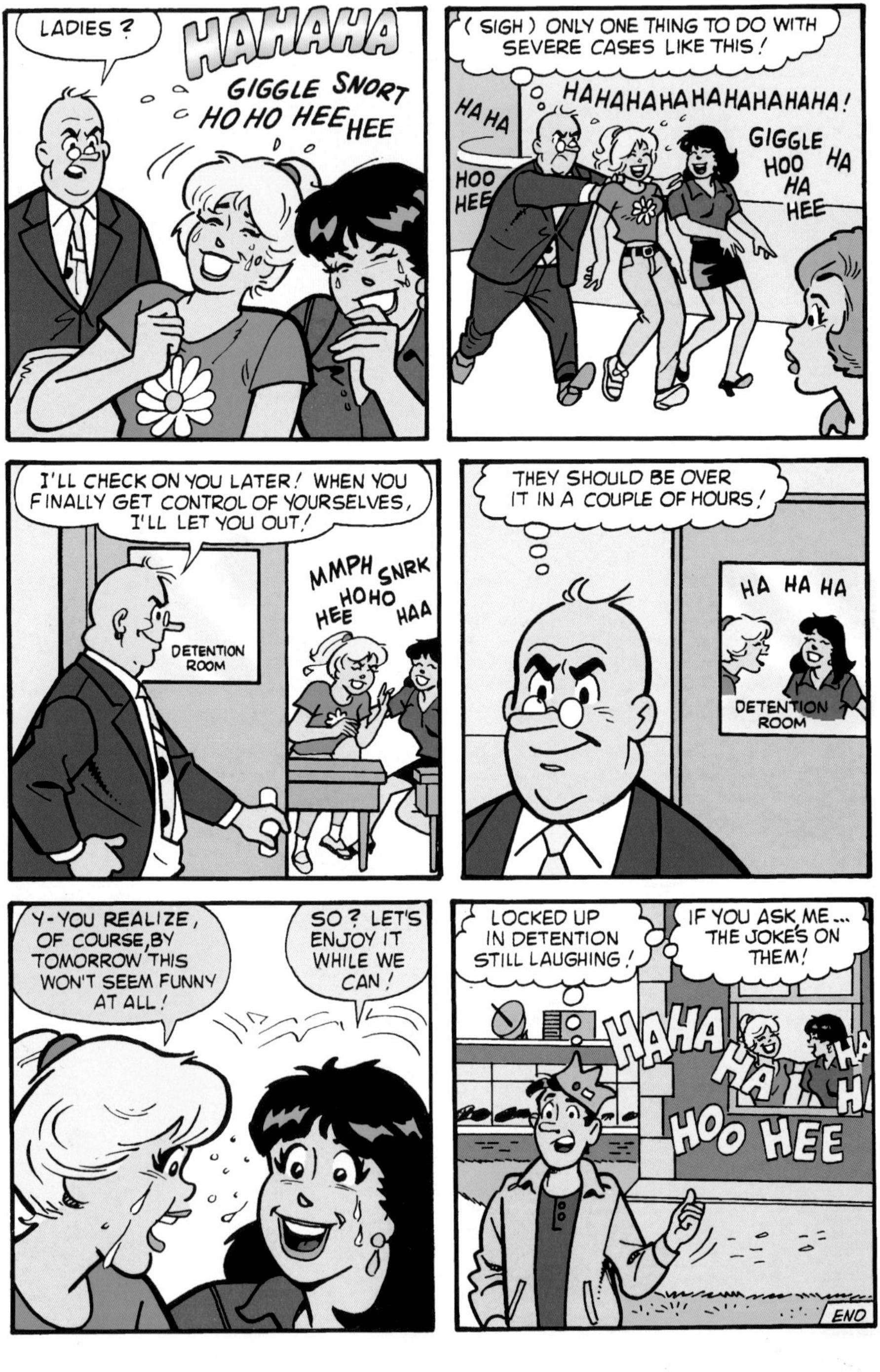
LADIES ?
HAHAHA
GIGGLE SNORT
HO HO HEE HEE
(SIGH) ONLY ONE THING TO DO WITH SEVERE CASES LIKE THIS!
HAHAHAHAHAHAHAHAHA!
HA HA
HOO HEE
GIGGLE HOO HA HEE HA
I'LL CHECK ON YOU LATER! WHEN YOU FINALLY GET CONTROL OF YOURSELVES, I'LL LET YOU OUT!
MMPH SNRK
HEE HOHO HAA
DETENTION ROOM
THEY SHOULD BE OVER IT IN A COUPLE OF HOURS!
HA HA HA
DETENTION ROOM
Y-YOU REALIZE, OF COURSE, BY TOMORROW THIS WON'T SEEM FUNNY AT ALL!
SO? LET'S ENJOY IT WHILE WE CAN!
LOCKED UP IN DETENTION STILL LAUGHING!
IF YOU ASK ME... THE JOKE'S ON THEM!
HAHA HA
HOO HEE
END

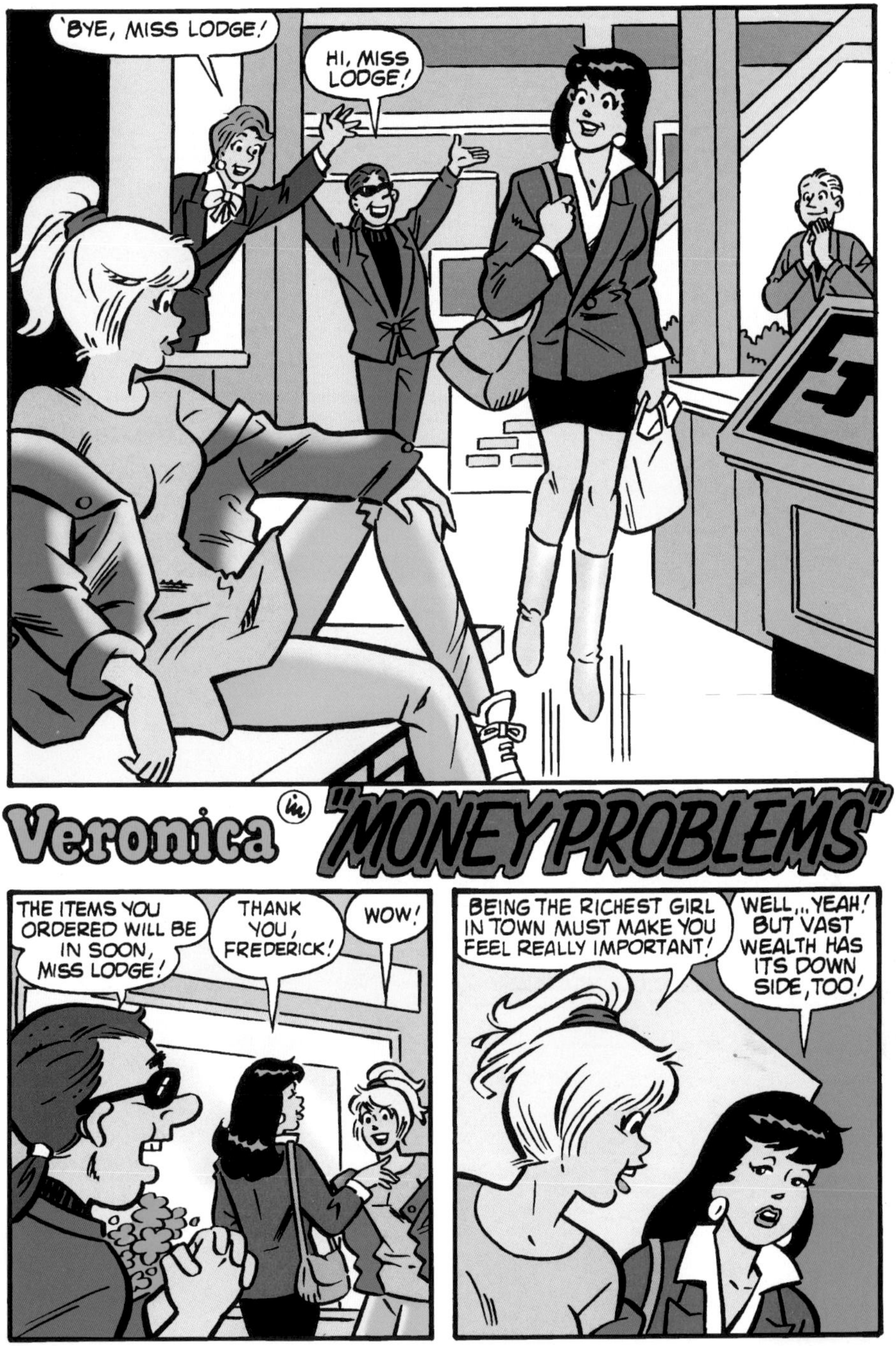
'BYE, MISS LODGE!
HI, MISS LODGE!
Veronica in "MONEY PROBLEMS"
THE ITEMS YOU ORDERED WILL BE IN SOON, MISS LODGE!
THANK YOU, FREDERICK!
WOW!
BEING THE RICHEST GIRL IN TOWN MUST MAKE YOU FEEL REALLY IMPORTANT!
WELL... YEAH! BUT VAST WEALTH HAS ITS DOWN SIDE, TOO!

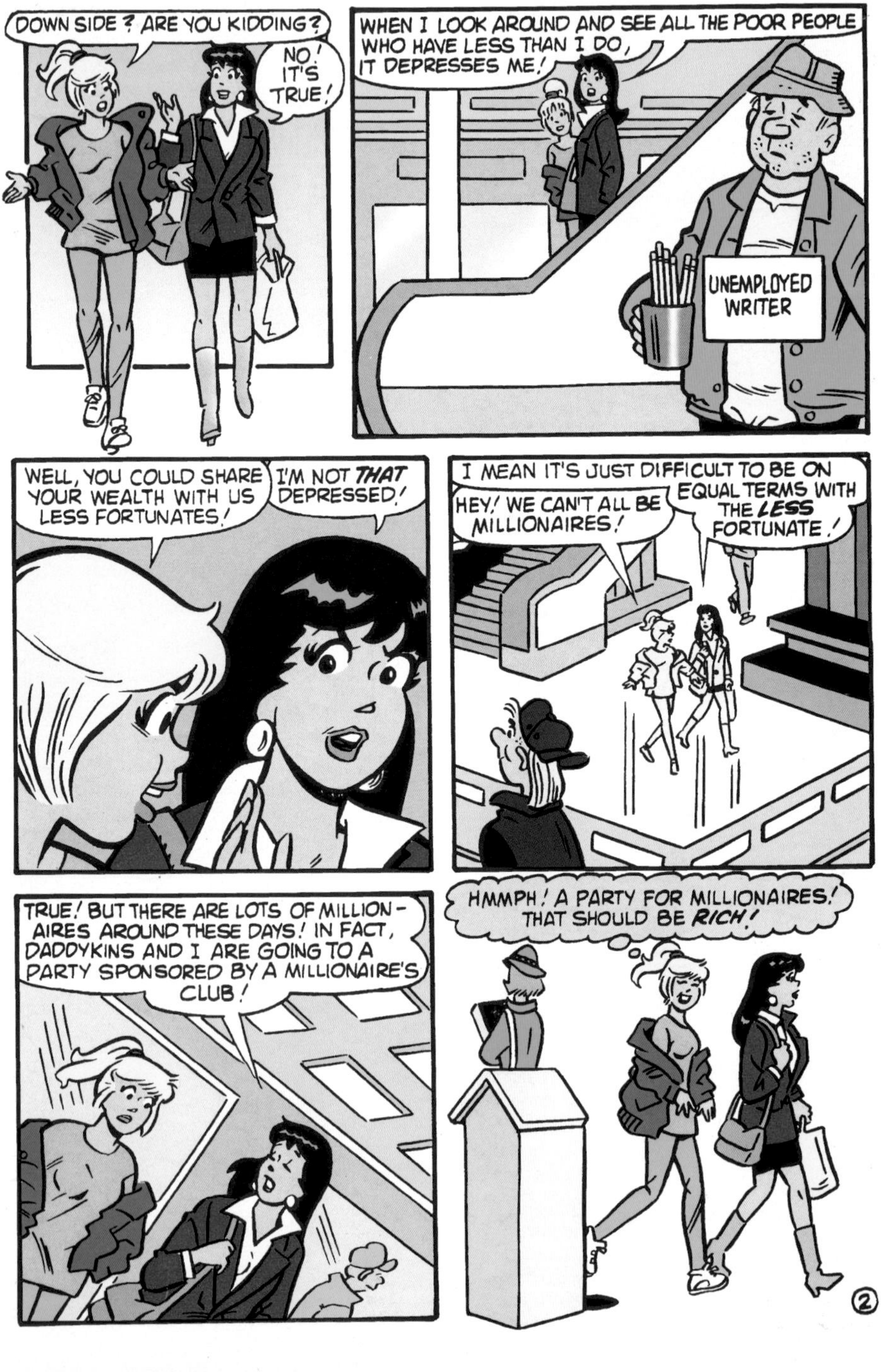
DOWN SIDE? ARE YOU KIDDING?
NO! IT'S TRUE!
WHEN I LOOK AROUND AND SEE ALL THE POOR PEOPLE WHO HAVE LESS THAN I DO, IT DEPRESSES ME!
UNEMPLOYED WRITER
WELL, YOU COULD SHARE YOUR WEALTH WITH US LESS FORTUNATES!
I'M NOT *THAT* DEPRESSED!
I MEAN IT'S JUST DIFFICULT TO BE ON EQUAL TERMS WITH THE *LESS* FORTUNATE!
HEY! WE CAN'T ALL BE MILLIONAIRES!
TRUE! BUT THERE ARE LOTS OF MILLION-AIRES AROUND THESE DAYS! IN FACT, DADDYKINS AND I ARE GOING TO A PARTY SPONSORED BY A MILLIONAIRE'S CLUB!
HMMPH! A PARTY FOR MILLIONAIRES! THAT SHOULD BE *RICH*!
2

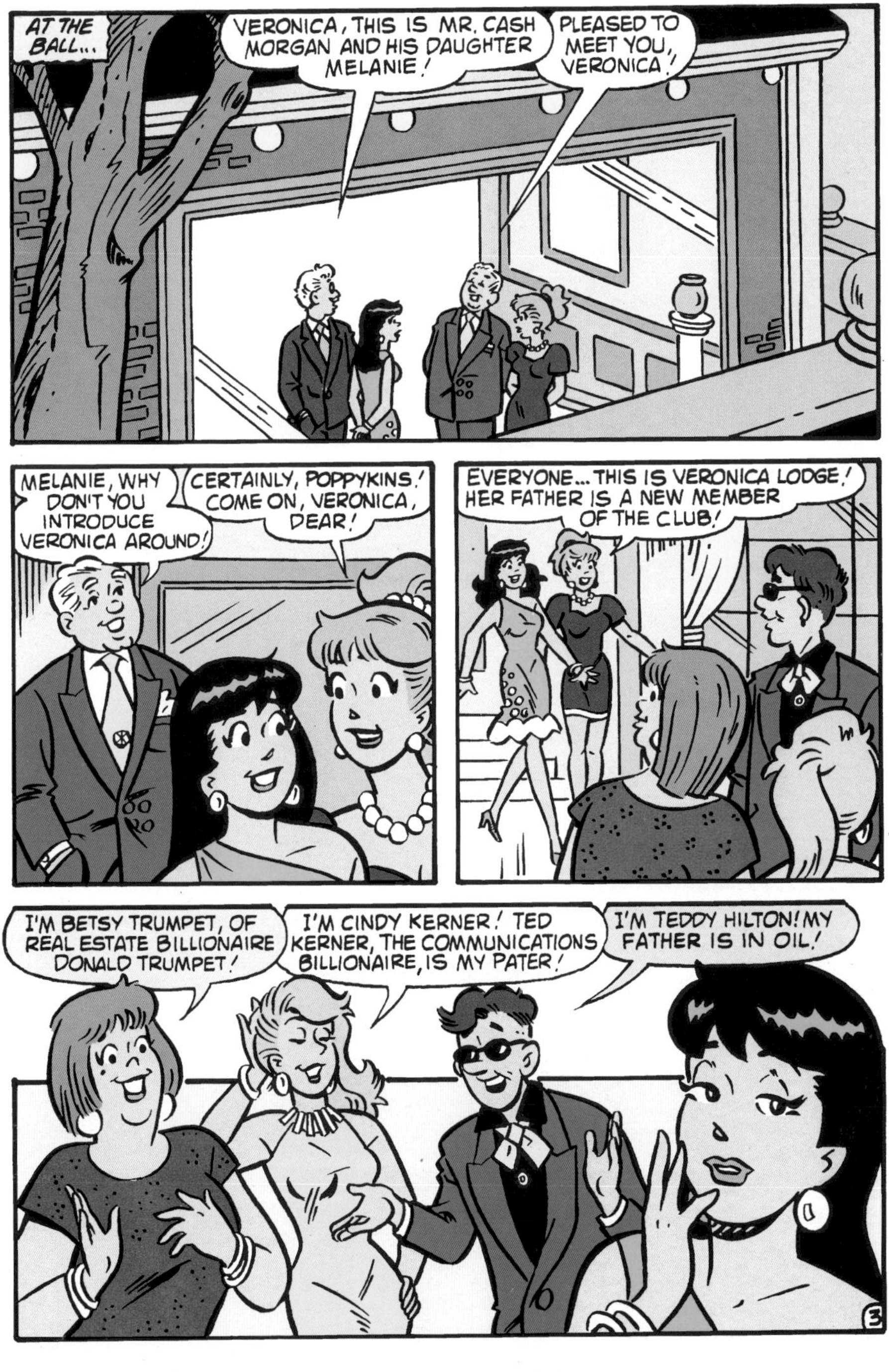
AT THE BALL...
VERONICA, THIS IS MR. CASH MORGAN AND HIS DAUGHTER MELANIE!
PLEASED TO MEET YOU, VERONICA!
MELANIE, WHY DON'T YOU INTRODUCE VERONICA AROUND!
CERTAINLY, POPPYKINS! COME ON, VERONICA, DEAR!
EVERYONE... THIS IS VERONICA LODGE! HER FATHER IS A NEW MEMBER OF THE CLUB!
I'M BETSY TRUMPET, OF REAL ESTATE BILLIONAIRE DONALD TRUMPET!
I'M CINDY KERNER! TED KERNER, THE COMMUNICATIONS BILLIONAIRE, IS MY PATER!
I'M TEDDY HILTON! MY FATHER IS IN OIL!
3

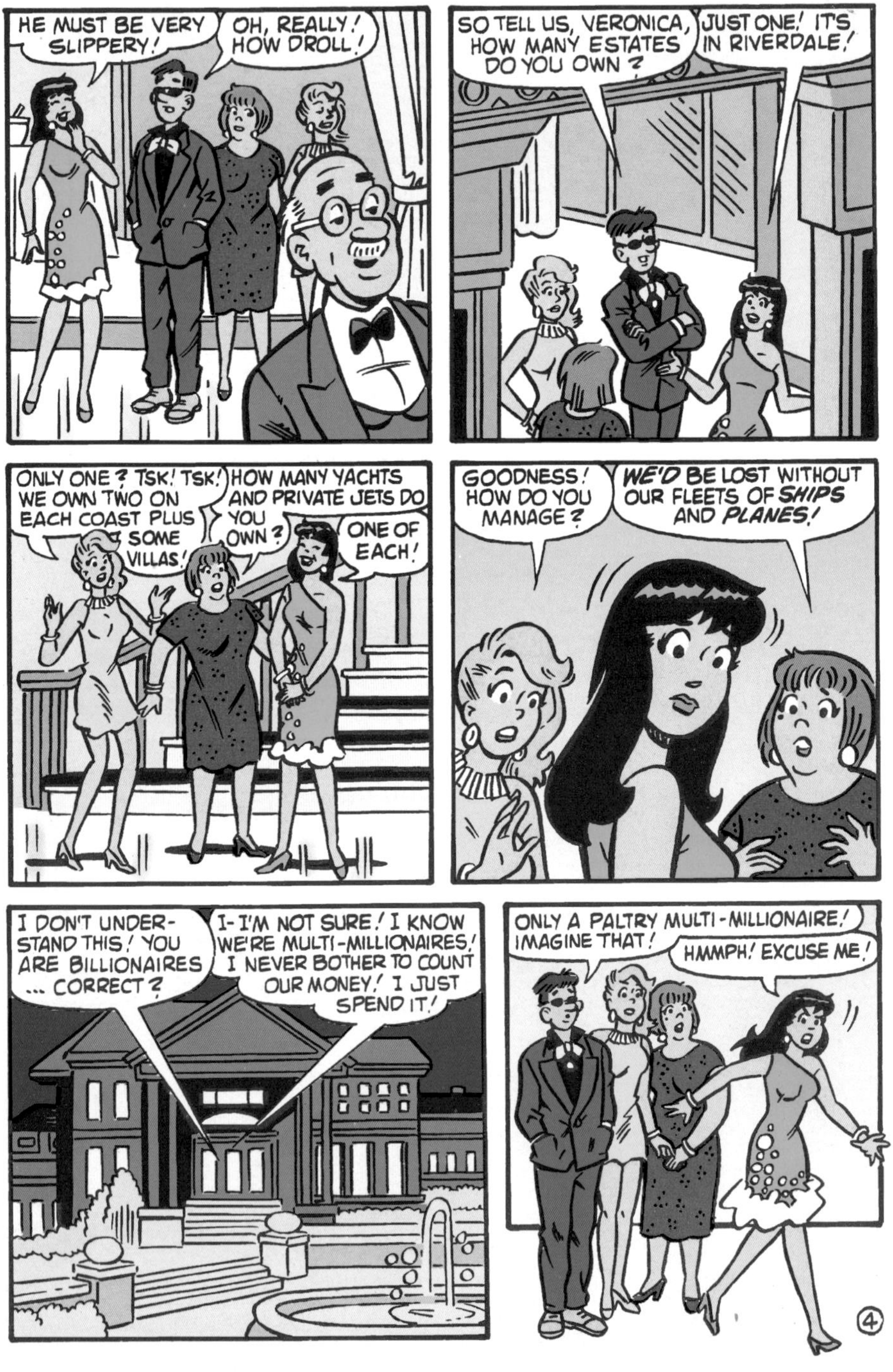
HE MUST BE VERY SLIPPERY!
OH, REALLY! HOW DROLL!
SO TELL US, VERONICA, HOW MANY ESTATES DO YOU OWN?
JUST ONE! IT'S IN RIVERDALE!
ONLY ONE? TSK! TSK! WE OWN TWO ON EACH COAST PLUS SOME VILLAS!
HOW MANY YACHTS AND PRIVATE JETS DO YOU OWN?
ONE OF EACH!
GOODNESS! HOW DO YOU MANAGE?
WE'D BE LOST WITHOUT OUR FLEETS OF SHIPS AND PLANES!
I DON'T UNDERSTAND THIS! YOU ARE BILLIONAIRES ... CORRECT?
I-I'M NOT SURE! I KNOW WE'RE MULTI-MILLIONAIRES! I NEVER BOTHER TO COUNT OUR MONEY! I JUST SPEND IT!
ONLY A PALTRY MULTI-MILLIONAIRE! IMAGINE THAT!
HMMPH! EXCUSE ME!
4

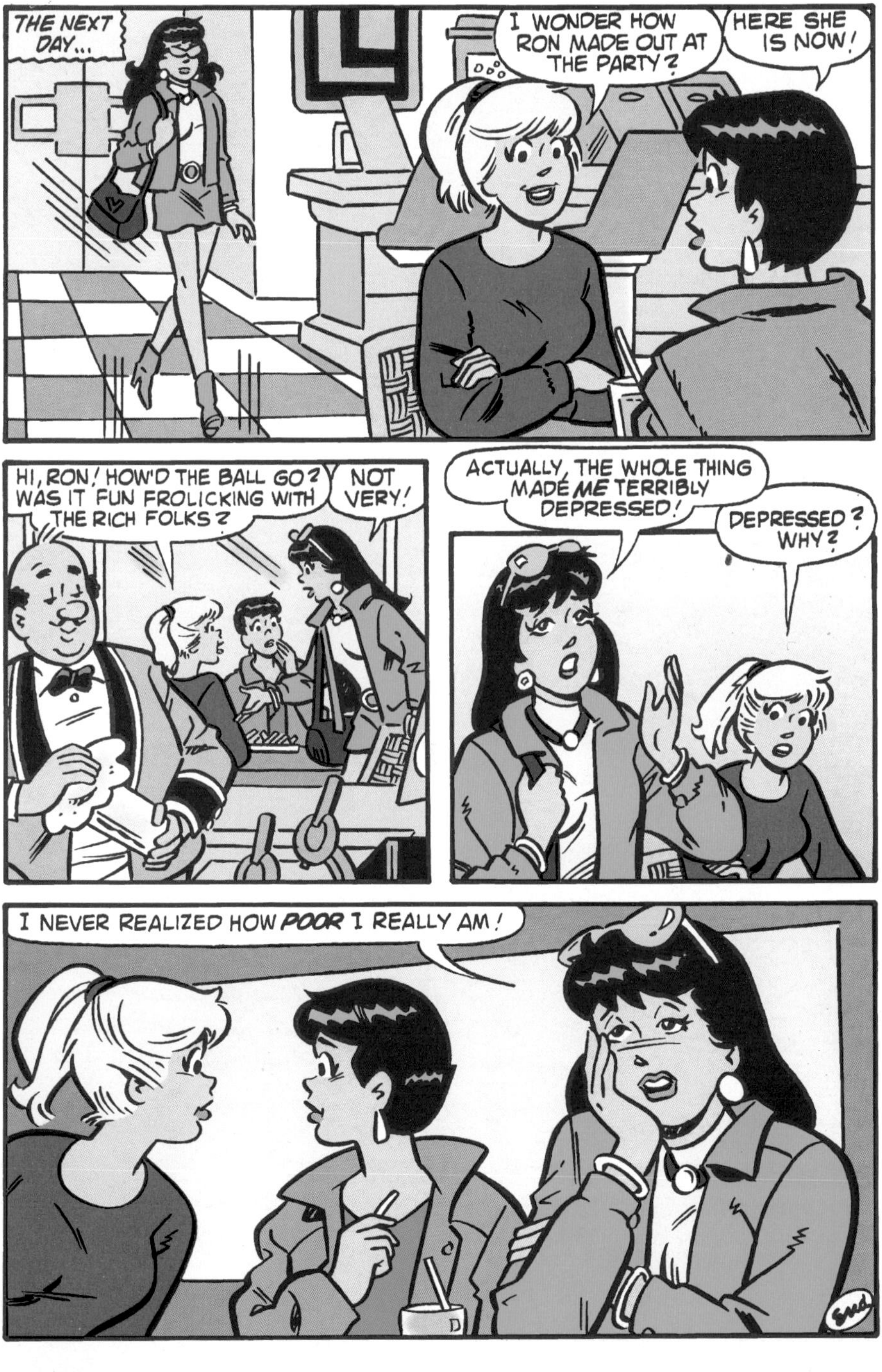
THE NEXT DAY...
I WONDER HOW RON MADE OUT AT THE PARTY?
HERE SHE IS NOW!
HI, RON! HOW'D THE BALL GO? WAS IT FUN FROLICKING WITH THE RICH FOLKS?
NOT VERY!
ACTUALLY, THE WHOLE THING MADE *ME* TERRIBLY DEPRESSED!
DEPRESSED? WHY?
I NEVER REALIZED HOW *POOR* I REALLY AM!
END

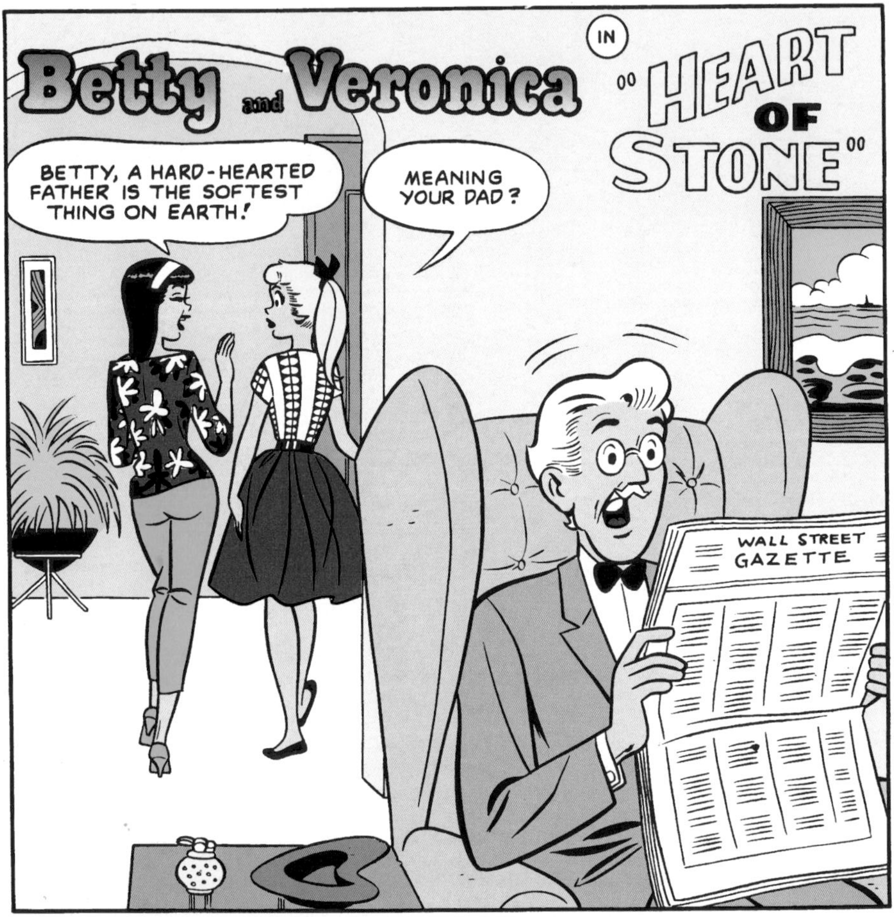
Betty and Veronica
IN
"HEART OF STONE"
BETTY, A HARD-HEARTED FATHER IS THE SOFTEST THING ON EARTH!
MEANING YOUR DAD?
WALL STREET GAZETTE

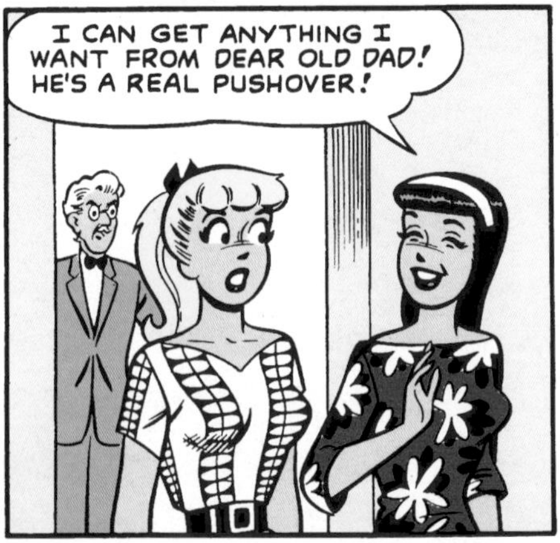
I CAN GET ANYTHING I WANT FROM DEAR OLD DAD! HE'S A REAL PUSHOVER!

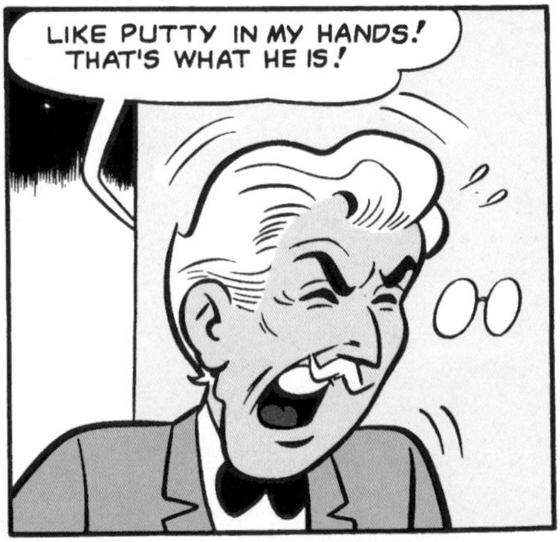
LIKE PUTTY IN MY HANDS! THAT'S WHAT HE IS!

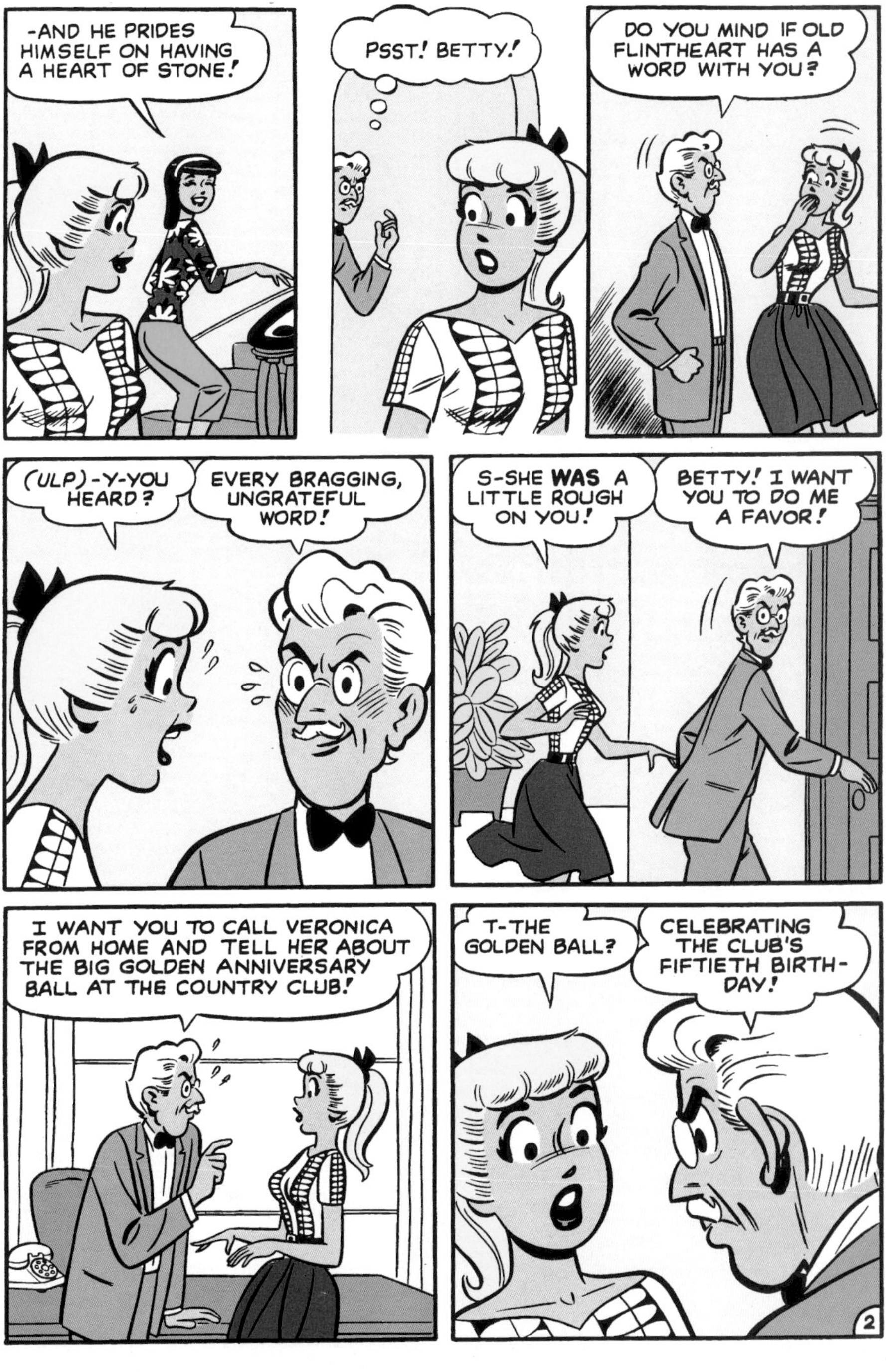
-AND HE PRIDES HIMSELF ON HAVING A HEART OF STONE!
PSST! BETTY!
DO YOU MIND IF OLD FLINTHEART HAS A WORD WITH YOU?
(ULP)-Y-YOU HEARD?
EVERY BRAGGING, UNGRATEFUL WORD!
S-SHE **WAS** A LITTLE ROUGH ON YOU!
BETTY! I WANT YOU TO DO ME A FAVOR!
I WANT YOU TO CALL VERONICA FROM HOME AND TELL HER ABOUT THE BIG GOLDEN ANNIVERSARY BALL AT THE COUNTRY CLUB!
T-THE GOLDEN BALL?
CELEBRATING THE CLUB'S FIFTIETH BIRTH-DAY!
2

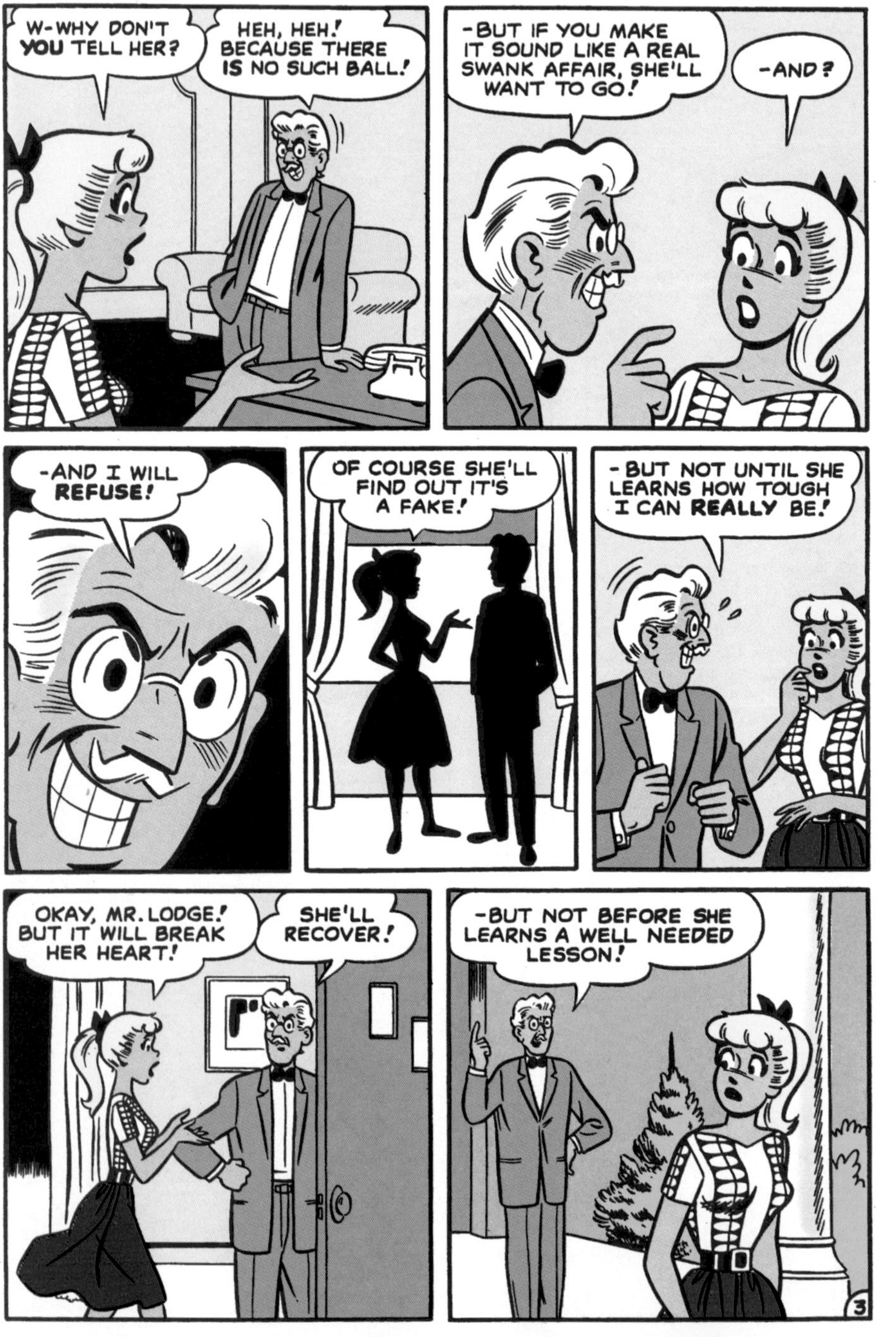
W-WHY DON'T **YOU** TELL HER?
HEH, HEH! BECAUSE THERE **IS** NO SUCH BALL!
-BUT IF YOU MAKE IT SOUND LIKE A REAL SWANK AFFAIR, SHE'LL WANT TO GO!
-AND?
-AND I WILL **REFUSE**!
OF COURSE SHE'LL FIND OUT IT'S A FAKE!
-BUT NOT UNTIL SHE LEARNS HOW TOUGH I CAN **REALLY** BE!
OKAY, MR. LODGE! BUT IT WILL BREAK HER HEART!
SHE'LL RECOVER!
-BUT NOT BEFORE SHE LEARNS A WELL NEEDED LESSON!
3

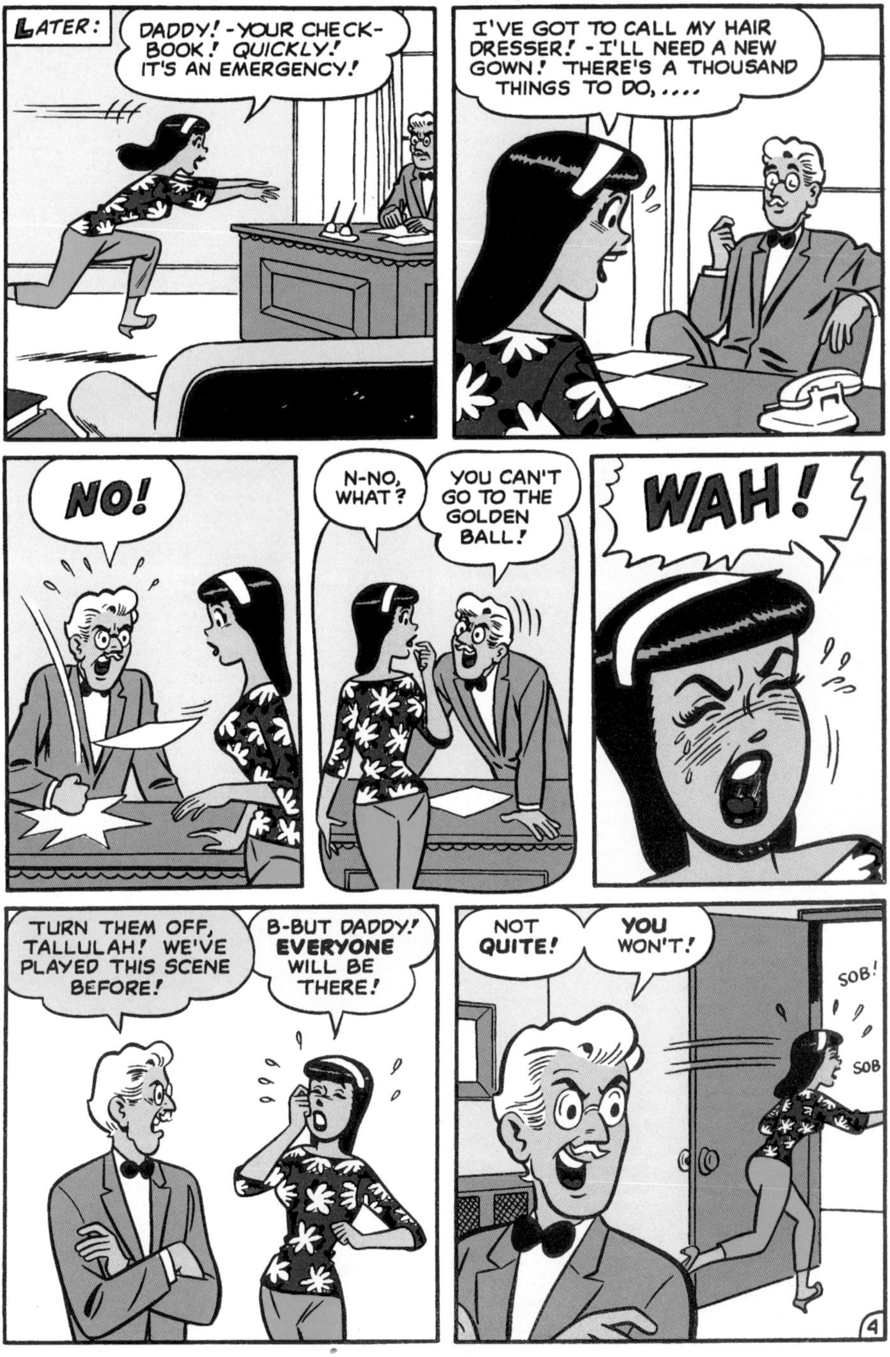
LATER:
DADDY! -YOUR CHECK-BOOK! QUICKLY! IT'S AN EMERGENCY!
I'VE GOT TO CALL MY HAIR DRESSER! - I'LL NEED A NEW GOWN! THERE'S A THOUSAND THINGS TO DO, ...
NO!
N-NO, WHAT?
YOU CAN'T GO TO THE GOLDEN BALL!
WAH!
TURN THEM OFF, TALLULAH! WE'VE PLAYED THIS SCENE BEFORE!
B-BUT DADDY! EVERYONE WILL BE THERE!
NOT QUITE!
YOU WON'T!
SOB!
SOB
4

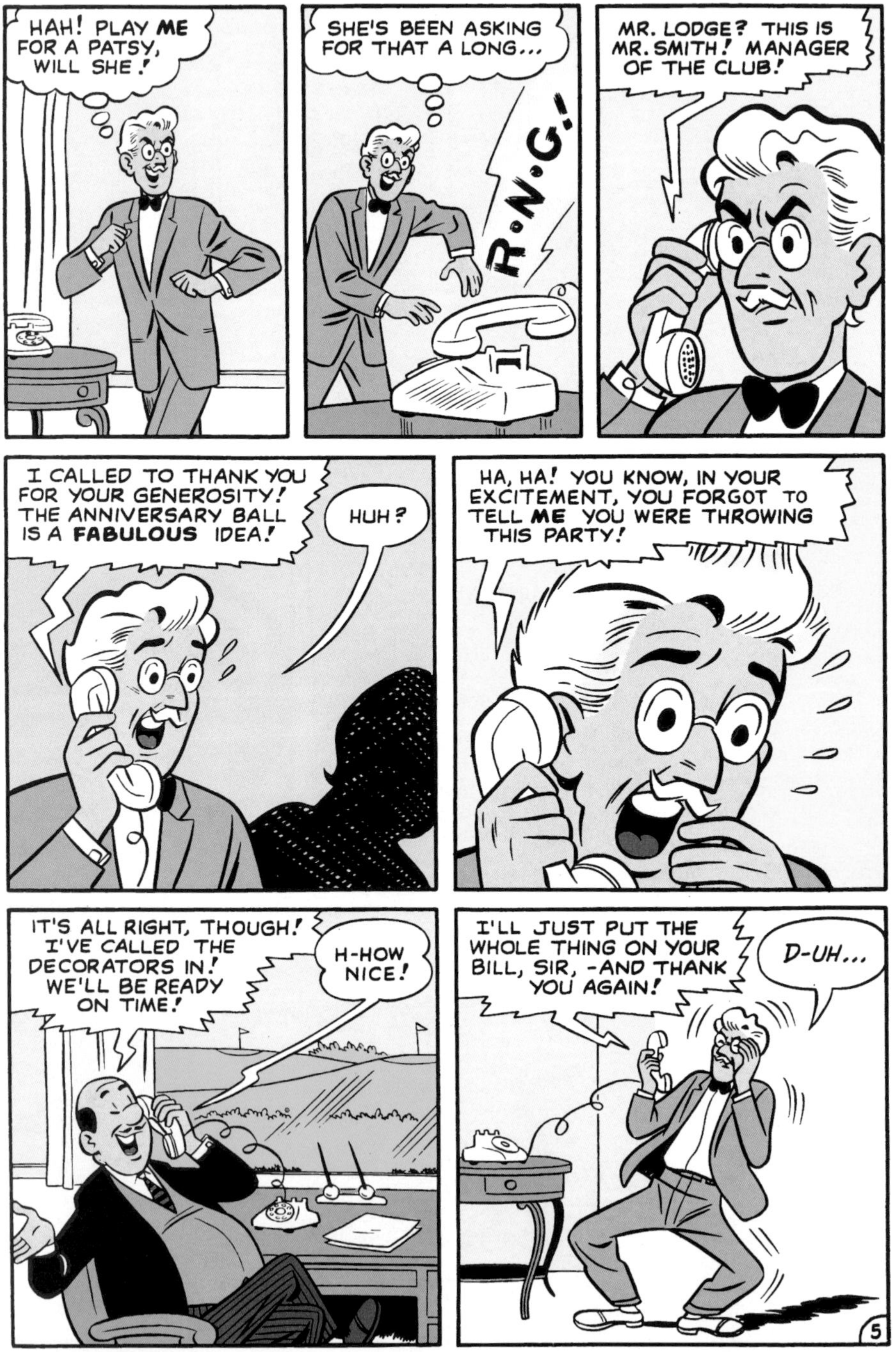
HAH! PLAY **ME** FOR A PATSY, WILL SHE!
SHE'S BEEN ASKING FOR THAT A LONG...
R-N-G!
MR. LODGE? THIS IS MR. SMITH! MANAGER OF THE CLUB!
I CALLED TO THANK YOU FOR YOUR GENEROSITY! THE ANNIVERSARY BALL IS A **FABULOUS** IDEA!
HUH?
HA, HA! YOU KNOW, IN YOUR EXCITEMENT, YOU FORGOT TO TELL **ME** YOU WERE THROWING THIS PARTY!
IT'S ALL RIGHT, THOUGH! I'VE CALLED THE DECORATORS IN! WE'LL BE READY ON TIME!
H-HOW NICE!
I'LL JUST PUT THE WHOLE THING ON YOUR BILL, SIR, -AND THANK YOU AGAIN!
D-UH...
5

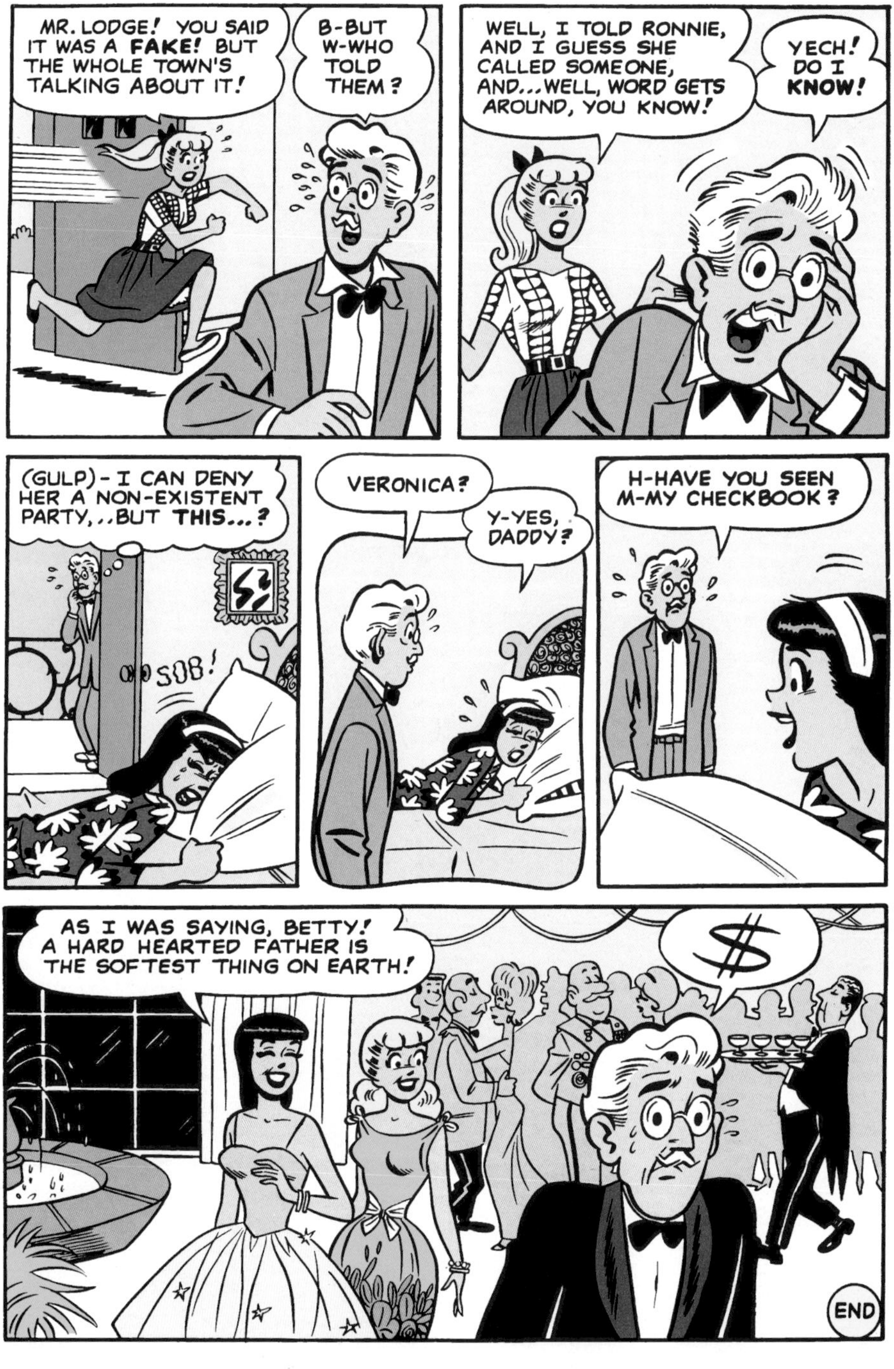
MR. LODGE! YOU SAID IT WAS A FAKE! BUT THE WHOLE TOWN'S TALKING ABOUT IT!
B-BUT W-WHO TOLD THEM?
WELL, I TOLD RONNIE, AND I GUESS SHE CALLED SOMEONE, AND...WELL, WORD GETS AROUND, YOU KNOW!
YECH! DO I KNOW!
(GULP)- I CAN DENY HER A NON-EXISTENT PARTY,..BUT THIS...?
SOB!
VERONICA?
Y-YES, DADDY?
H-HAVE YOU SEEN M-MY CHECKBOOK?
AS I WAS SAYING, BETTY! A HARD HEARTED FATHER IS THE SOFTEST THING ON EARTH!
$
END

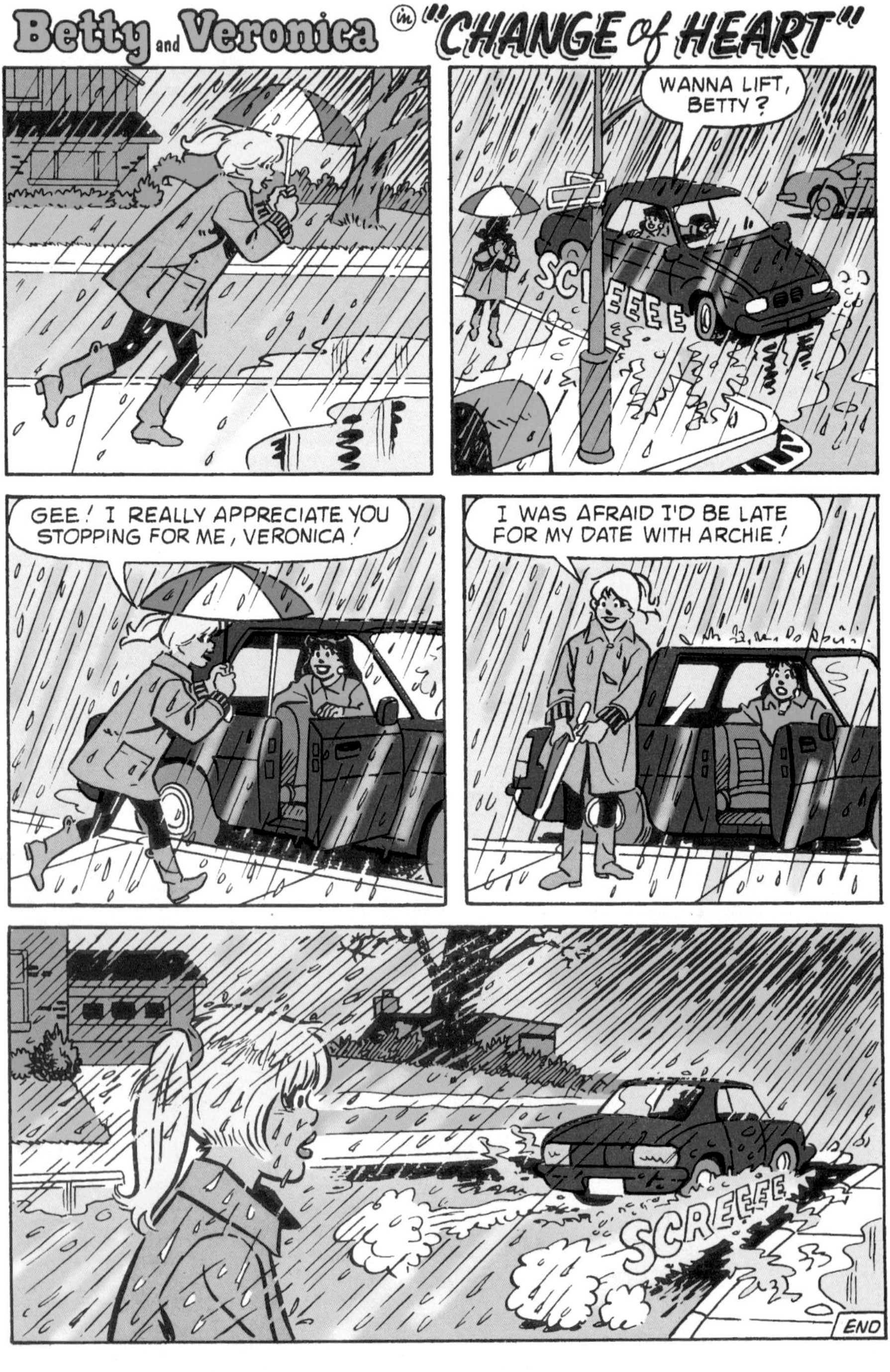
Betty and Veronica in "CHANGE of HEART"
WANNA LIFT, BETTY?
SCREEEEE
GEE! I REALLY APPRECIATE YOU STOPPING FOR ME, VERONICA!
I WAS AFRAID I'D BE LATE FOR MY DATE WITH ARCHIE!
SCREEEEE
END

Veronica in "Let's Veg Out"

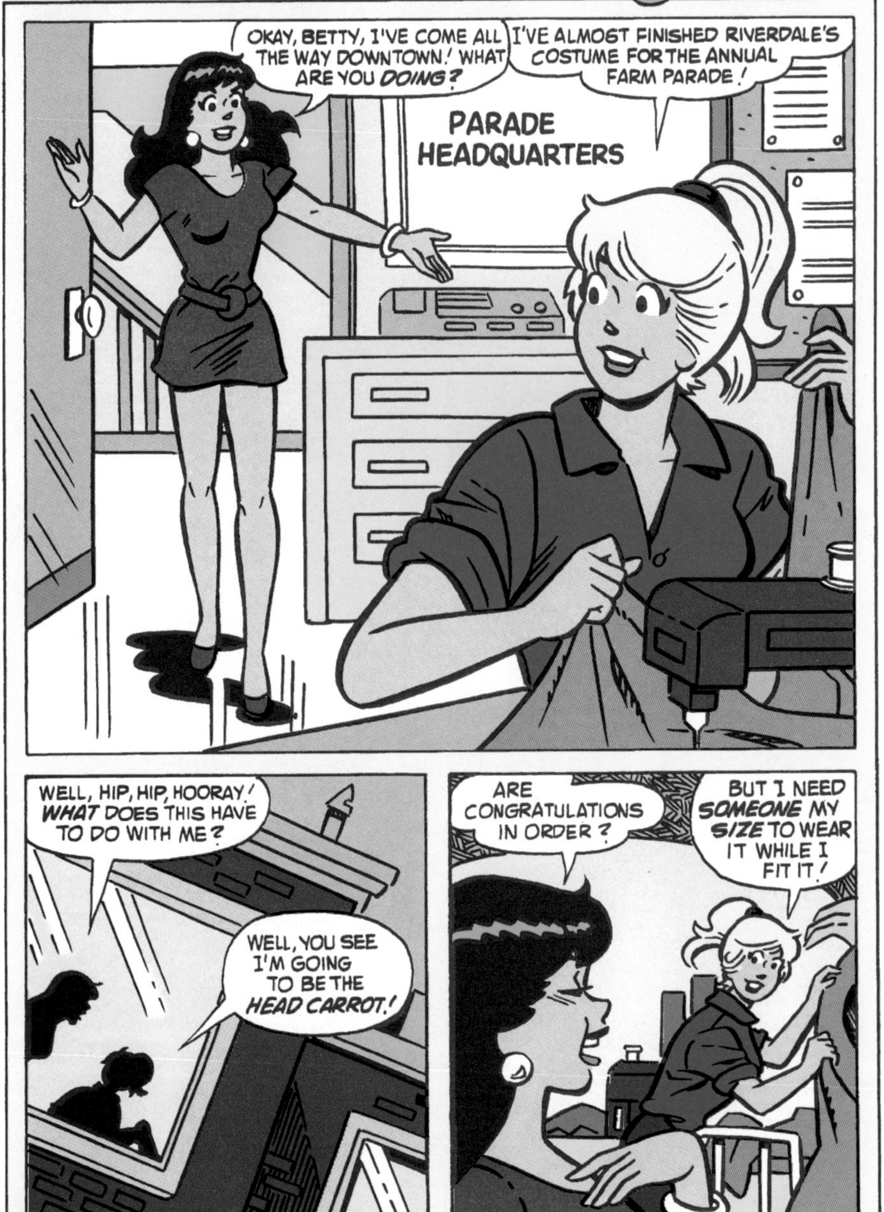
OKAY, BETTY, I'VE COME ALL THE WAY DOWNTOWN! WHAT ARE YOU DOING?
I'VE ALMOST FINISHED RIVERDALE'S COSTUME FOR THE ANNUAL FARM PARADE!
PARADE HEADQUARTERS
WELL, HIP, HIP, HOORAY! WHAT DOES THIS HAVE TO DO WITH ME?
WELL, YOU SEE I'M GOING TO BE THE HEAD CARROT!
ARE CONGRATULATIONS IN ORDER?
BUT I NEED SOMEONE MY SIZE TO WEAR IT WHILE I FIT IT!

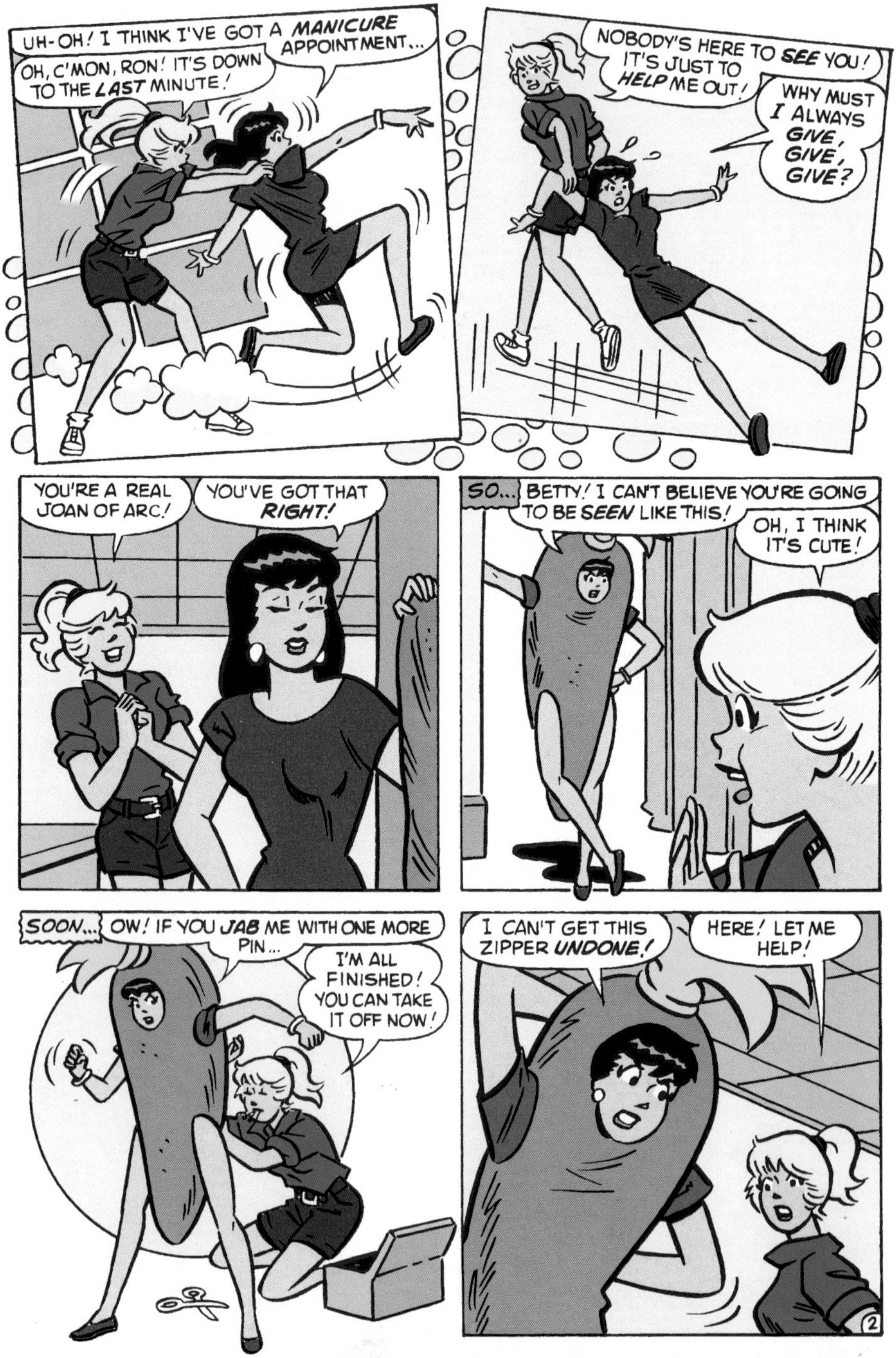
UH-OH! I THINK I'VE GOT A MANICURE APPOINTMENT...
OH, C'MON, RON! IT'S DOWN TO THE LAST MINUTE!
NOBODY'S HERE TO SEE YOU! IT'S JUST TO HELP ME OUT!
WHY MUST I ALWAYS GIVE, GIVE, GIVE?
YOU'RE A REAL JOAN OF ARC!
YOU'VE GOT THAT RIGHT!
SO...
BETTY! I CAN'T BELIEVE YOU'RE GOING TO BE SEEN LIKE THIS!
OH, I THINK IT'S CUTE!
SOON...
OW! IF YOU JAB ME WITH ONE MORE PIN...
I'M ALL FINISHED! YOU CAN TAKE IT OFF NOW!
I CAN'T GET THIS ZIPPER UNDONE!
HERE! LET ME HELP!
2

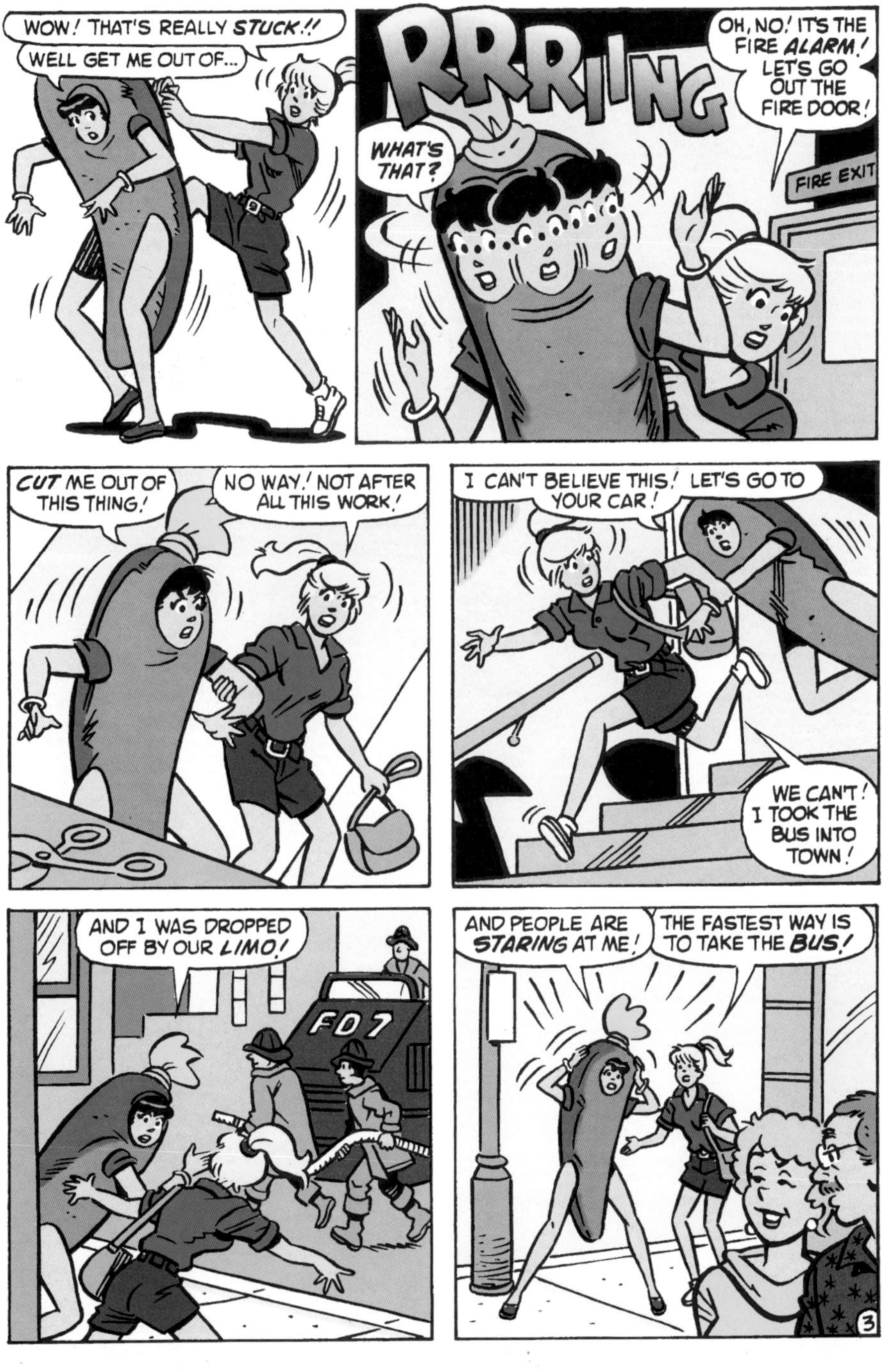
WOW! THAT'S REALLY STUCK!!
WELL GET ME OUT OF...
RRRIING
WHAT'S THAT?
OH, NO! IT'S THE FIRE ALARM! LET'S GO OUT THE FIRE DOOR!
FIRE EXIT
CUT ME OUT OF THIS THING!
NO WAY! NOT AFTER ALL THIS WORK!
I CAN'T BELIEVE THIS! LET'S GO TO YOUR CAR!
WE CAN'T! I TOOK THE BUS INTO TOWN!
AND I WAS DROPPED OFF BY OUR LIMO!
FD 7
AND PEOPLE ARE STARING AT ME!
THE FASTEST WAY IS TO TAKE THE BUS!
3

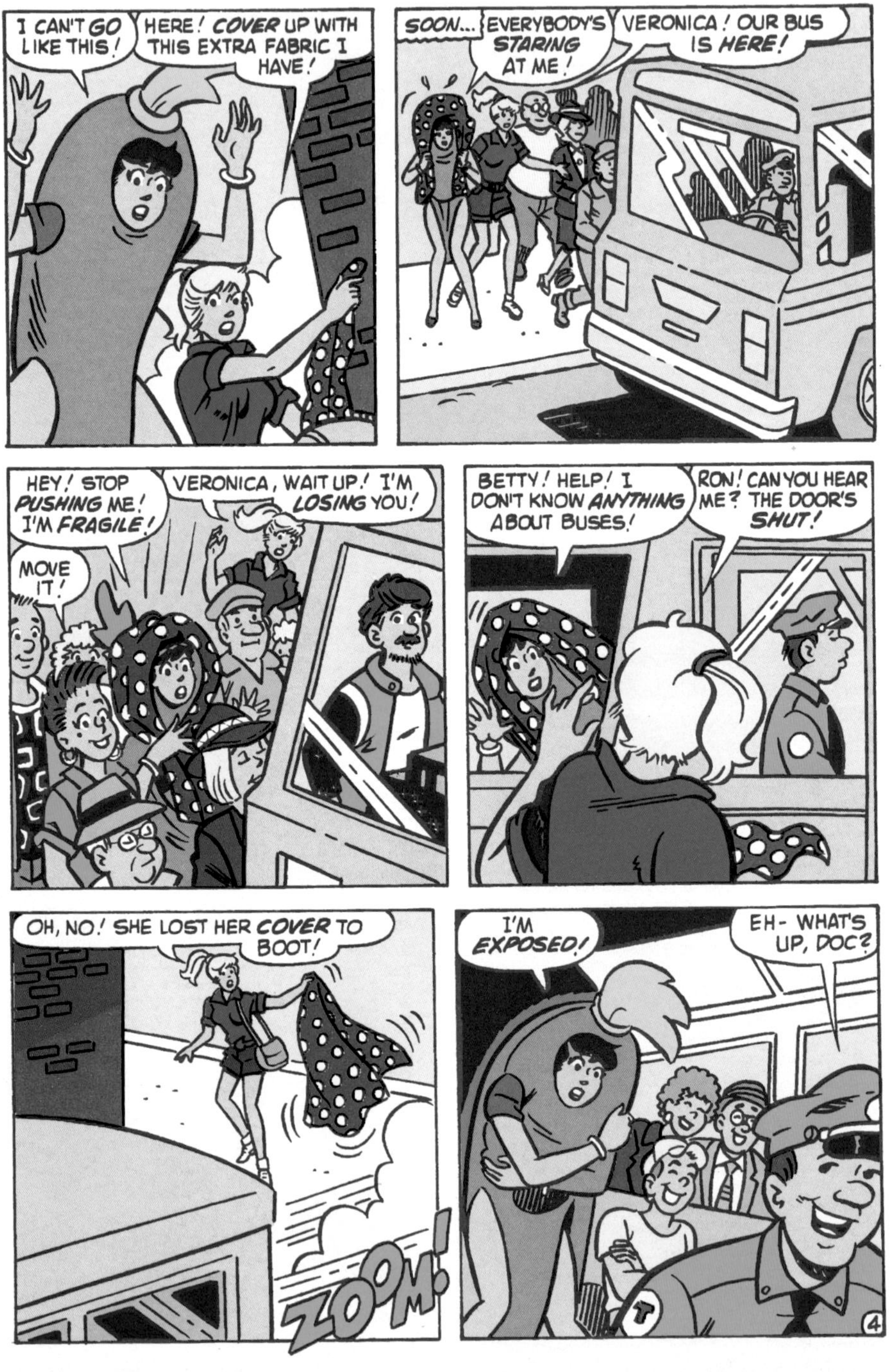
I CAN'T GO LIKE THIS!
HERE! COVER UP WITH THIS EXTRA FABRIC I HAVE!
SOON...
EVERYBODY'S STARING AT ME!
VERONICA! OUR BUS IS HERE!
HEY! STOP PUSHING ME! I'M FRAGILE!
VERONICA, WAIT UP! I'M LOSING YOU!
MOVE IT!
BETTY! HELP! I DON'T KNOW ANYTHING ABOUT BUSES!
RON! CAN YOU HEAR ME? THE DOOR'S SHUT!
OH, NO! SHE LOST HER COVER TO BOOT!
ZOOM!
I'M EXPOSED!
EH- WHAT'S UP, DOC?
4

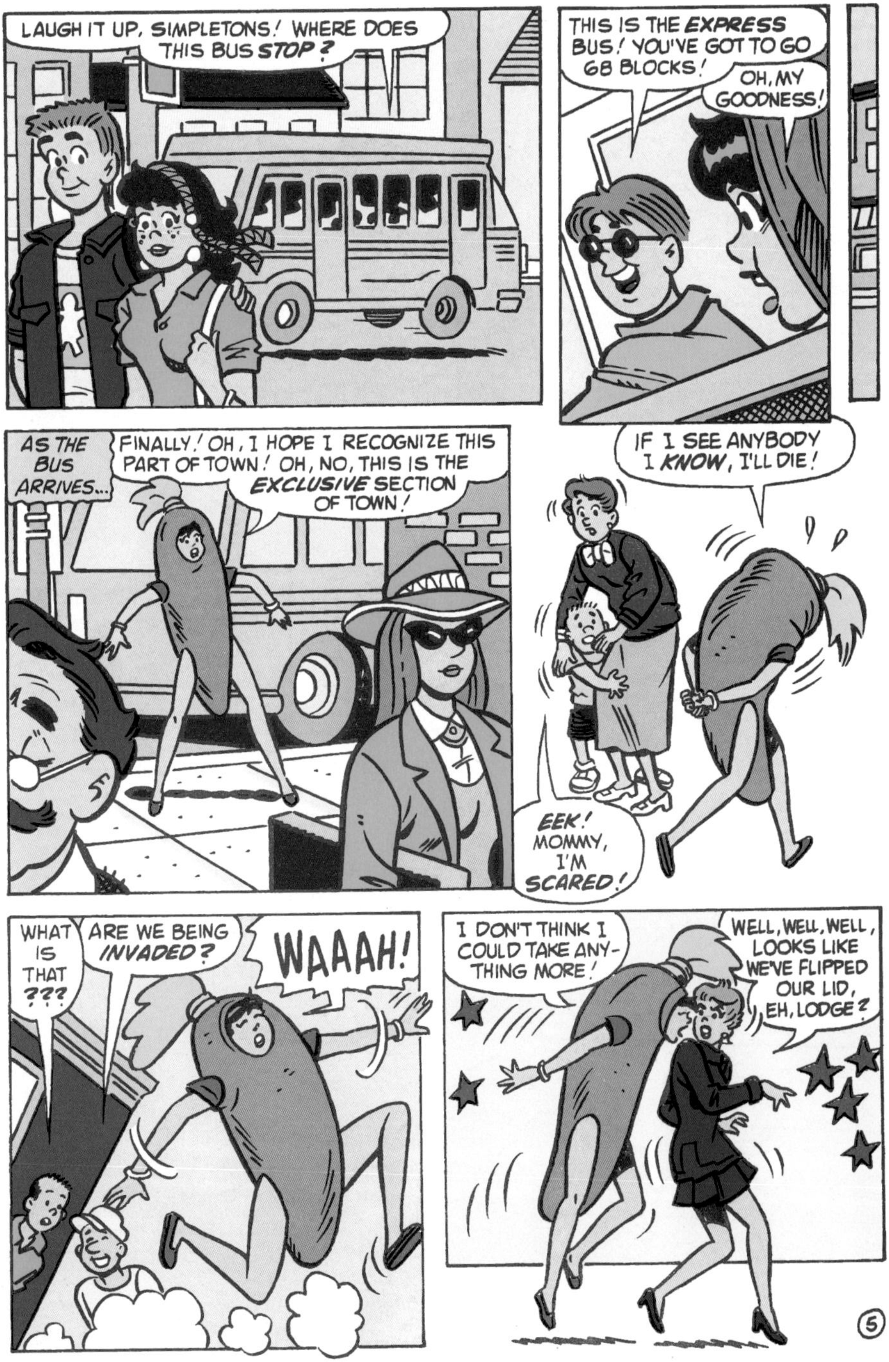
LAUGH IT UP, SIMPLETONS! WHERE DOES THIS BUS STOP?
THIS IS THE EXPRESS BUS! YOU'VE GOT TO GO 68 BLOCKS!
OH, MY GOODNESS!
AS THE BUS ARRIVES...
FINALLY! OH, I HOPE I RECOGNIZE THIS PART OF TOWN! OH, NO, THIS IS THE EXCLUSIVE SECTION OF TOWN!
IF I SEE ANYBODY I KNOW, I'LL DIE!
EEK! MOMMY, I'M SCARED!
WHAT IS THAT???
ARE WE BEING INVADED?
WAAAH!
I DON'T THINK I COULD TAKE ANYTHING MORE!
WELL, WELL, WELL, LOOKS LIKE WE'VE FLIPPED OUR LID, EH, LODGE?

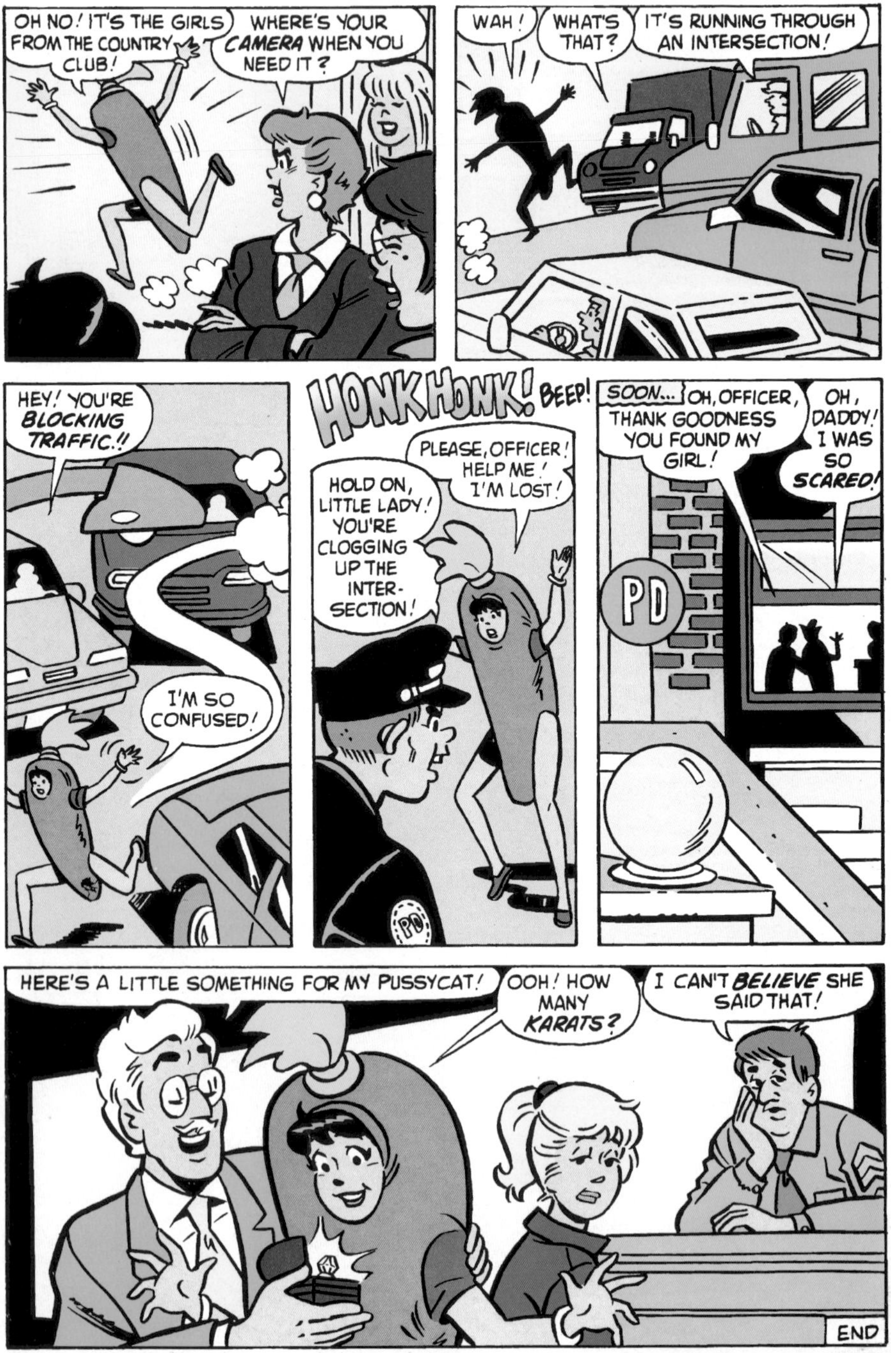
OH NO! IT'S THE GIRLS FROM THE COUNTRY CLUB!
WHERE'S YOUR *CAMERA* WHEN YOU NEED IT?
WAH!
WHAT'S THAT?
IT'S RUNNING THROUGH AN INTERSECTION!
HEY! YOU'RE *BLOCKING TRAFFIC!!*
I'M SO CONFUSED!
HONK HONK! BEEP!
PLEASE, OFFICER! HELP ME! I'M LOST!
HOLD ON, LITTLE LADY! YOU'RE CLOGGING UP THE INTER-SECTION!
PD
SOON...
OH, OFFICER, THANK GOODNESS YOU FOUND MY GIRL!
OH, DADDY! I WAS SO *SCARED!*
PD
HERE'S A LITTLE SOMETHING FOR MY PUSSYCAT!
OOH! HOW MANY *KARATS?*
I CAN'T *BELIEVE* SHE SAID THAT!
END

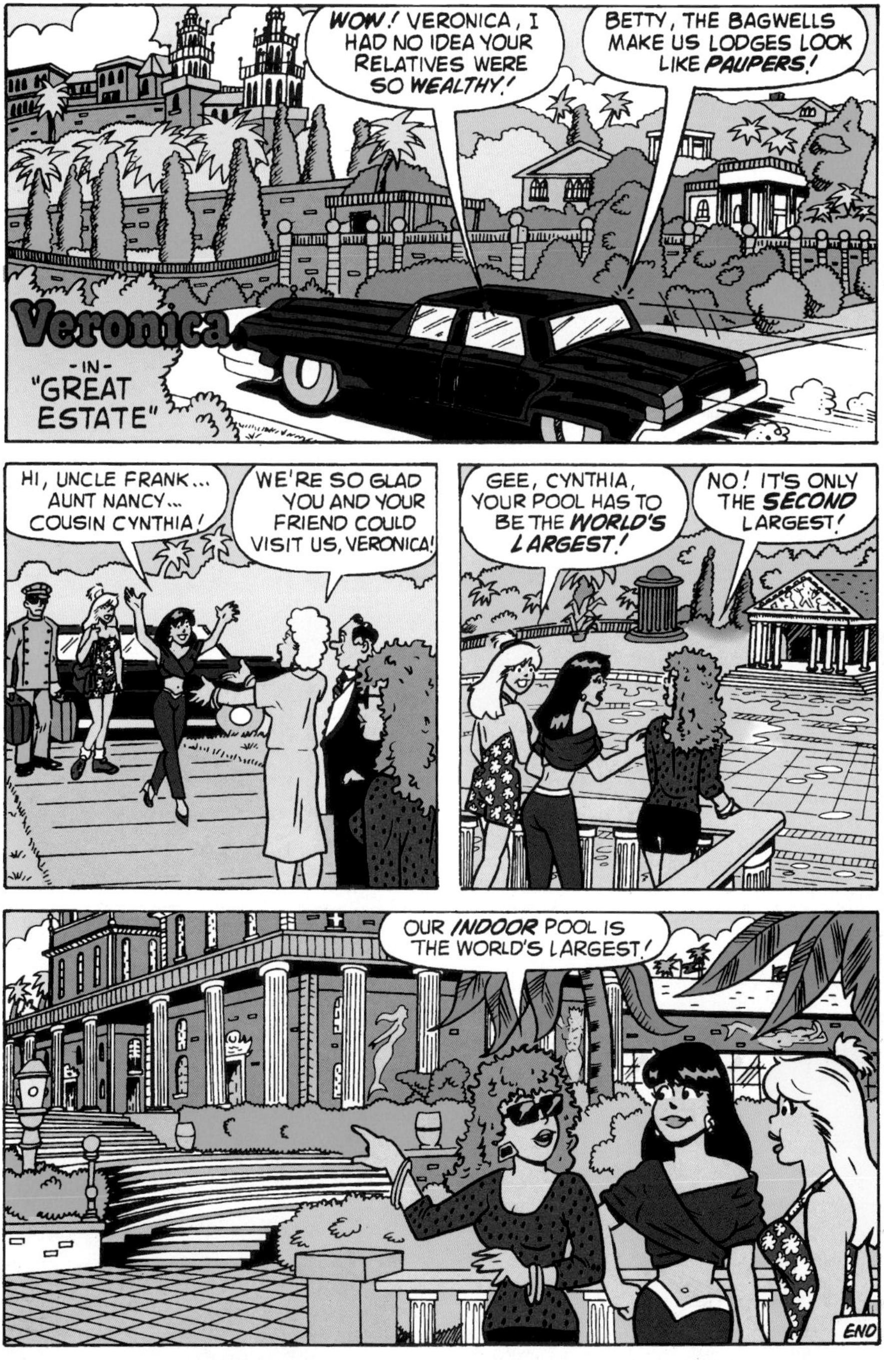
WOW! VERONICA, I HAD NO IDEA YOUR RELATIVES WERE SO WEALTHY!
BETTY, THE BAGWELLS MAKE US LODGES LOOK LIKE PAUPERS!
Veronica
-IN-
"GREAT ESTATE"
HI, UNCLE FRANK... AUNT NANCY... COUSIN CYNTHIA!
WE'RE SO GLAD YOU AND YOUR FRIEND COULD VISIT US, VERONICA!
GEE, CYNTHIA, YOUR POOL HAS TO BE THE WORLD'S LARGEST!
NO! IT'S ONLY THE SECOND LARGEST!
OUR INDOOR POOL IS THE WORLD'S LARGEST!
END

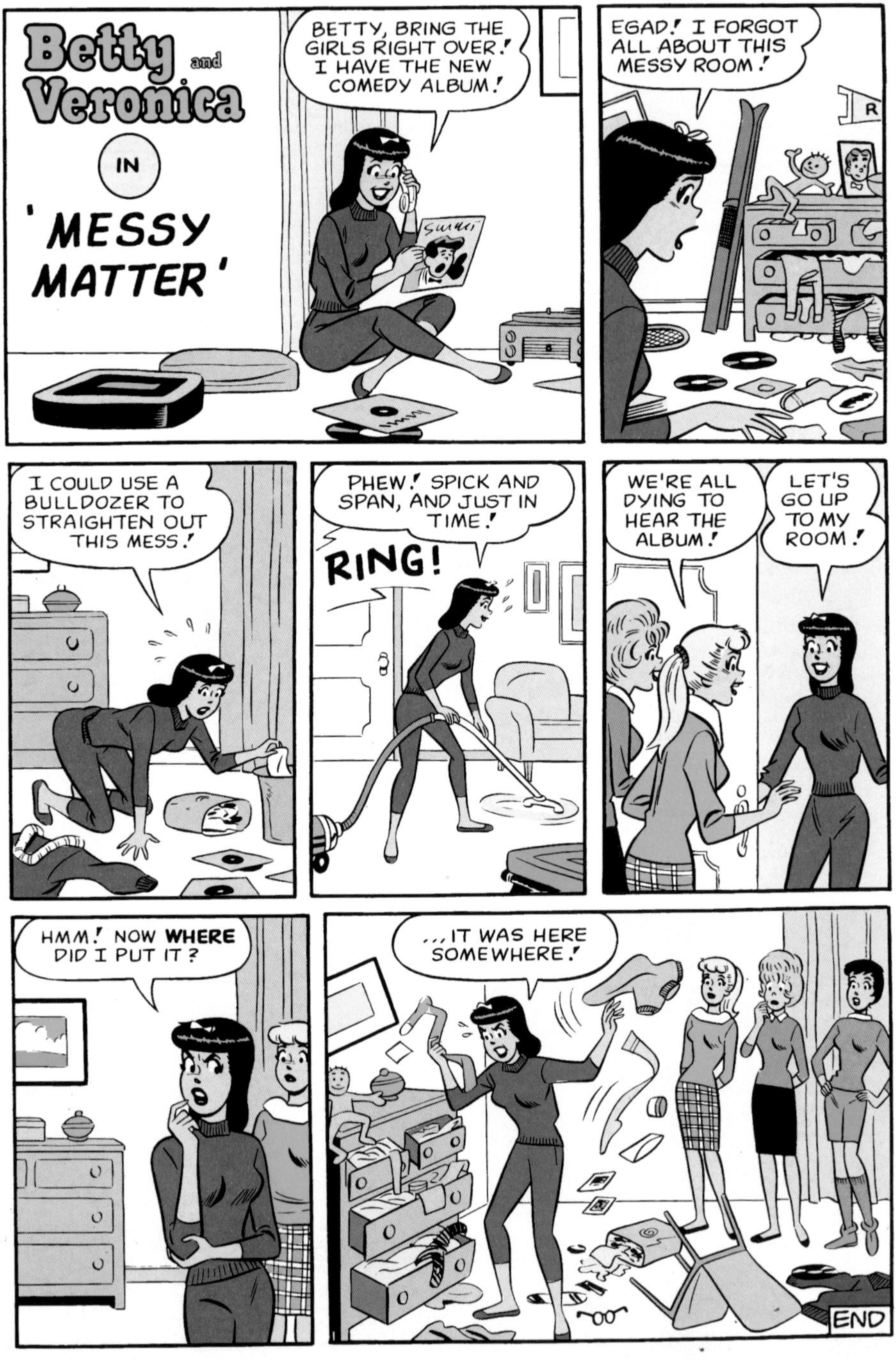
Betty and Veronica
IN
'MESSY MATTER'
BETTY, BRING THE GIRLS RIGHT OVER! I HAVE THE NEW COMEDY ALBUM!
EGAD! I FORGOT ALL ABOUT THIS MESSY ROOM!
I COULD USE A BULLDOZER TO STRAIGHTEN OUT THIS MESS!
PHEW! SPICK AND SPAN, AND JUST IN TIME!
RING!
WE'RE ALL DYING TO HEAR THE ALBUM!
LET'S GO UP TO MY ROOM!
HMM! NOW **WHERE** DID I PUT IT?
...IT WAS HERE SOMEWHERE!
END

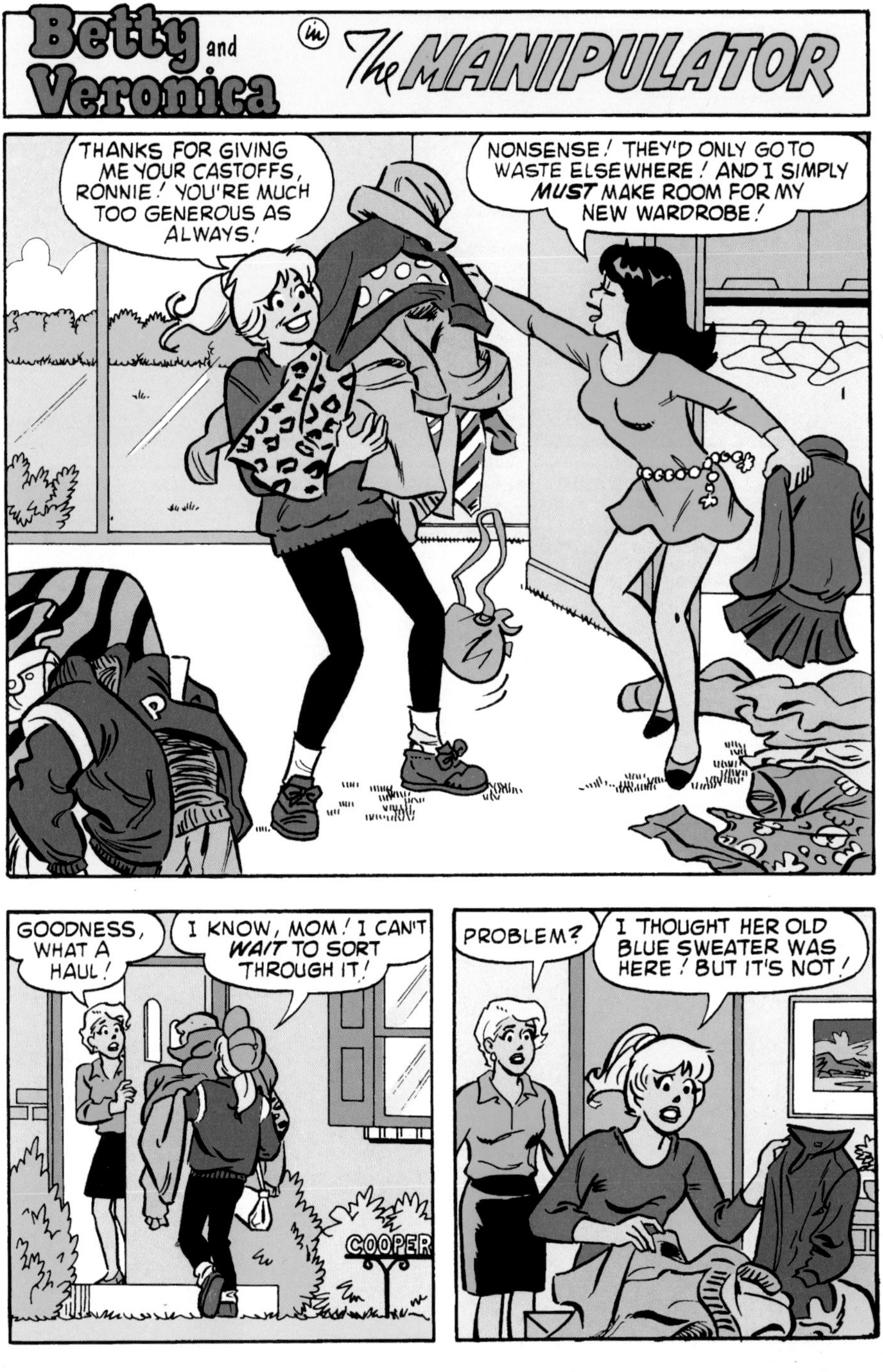
Betty and Veronica
in
The MANIPULATOR
THANKS FOR GIVING ME YOUR CASTOFFS, RONNIE! YOU'RE MUCH TOO GENEROUS AS ALWAYS!
NONSENSE! THEY'D ONLY GO TO WASTE ELSEWHERE! AND I SIMPLY MUST MAKE ROOM FOR MY NEW WARDROBE!
GOODNESS, WHAT A HAUL!
I KNOW, MOM! I CAN'T WAIT TO SORT THROUGH IT!
COOPER
PROBLEM?
I THOUGHT HER OLD BLUE SWEATER WAS HERE! BUT IT'S NOT!

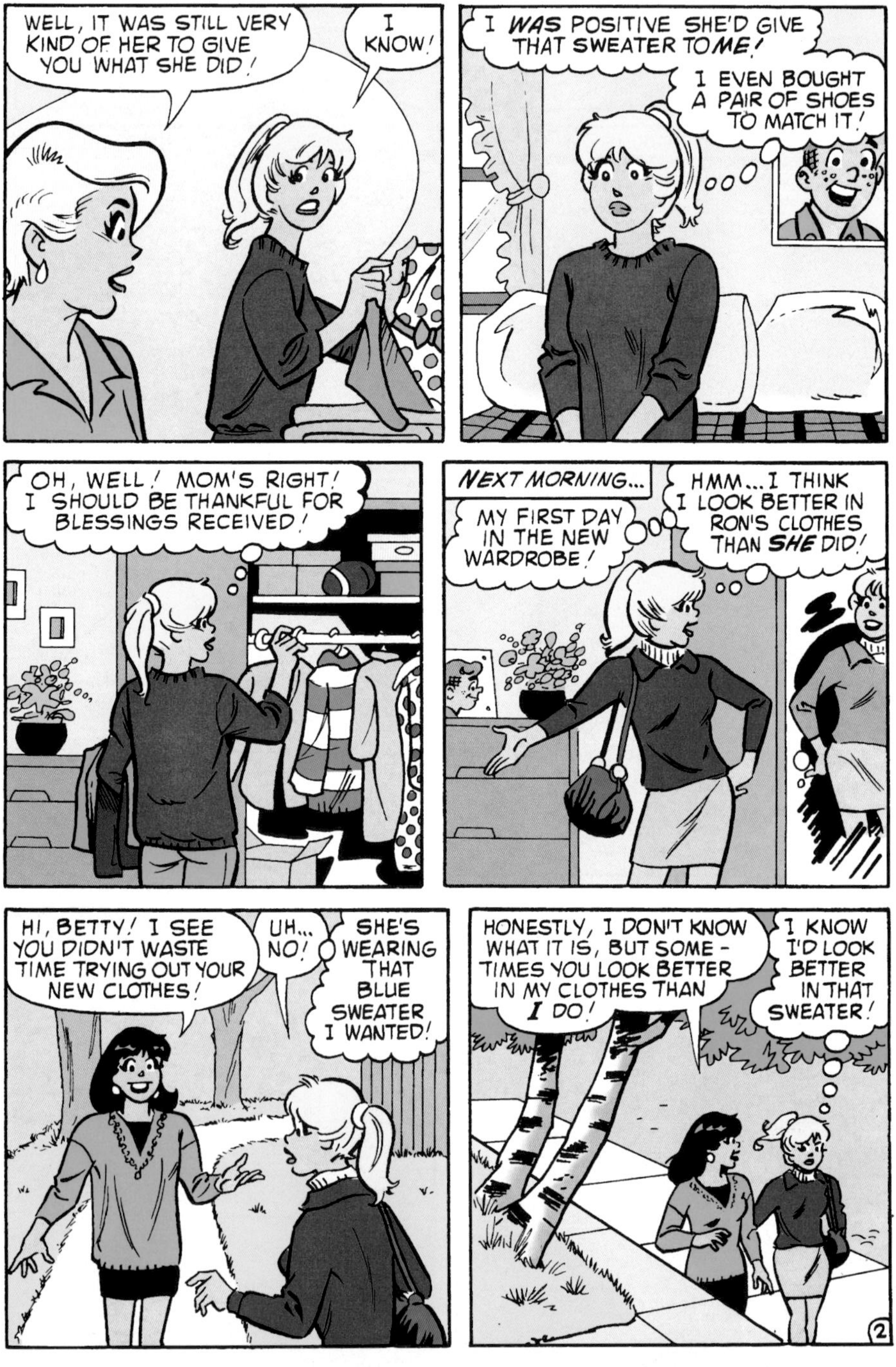
WELL, IT WAS STILL VERY KIND OF HER TO GIVE YOU WHAT SHE DID!
I KNOW!
I WAS POSITIVE SHE'D GIVE THAT SWEATER TO ME!
I EVEN BOUGHT A PAIR OF SHOES TO MATCH IT!
OH, WELL! MOM'S RIGHT! I SHOULD BE THANKFUL FOR BLESSINGS RECEIVED!
NEXT MORNING...
MY FIRST DAY IN THE NEW WARDROBE!
HMM... I THINK I LOOK BETTER IN RON'S CLOTHES THAN SHE DID!
HI, BETTY! I SEE YOU DIDN'T WASTE TIME TRYING OUT YOUR NEW CLOTHES!
UH... NO!
SHE'S WEARING THAT BLUE SWEATER I WANTED!
HONESTLY, I DON'T KNOW WHAT IT IS, BUT SOME-TIMES YOU LOOK BETTER IN MY CLOTHES THAN I DO!
I KNOW I'D LOOK BETTER IN THAT SWEATER!
2

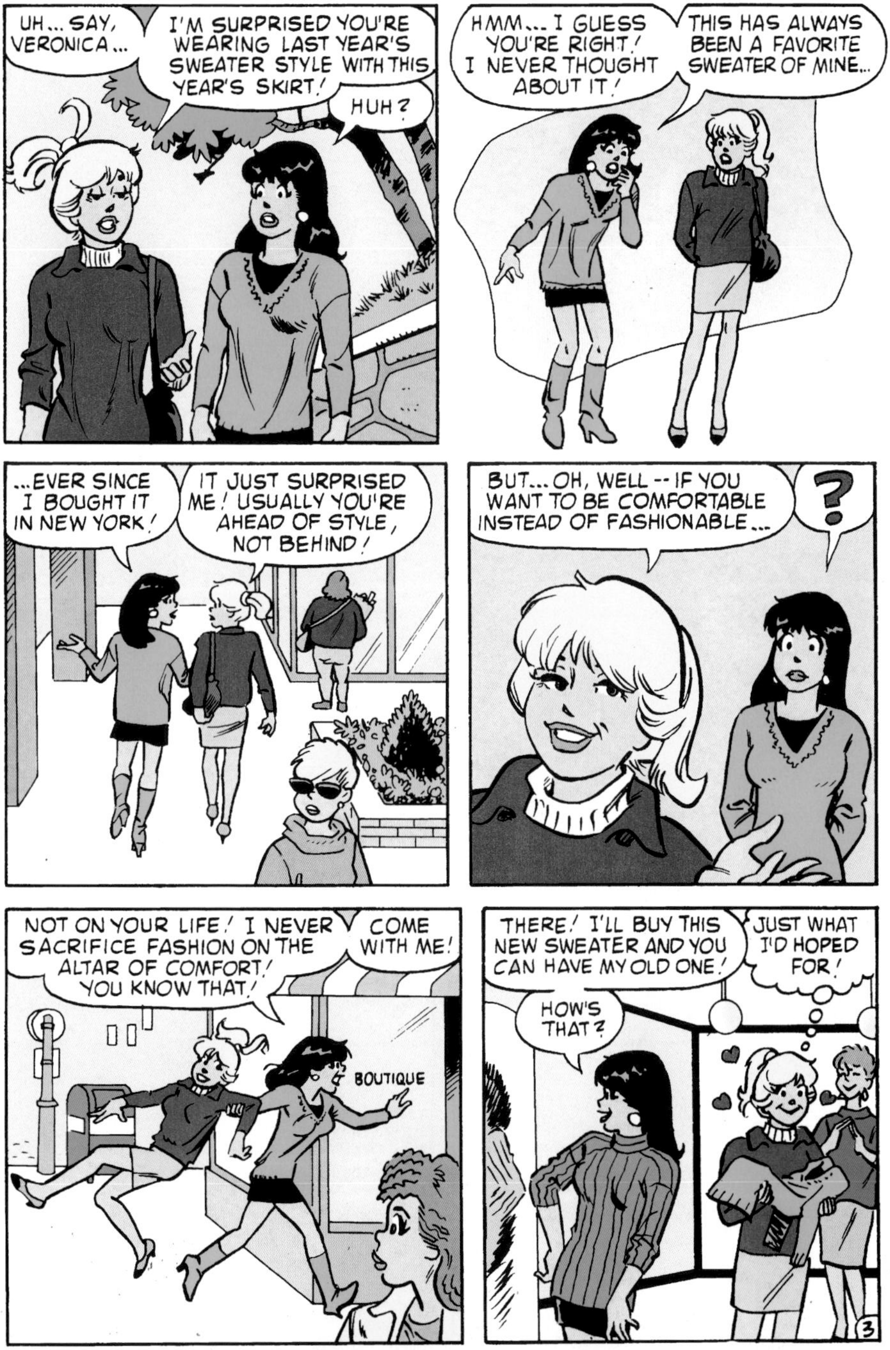
UH... SAY, VERONICA...
I'M SURPRISED YOU'RE WEARING LAST YEAR'S SWEATER STYLE WITH THIS YEAR'S SKIRT!
HUH?
HMM... I GUESS YOU'RE RIGHT! I NEVER THOUGHT ABOUT IT!
THIS HAS ALWAYS BEEN A FAVORITE SWEATER OF MINE...
...EVER SINCE I BOUGHT IT IN NEW YORK!
IT JUST SURPRISED ME! USUALLY YOU'RE AHEAD OF STYLE, NOT BEHIND!
BUT... OH, WELL -- IF YOU WANT TO BE COMFORTABLE INSTEAD OF FASHIONABLE...
?
NOT ON YOUR LIFE! I NEVER SACRIFICE FASHION ON THE ALTAR OF COMFORT! YOU KNOW THAT!
COME WITH ME!
BOUTIQUE
THERE! I'LL BUY THIS NEW SWEATER AND YOU CAN HAVE MY OLD ONE!
HOW'S THAT?
JUST WHAT I'D HOPED FOR!
3

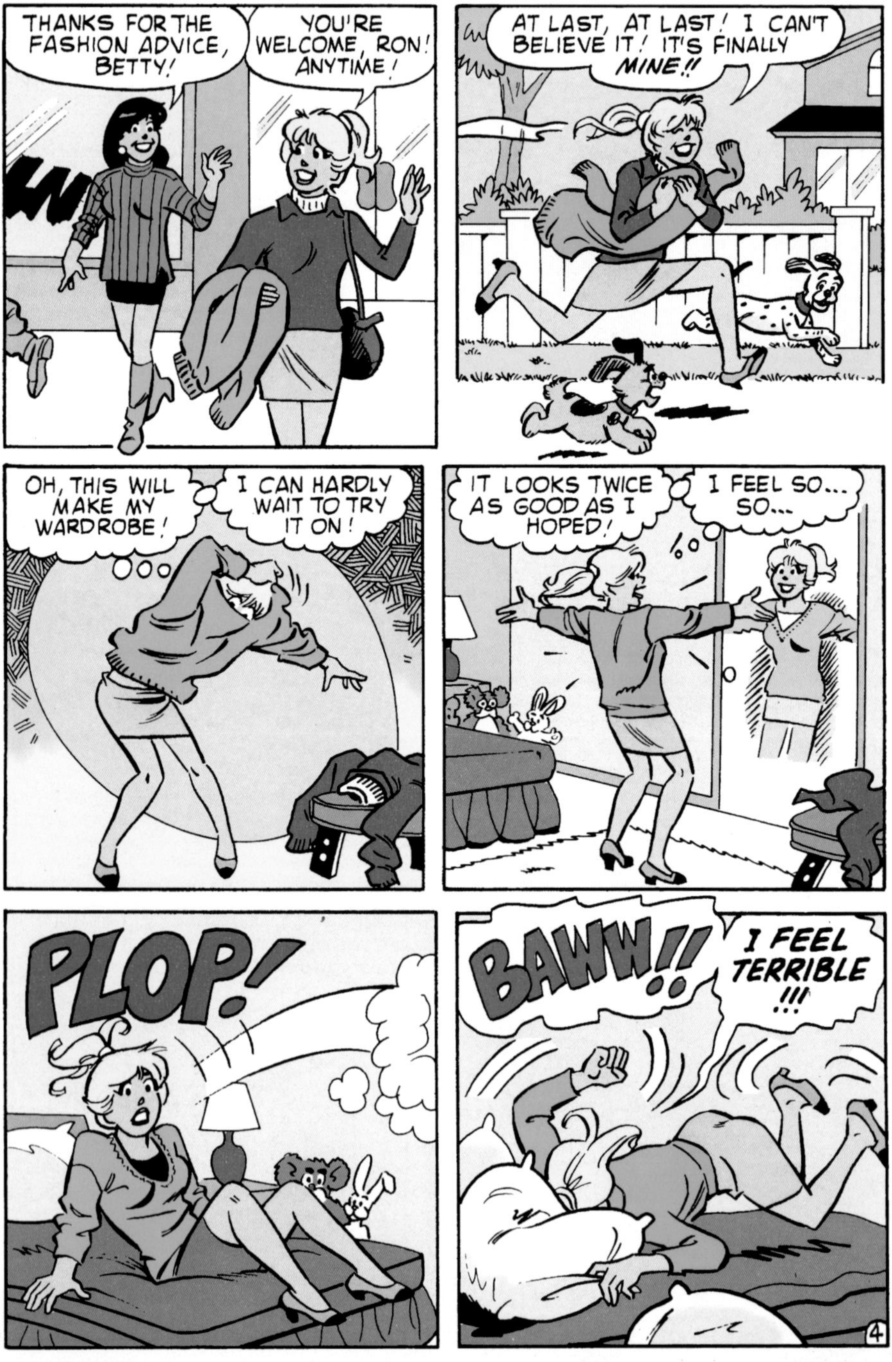
THANKS FOR THE FASHION ADVICE, BETTY!
YOU'RE WELCOME, RON! ANYTIME!
AT LAST, AT LAST! I CAN'T BELIEVE IT! IT'S FINALLY MINE!!
OH, THIS WILL MAKE MY WARDROBE!
I CAN HARDLY WAIT TO TRY IT ON!
IT LOOKS TWICE AS GOOD AS I HOPED!
I FEEL SO... SO...
PLOP!
BAWW!!
I FEEL TERRIBLE!!!
4

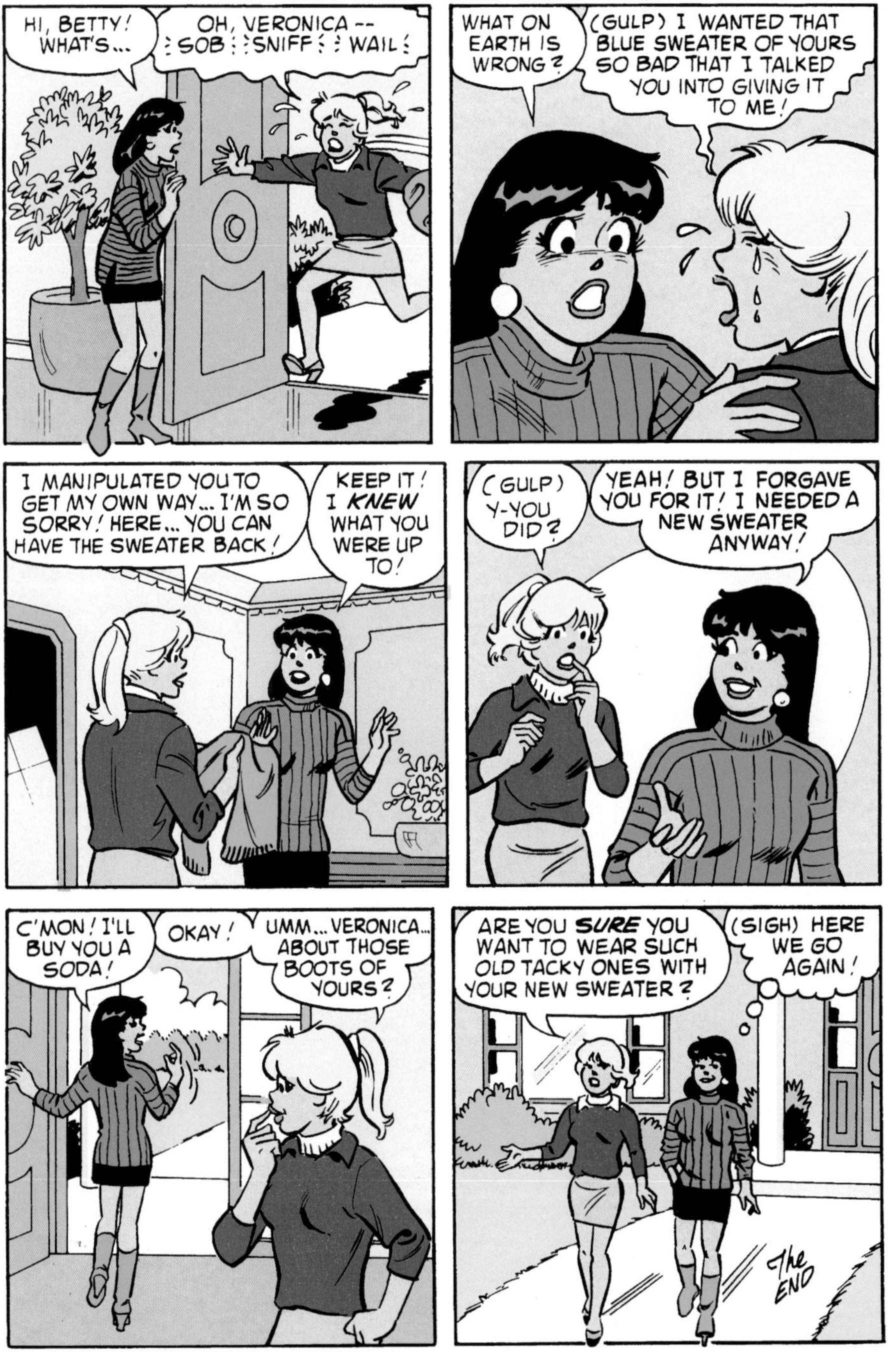
HI, BETTY! WHAT'S...
OH, VERONICA -- SOB SNIFF WAIL
WHAT ON EARTH IS WRONG?
(GULP) I WANTED THAT BLUE SWEATER OF YOURS SO BAD THAT I TALKED YOU INTO GIVING IT TO ME!
I MANIPULATED YOU TO GET MY OWN WAY... I'M SO SORRY! HERE... YOU CAN HAVE THE SWEATER BACK!
KEEP IT! I KNEW WHAT YOU WERE UP TO!
(GULP) Y-YOU DID?
YEAH! BUT I FORGAVE YOU FOR IT! I NEEDED A NEW SWEATER ANYWAY!
C'MON! I'LL BUY YOU A SODA!
OKAY!
UMM... VERONICA... ABOUT THOSE BOOTS OF YOURS?
ARE YOU SURE YOU WANT TO WEAR SUCH OLD TACKY ONES WITH YOUR NEW SWEATER?
(SIGH) HERE WE GO AGAIN!
The END

MR. LODGE EXPLAINS.... The LASS WORD

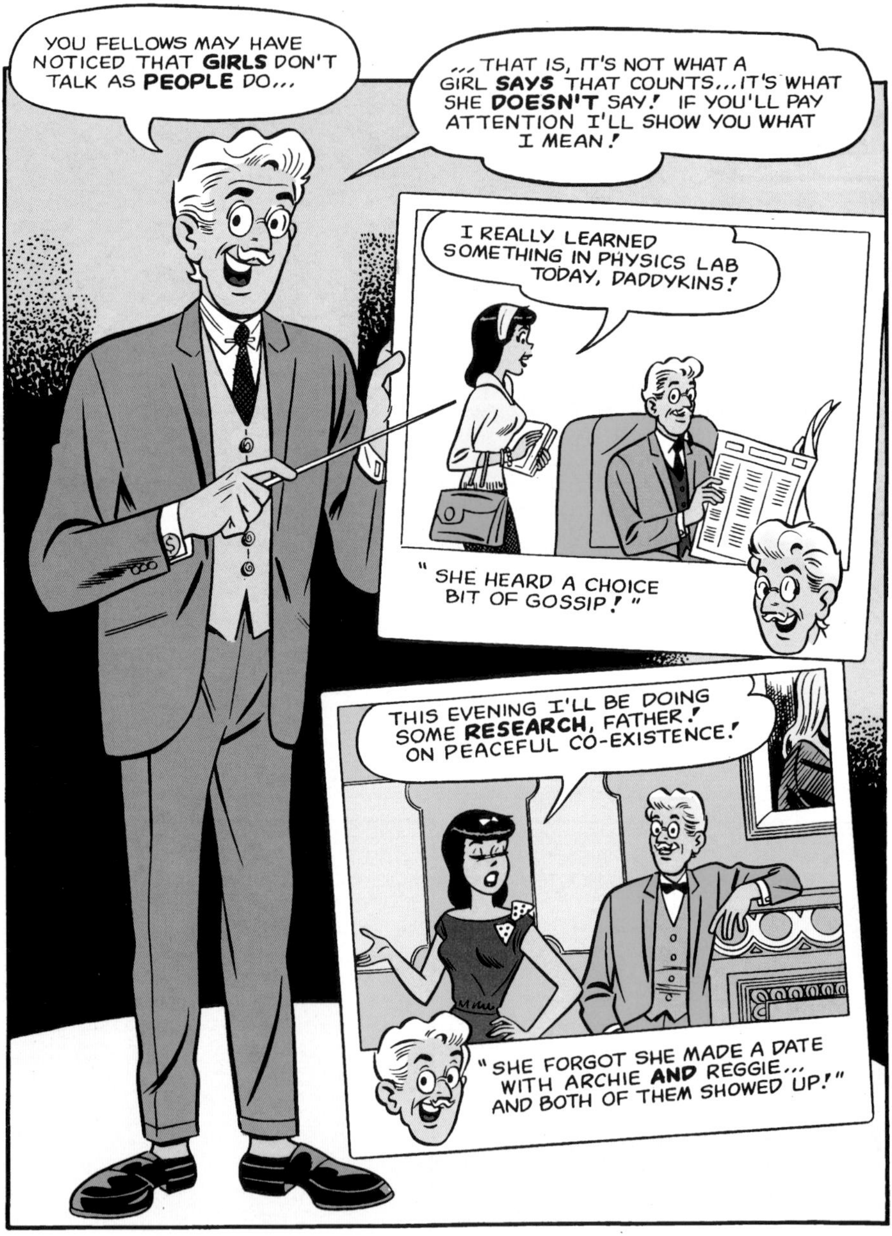
YOU FELLOWS MAY HAVE NOTICED THAT **GIRLS** DON'T TALK AS **PEOPLE** DO...
...THAT IS, IT'S NOT WHAT A GIRL **SAYS** THAT COUNTS...IT'S WHAT SHE **DOESN'T** SAY! IF YOU'LL PAY ATTENTION I'LL SHOW YOU WHAT I MEAN!
I REALLY LEARNED SOMETHING IN PHYSICS LAB TODAY, DADDYKINS!
" SHE HEARD A CHOICE BIT OF GOSSIP! "
THIS EVENING I'LL BE DOING SOME **RESEARCH**, FATHER! ON PEACEFUL CO-EXISTENCE!
" SHE FORGOT SHE MADE A DATE WITH ARCHIE **AND** REGGIE... AND BOTH OF THEM SHOWED UP! "

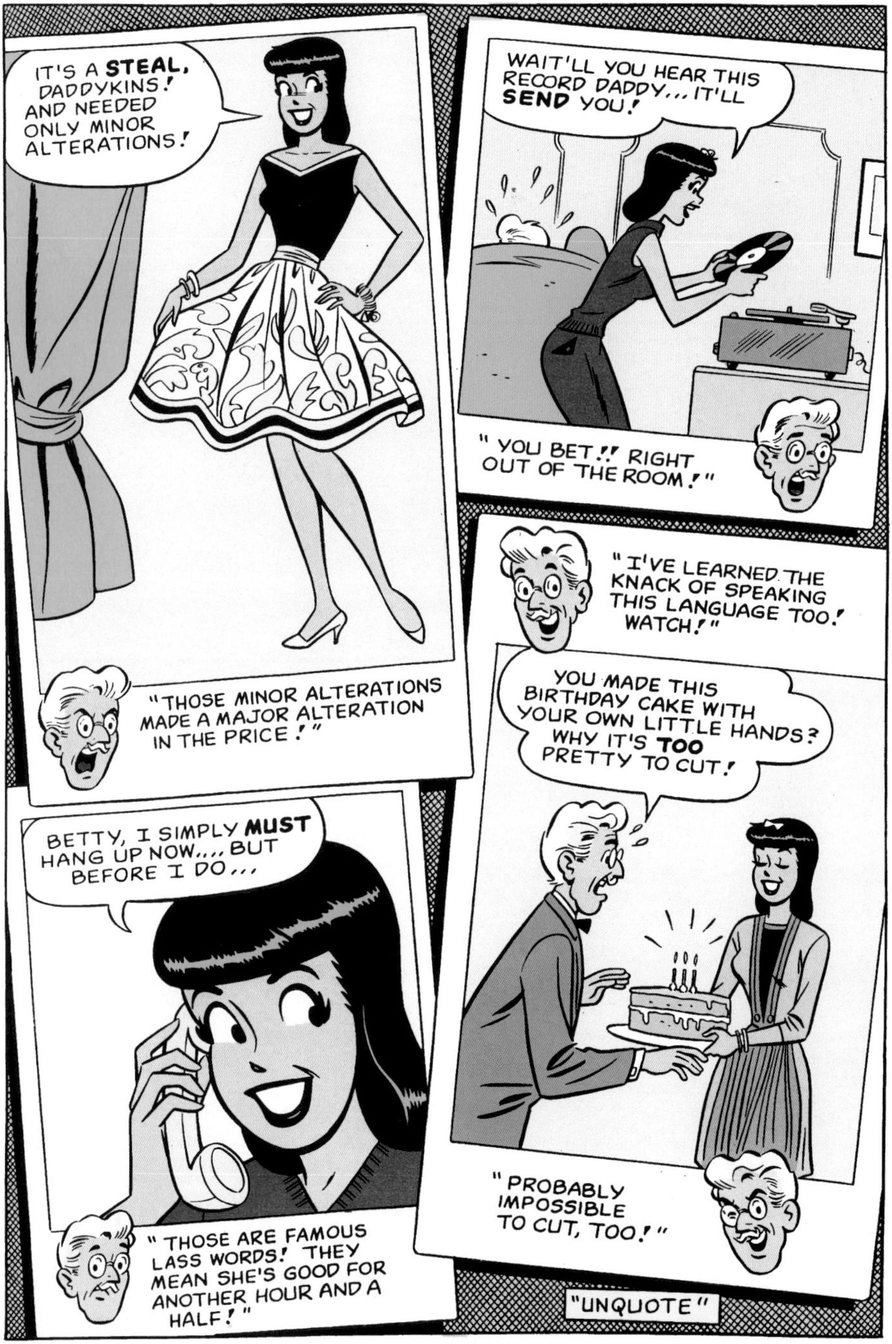
IT'S A STEAL, DADDYKINS! AND NEEDED ONLY MINOR ALTERATIONS!
"THOSE MINOR ALTERATIONS MADE A MAJOR ALTERATION IN THE PRICE!"
WAIT'LL YOU HEAR THIS RECORD DADDY... IT'LL SEND YOU!
"YOU BET!! RIGHT OUT OF THE ROOM!"
BETTY, I SIMPLY MUST HANG UP NOW.... BUT BEFORE I DO...
"THOSE ARE FAMOUS LASS WORDS! THEY MEAN SHE'S GOOD FOR ANOTHER HOUR AND A HALF!"
"I'VE LEARNED THE KNACK OF SPEAKING THIS LANGUAGE TOO! WATCH!"
YOU MADE THIS BIRTHDAY CAKE WITH YOUR OWN LITTLE HANDS? WHY IT'S TOO PRETTY TO CUT!
"PROBABLY IMPOSSIBLE TO CUT, TOO!"
"UNQUOTE"

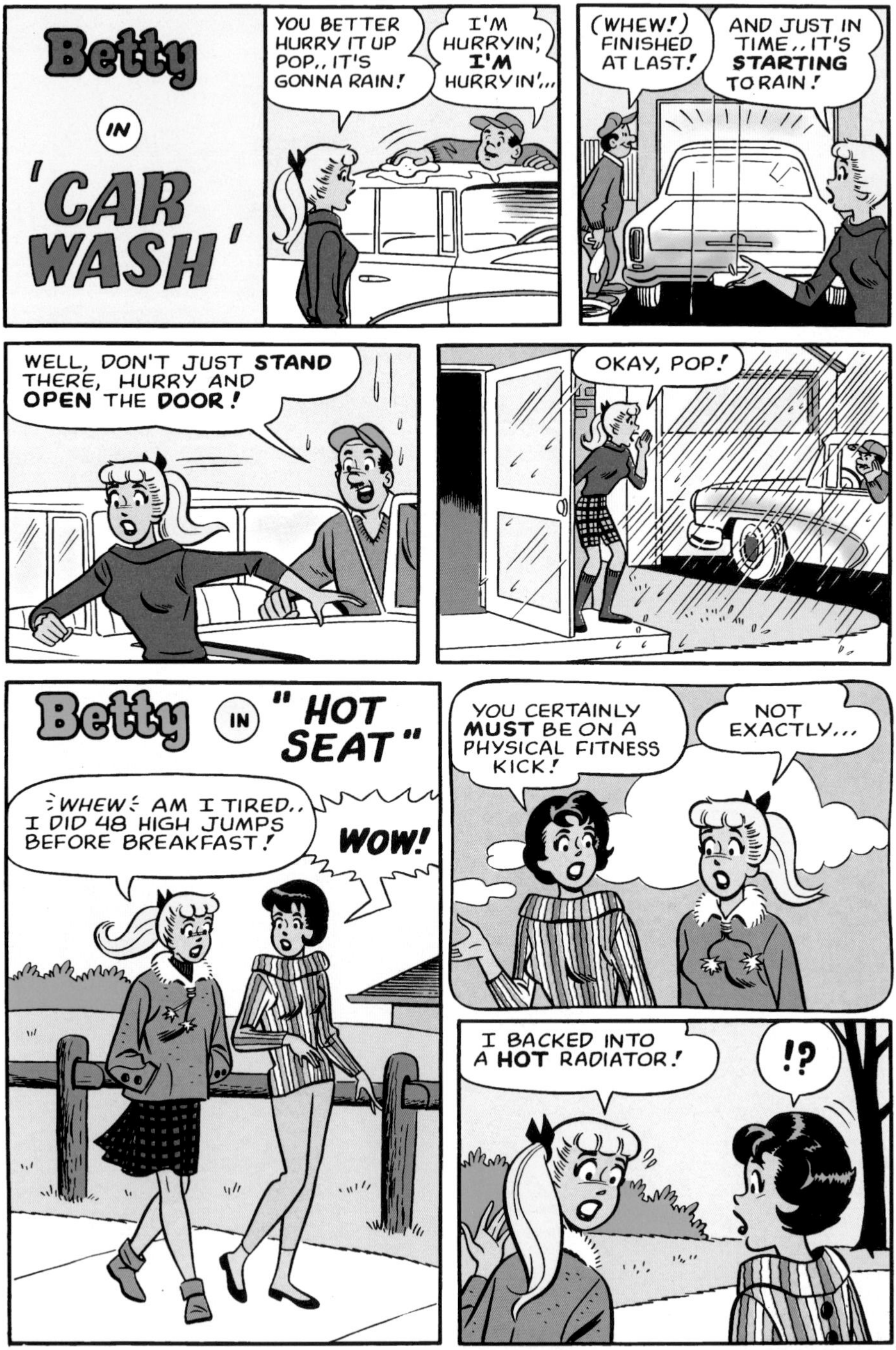
Betty
IN
'CAR WASH'
YOU BETTER HURRY IT UP POP,, IT'S GONNA RAIN!
I'M HURRYIN', I'M HURRYIN',,,
(WHEW!) FINISHED AT LAST!
AND JUST IN TIME,, IT'S STARTING TO RAIN!
WELL, DON'T JUST STAND THERE, HURRY AND OPEN THE DOOR!
OKAY, POP!
Betty
IN
"HOT SEAT"
WHEW AM I TIRED,, I DID 48 HIGH JUMPS BEFORE BREAKFAST!
WOW!
YOU CERTAINLY MUST BE ON A PHYSICAL FITNESS KICK!
NOT EXACTLY...
I BACKED INTO A HOT RADIATOR!
!?

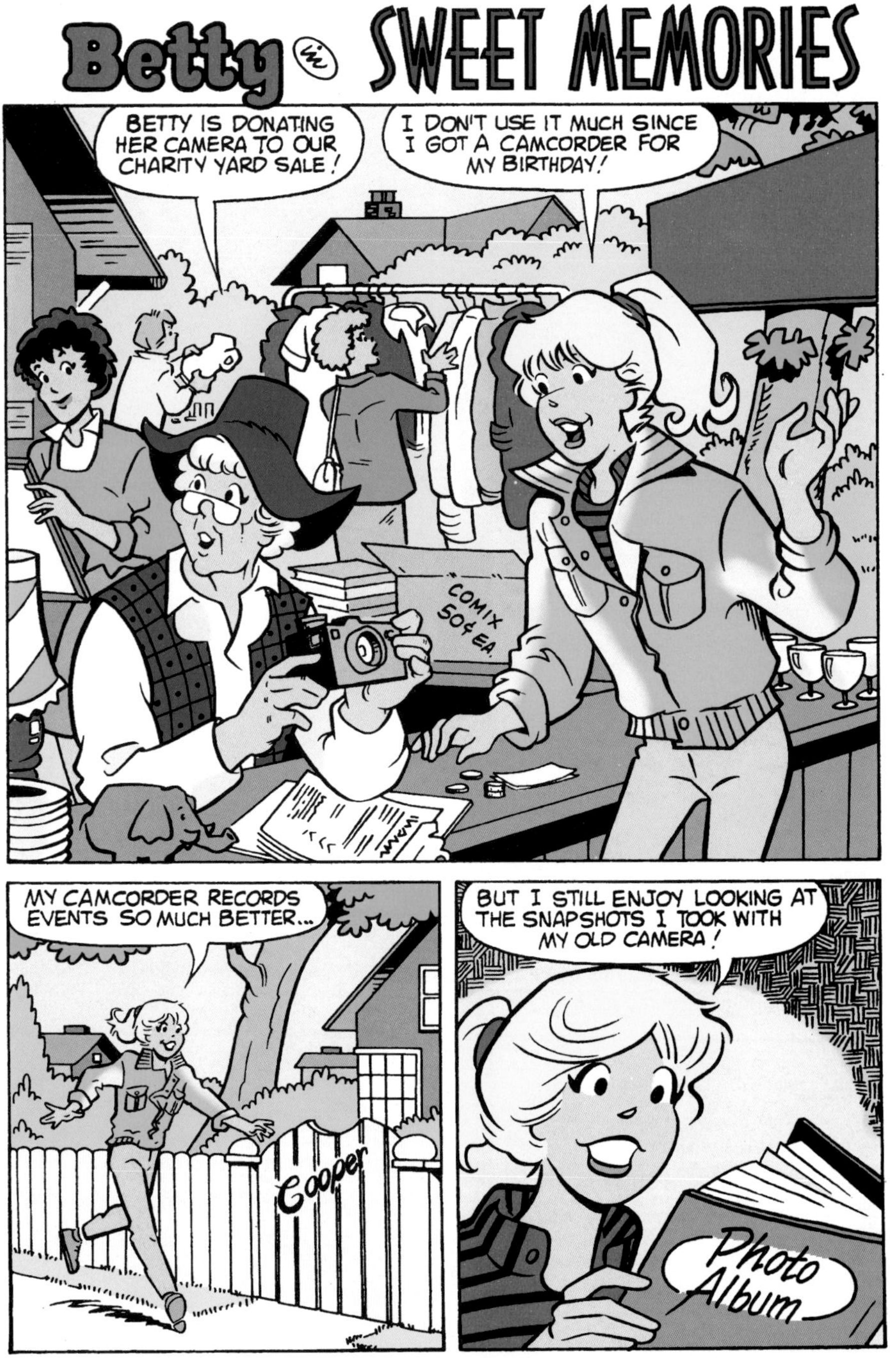
Betty in SWEET MEMORIES
BETTY IS DONATING HER CAMERA TO OUR CHARITY YARD SALE!
I DON'T USE IT MUCH SINCE I GOT A CAMCORDER FOR MY BIRTHDAY!
COMIX 50¢ EA.
MY CAMCORDER RECORDS EVENTS SO MUCH BETTER...
Cooper
BUT I STILL ENJOY LOOKING AT THE SNAPSHOTS I TOOK WITH MY OLD CAMERA!
Photo Album

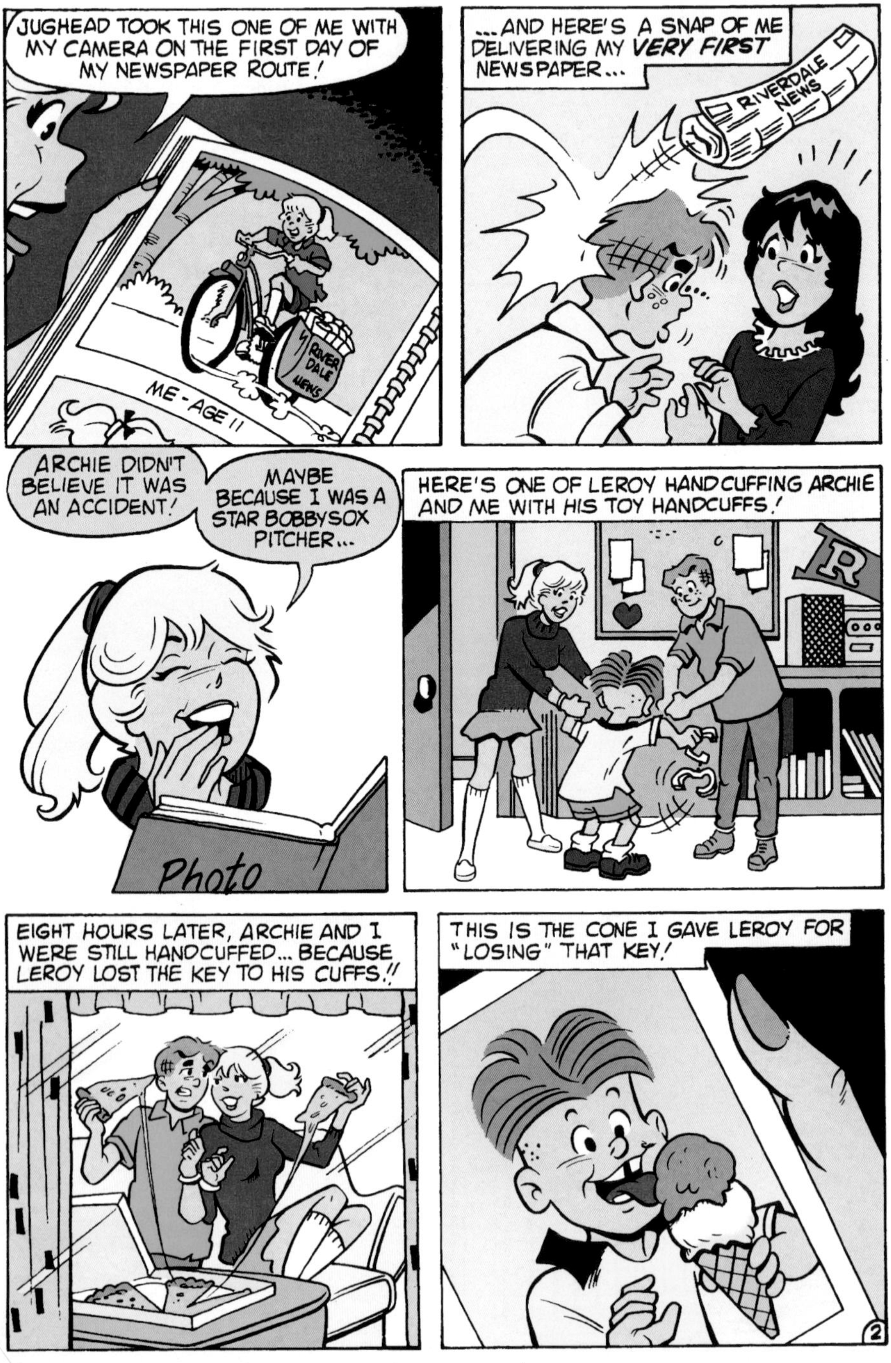
JUGHEAD TOOK THIS ONE OF ME WITH MY CAMERA ON THE FIRST DAY OF MY NEWSPAPER ROUTE!
RIVER DALE NEWS
ME - AGE 11
...AND HERE'S A SNAP OF ME DELIVERING MY VERY FIRST NEWSPAPER...
RIVERDALE NEWS
ARCHIE DIDN'T BELIEVE IT WAS AN ACCIDENT!
MAYBE BECAUSE I WAS A STAR BOBBYSOX PITCHER...
Photo
HERE'S ONE OF LEROY HANDCUFFING ARCHIE AND ME WITH HIS TOY HANDCUFFS!
R
EIGHT HOURS LATER, ARCHIE AND I WERE STILL HANDCUFFED... BECAUSE LEROY LOST THE KEY TO HIS CUFFS!!
THIS IS THE CONE I GAVE LEROY FOR "LOSING" THAT KEY!
2

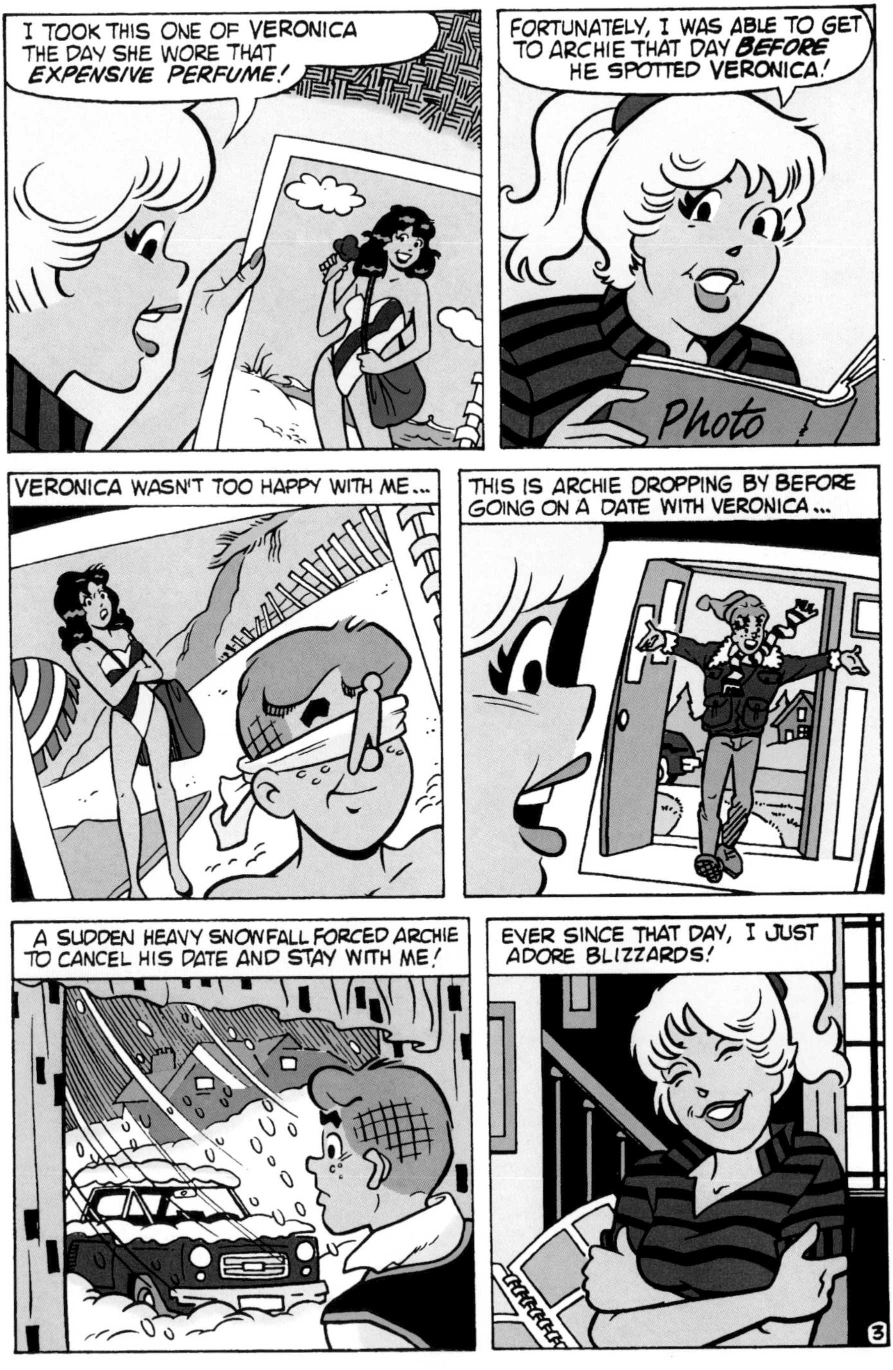
I TOOK THIS ONE OF VERONICA THE DAY SHE WORE THAT *EXPENSIVE PERFUME!*
FORTUNATELY, I WAS ABLE TO GET TO ARCHIE THAT DAY *BEFORE* HE SPOTTED VERONICA!
Photo
VERONICA WASN'T TOO HAPPY WITH ME...
THIS IS ARCHIE DROPPING BY BEFORE GOING ON A DATE WITH VERONICA...
A SUDDEN HEAVY SNOWFALL FORCED ARCHIE TO CANCEL HIS DATE AND STAY WITH ME!
EVER SINCE THAT DAY, I JUST ADORE BLIZZARDS!
3

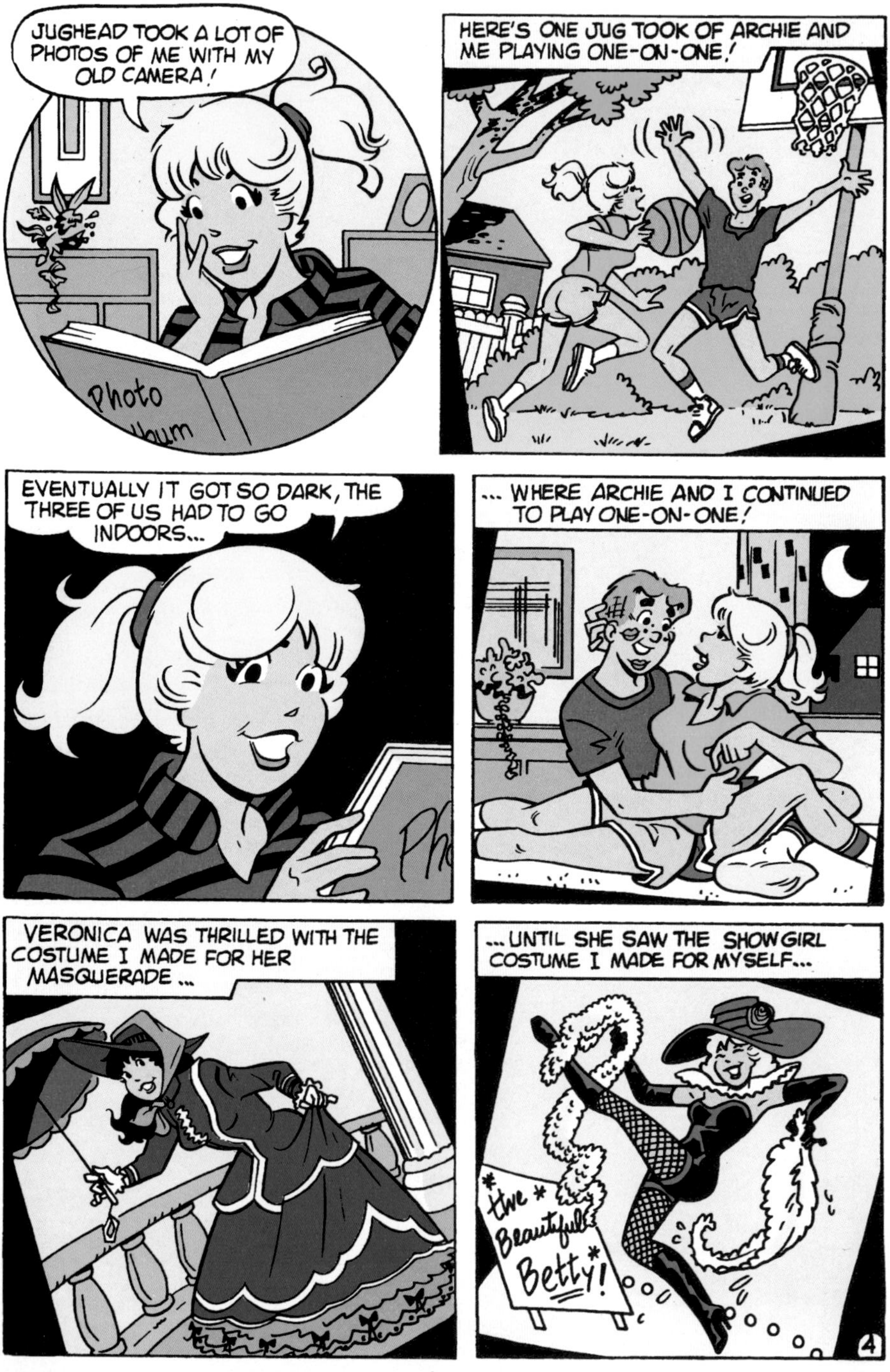
JUGHEAD TOOK A LOT OF PHOTOS OF ME WITH MY OLD CAMERA!
Photo Album
HERE'S ONE JUG TOOK OF ARCHIE AND ME PLAYING ONE-ON-ONE!
EVENTUALLY IT GOT SO DARK, THE THREE OF US HAD TO GO INDOORS...
... WHERE ARCHIE AND I CONTINUED TO PLAY ONE-ON-ONE!
VERONICA WAS THRILLED WITH THE COSTUME I MADE FOR HER MASQUERADE ...
... UNTIL SHE SAW THE SHOWGIRL COSTUME I MADE FOR MYSELF...
the Beautiful Betty!*
4

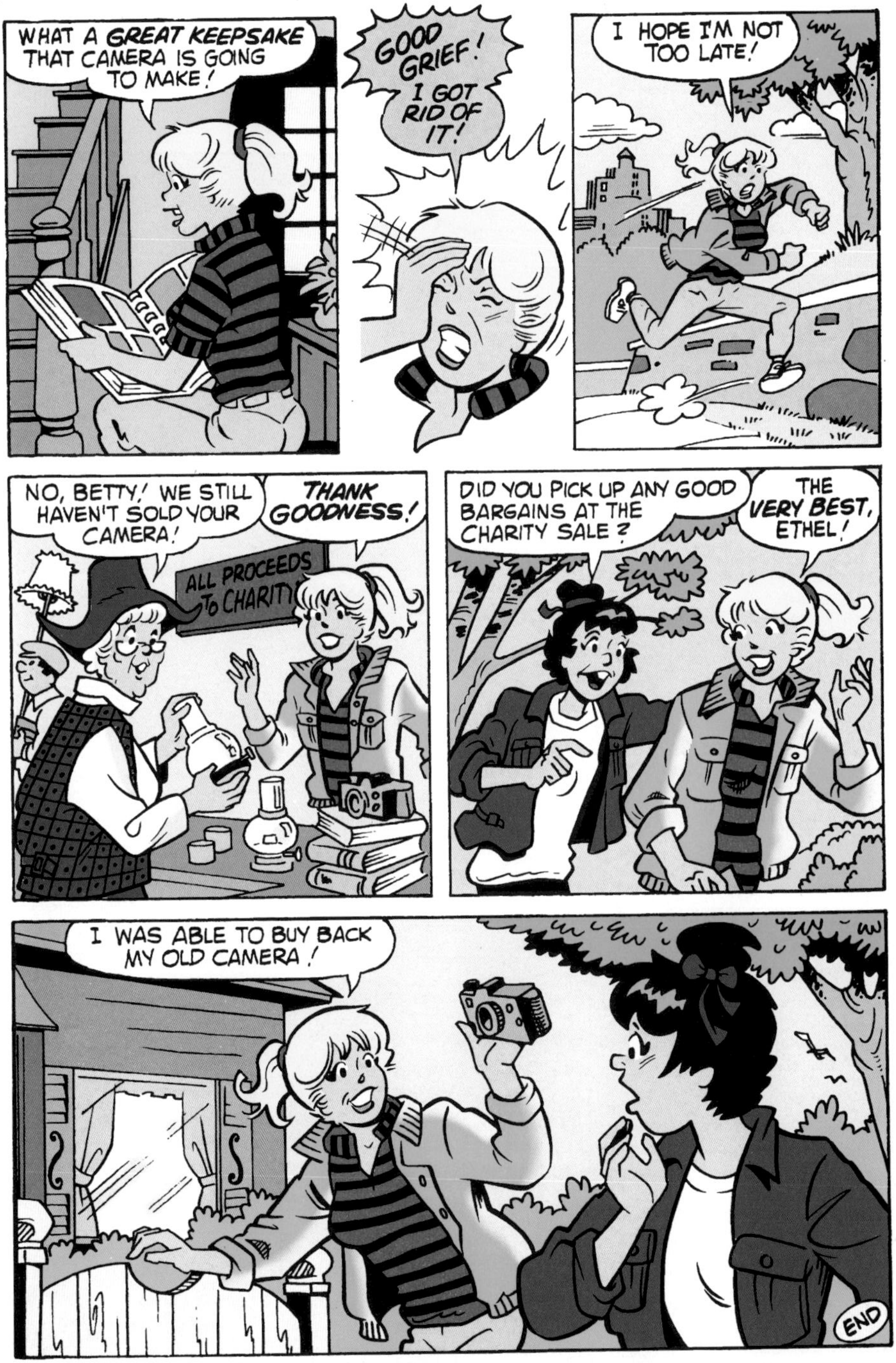
WHAT A GREAT KEEPSAKE THAT CAMERA IS GOING TO MAKE!
GOOD GRIEF! I GOT RID OF IT!
I HOPE I'M NOT TOO LATE!
NO, BETTY! WE STILL HAVEN'T SOLD YOUR CAMERA!
THANK GOODNESS!
ALL PROCEEDS TO CHARITY
DID YOU PICK UP ANY GOOD BARGAINS AT THE CHARITY SALE?
THE VERY BEST, ETHEL!
I WAS ABLE TO BUY BACK MY OLD CAMERA!
END

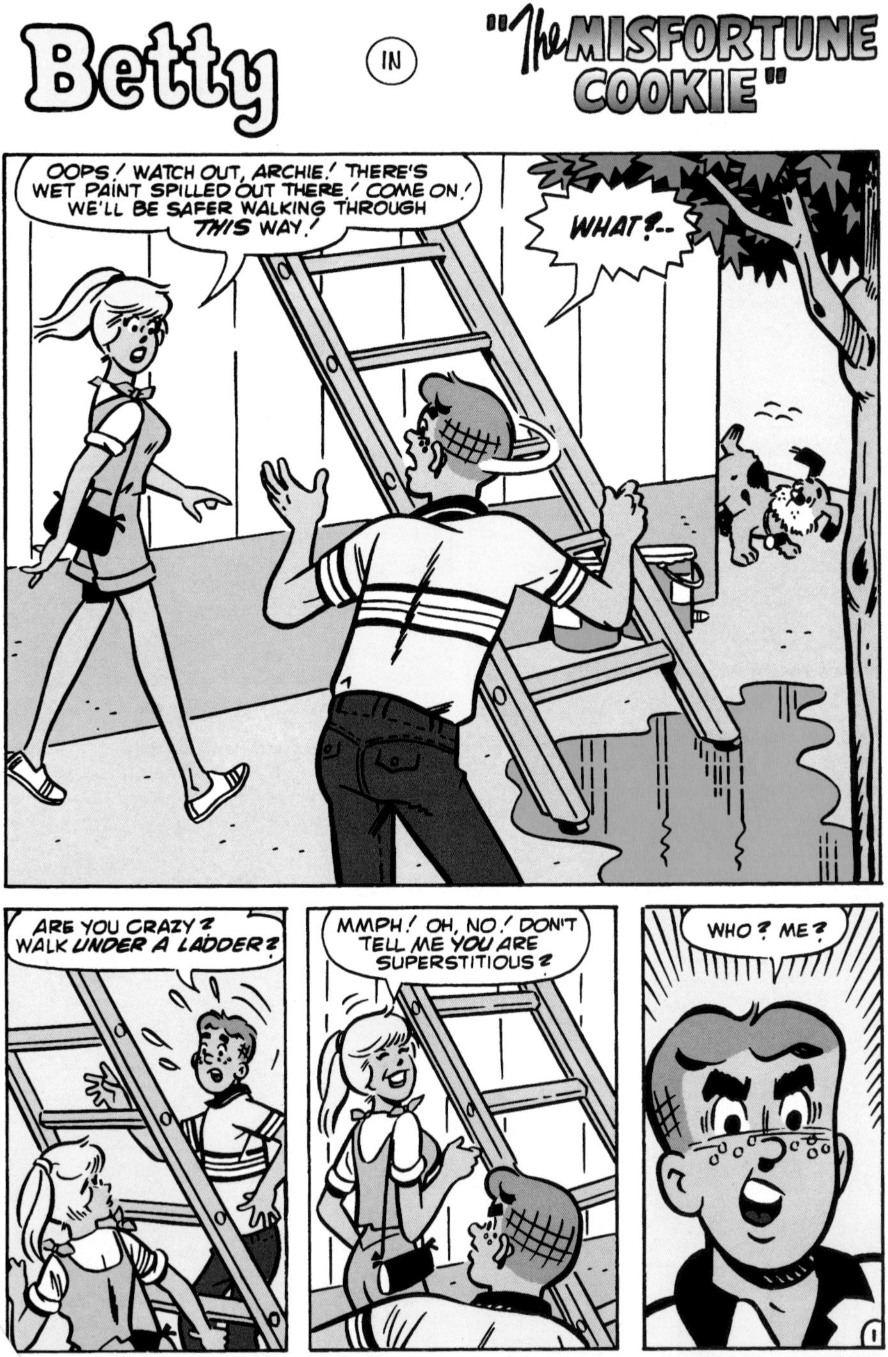
Betty
IN
"The MISFORTUNE COOKIE"
OOPS! WATCH OUT, ARCHIE! THERE'S WET PAINT SPILLED OUT THERE! COME ON! WE'LL BE SAFER WALKING THROUGH THIS WAY!
WHAT?--
ARE YOU CRAZY? WALK UNDER A LADDER?
MMPH! OH, NO! DON'T TELL ME YOU ARE SUPERSTITIOUS?
WHO? ME?
1

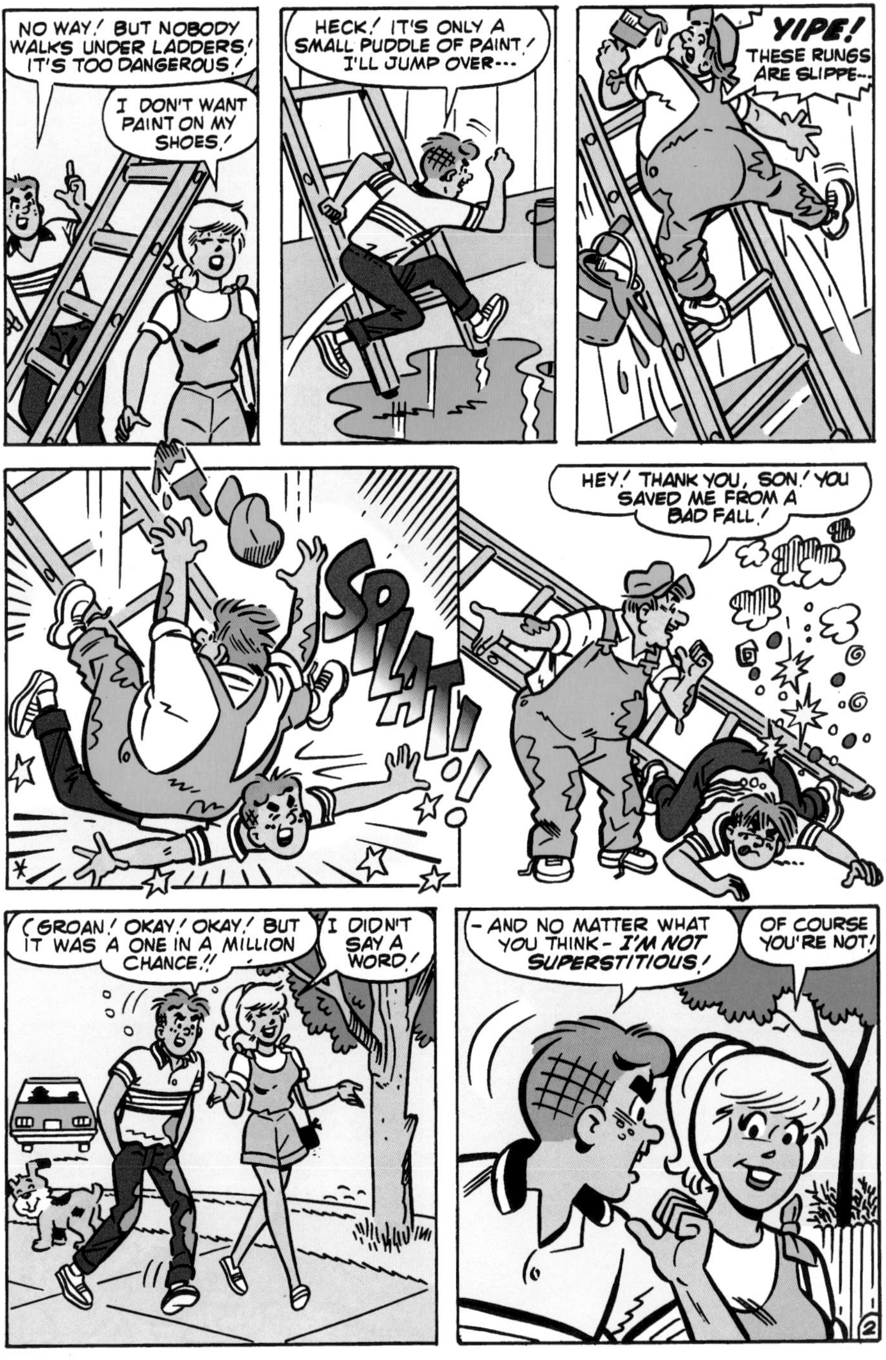
NO WAY! BUT NOBODY WALKS UNDER LADDERS! IT'S TOO DANGEROUS!
I DON'T WANT PAINT ON MY SHOES!
HECK! IT'S ONLY A SMALL PUDDLE OF PAINT! I'LL JUMP OVER---
YIPE! THESE RUNGS ARE SLIPPE--
SPLAT!
O!
HEY! THANK YOU, SON! YOU SAVED ME FROM A BAD FALL!
(GROAN! OKAY! OKAY! BUT IT WAS A ONE IN A MILLION CHANCE!!
I DIDN'T SAY A WORD!
- AND NO MATTER WHAT YOU THINK - I'M NOT SUPERSTITIOUS!
OF COURSE YOU'RE NOT!
2

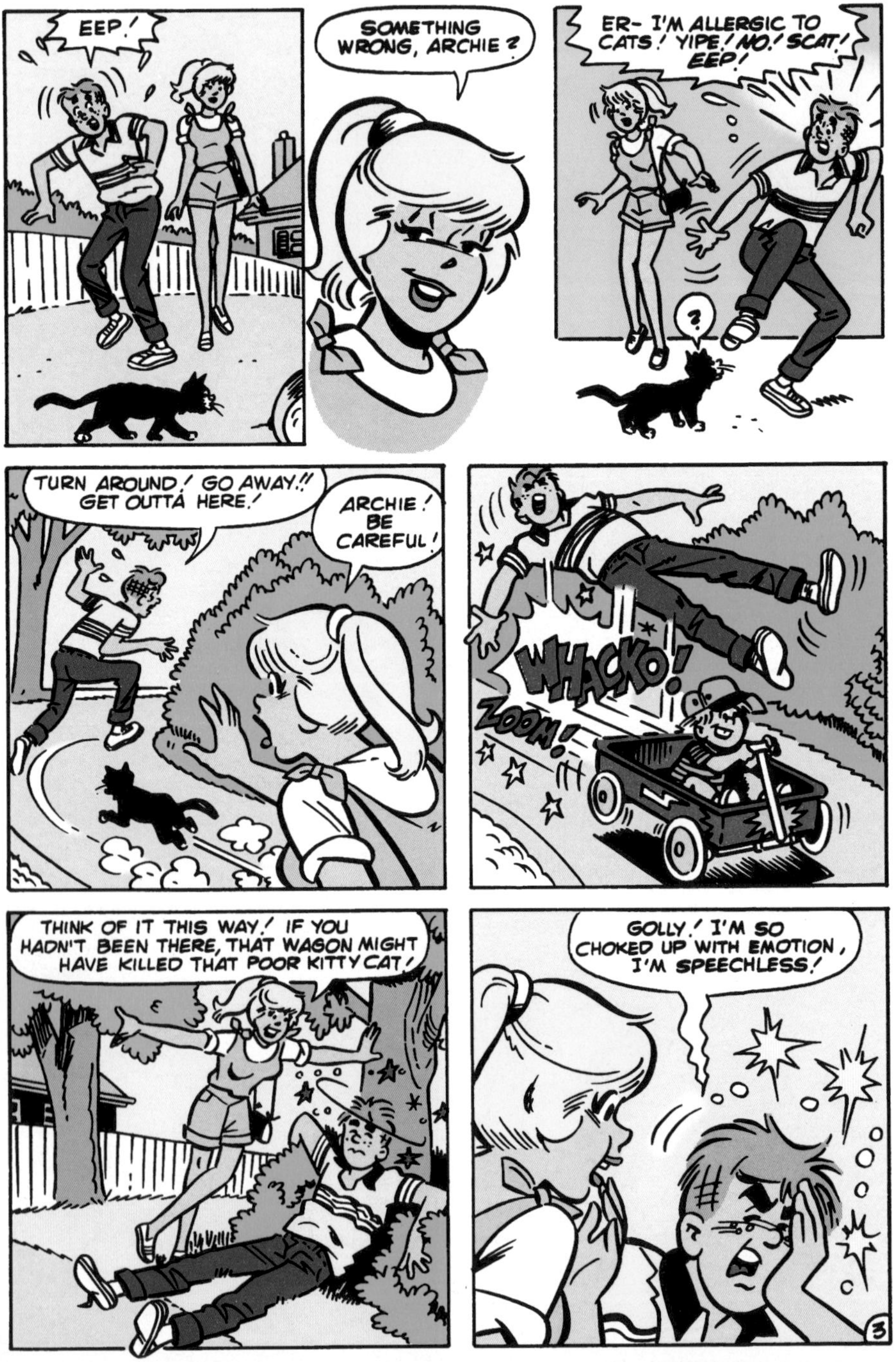
EEP!
SOMETHING WRONG, ARCHIE?
ER- I'M ALLERGIC TO CATS! YIPE! NO! SCAT! EEP!
?
TURN AROUND! GO AWAY!! GET OUTTA HERE!
ARCHIE! BE CAREFUL!
WHACKO!
ZOOM!
THINK OF IT THIS WAY! IF YOU HADN'T BEEN THERE, THAT WAGON MIGHT HAVE KILLED THAT POOR KITTY CAT!
GOLLY! I'M SO CHOKED UP WITH EMOTION, I'M SPEECHLESS!
3

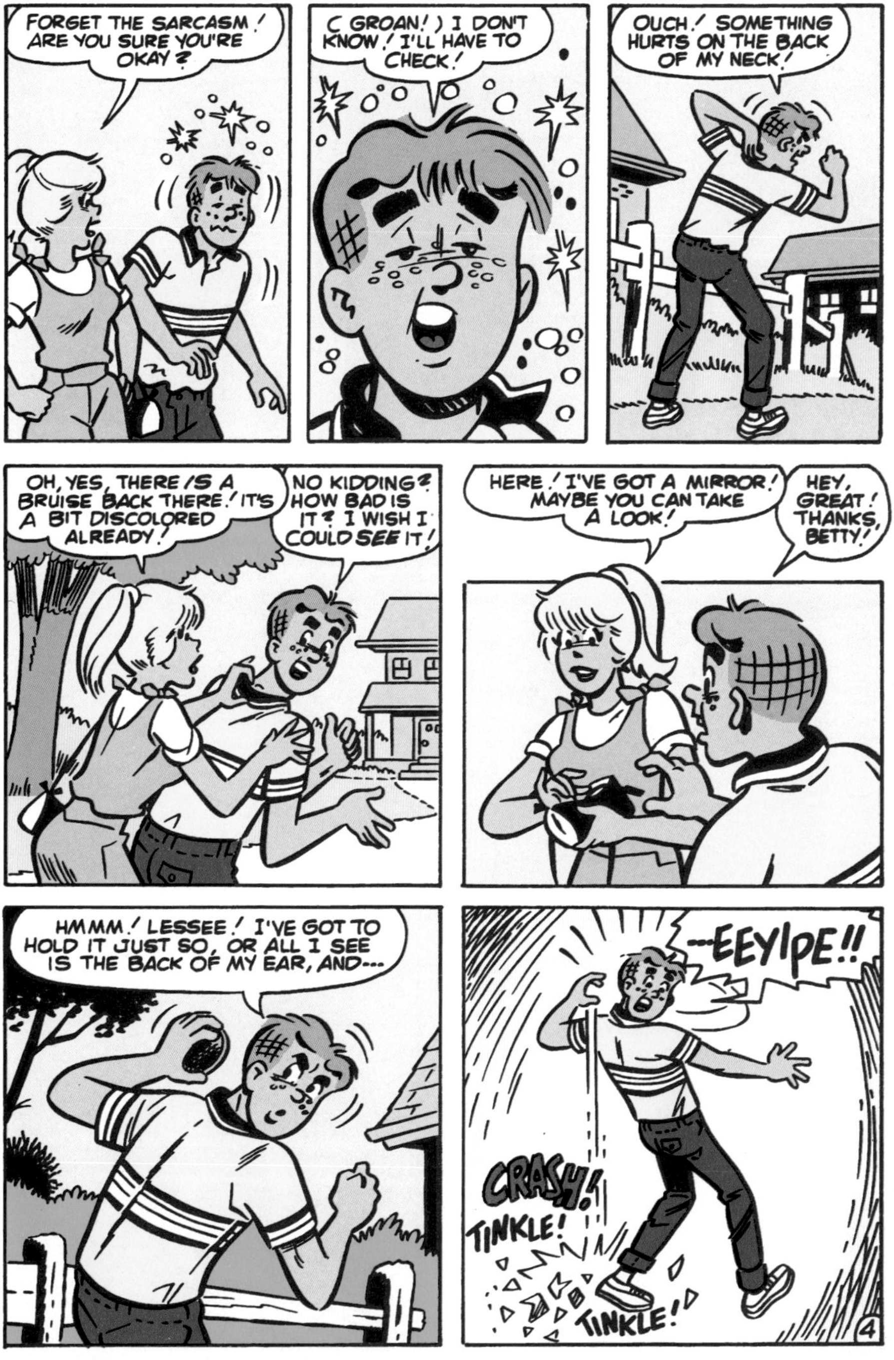
FORGET THE SARCASM! ARE YOU SURE YOU'RE OKAY?
(GROAN!) I DON'T KNOW! I'LL HAVE TO CHECK!
OUCH! SOMETHING HURTS ON THE BACK OF MY NECK!
OH, YES, THERE IS A BRUISE BACK THERE! IT'S A BIT DISCOLORED ALREADY!
NO KIDDING? HOW BAD IS IT? I WISH I COULD SEE IT!
HERE! I'VE GOT A MIRROR! MAYBE YOU CAN TAKE A LOOK!
HEY, GREAT! THANKS, BETTY!
HMMM! LESSEE! I'VE GOT TO HOLD IT JUST SO, OR ALL I SEE IS THE BACK OF MY EAR, AND---
---EEYIPE!!
CRASH!
TINKLE!
TINKLE!
4

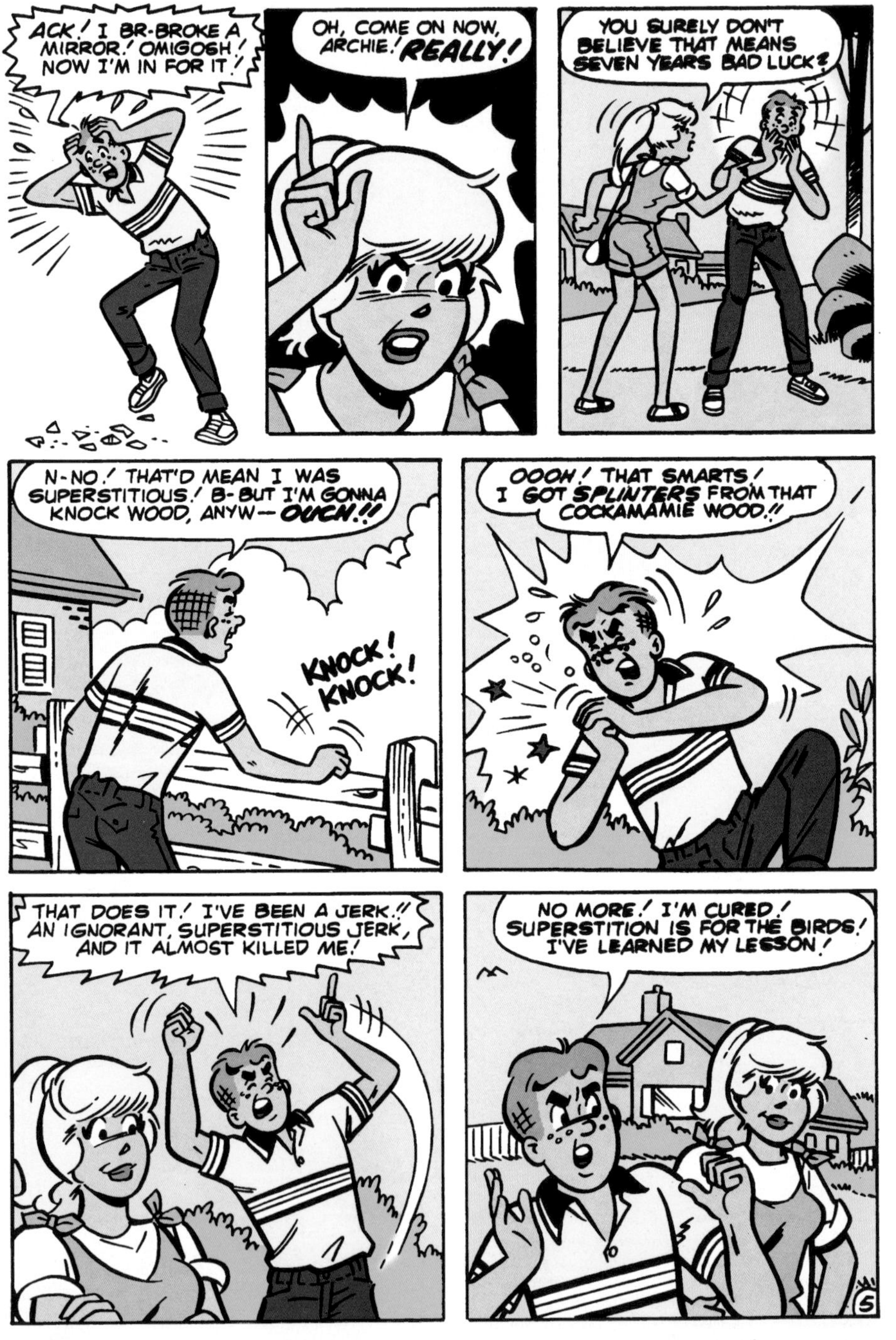
ACK! I BR-BROKE A MIRROR! OMIGOSH! NOW I'M IN FOR IT!
OH, COME ON NOW, ARCHIE! REALLY!
YOU SURELY DON'T BELIEVE THAT MEANS SEVEN YEARS BAD LUCK?
N-NO! THAT'D MEAN I WAS SUPERSTITIOUS! B-BUT I'M GONNA KNOCK WOOD, ANYW--OUCH!!
KNOCK! KNOCK!
OOOH! THAT SMARTS! I GOT SPLINTERS FROM THAT COCKAMAMIE WOOD!!
THAT DOES IT! I'VE BEEN A JERK!! AN IGNORANT, SUPERSTITIOUS JERK, AND IT ALMOST KILLED ME!
NO MORE! I'M CURED! SUPERSTITION IS FOR THE BIRDS! I'VE LEARNED MY LESSON!
5

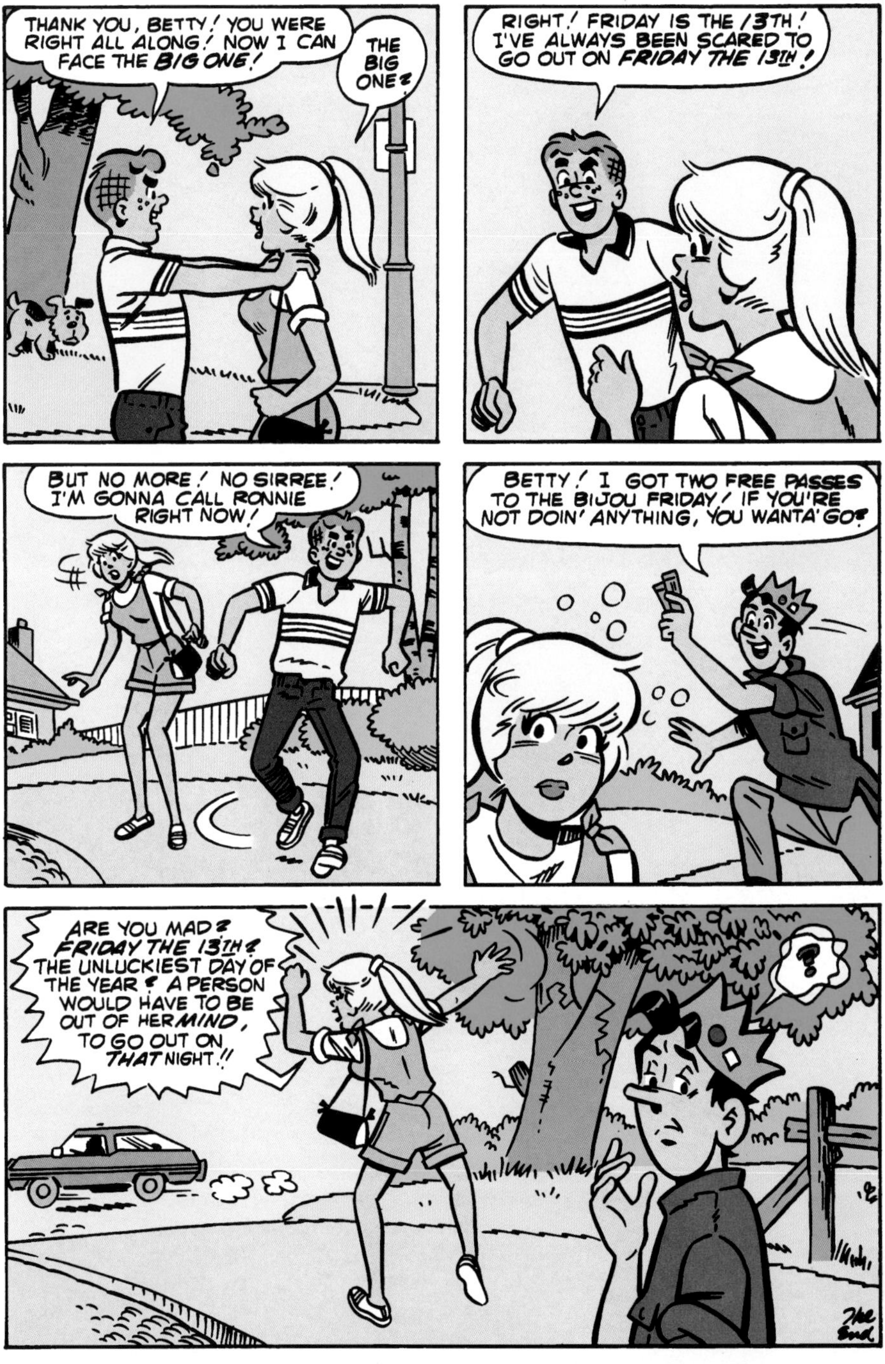
THANK YOU, BETTY! YOU WERE RIGHT ALL ALONG! NOW I CAN FACE THE BIG ONE!
THE BIG ONE?
RIGHT! FRIDAY IS THE 13TH! I'VE ALWAYS BEEN SCARED TO GO OUT ON FRIDAY THE 13TH!
BUT NO MORE! NO SIRREE! I'M GONNA CALL RONNIE RIGHT NOW!
BETTY! I GOT TWO FREE PASSES TO THE BIJOU FRIDAY! IF YOU'RE NOT DOIN' ANYTHING, YOU WANTA' GO?
ARE YOU MAD? FRIDAY THE 13TH? THE UNLUCKIEST DAY OF THE YEAR! A PERSON WOULD HAVE TO BE OUT OF HER MIND, TO GO OUT ON THAT NIGHT!!
The End

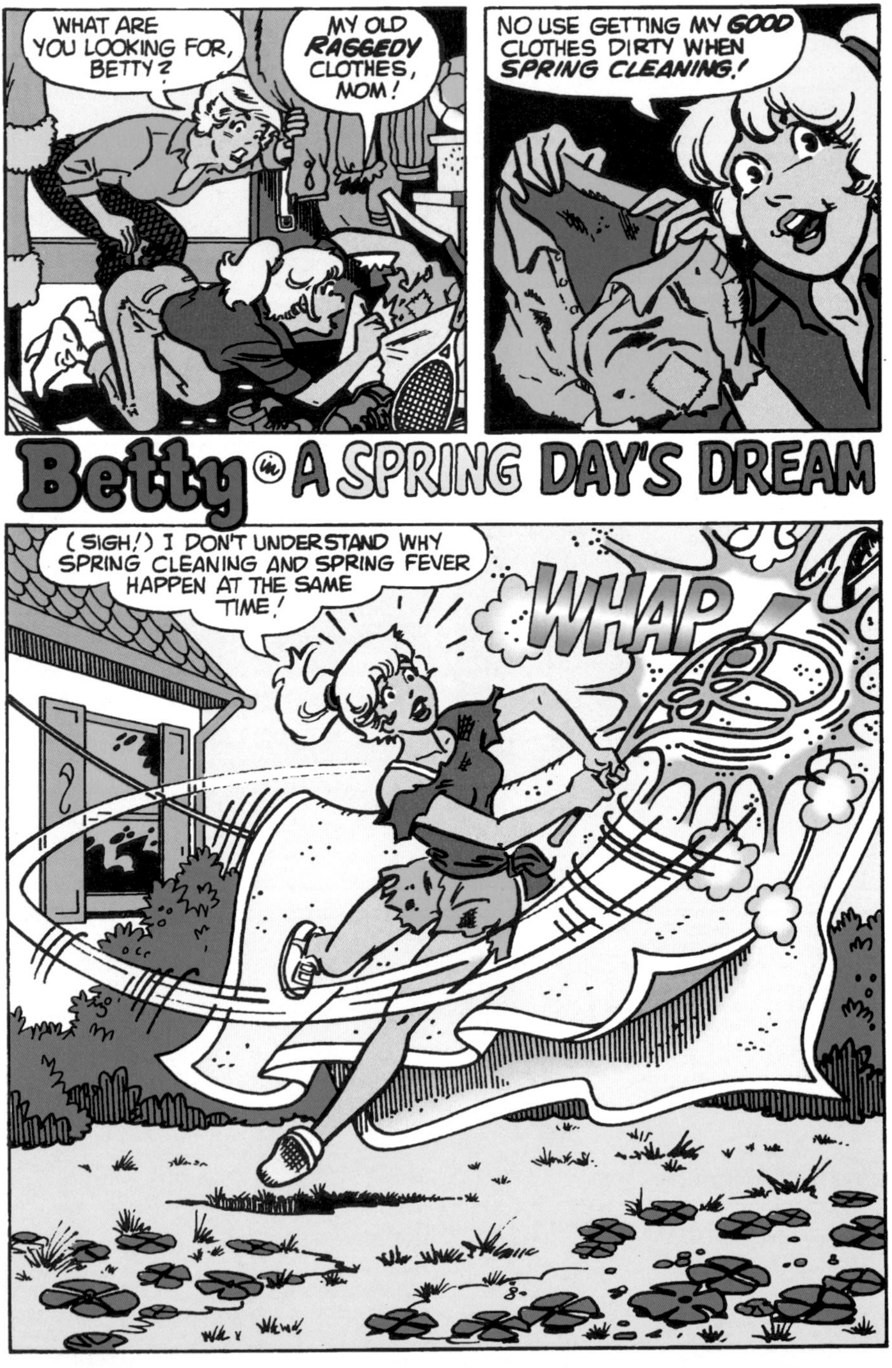
WHAT ARE YOU LOOKING FOR, BETTY?
MY OLD RAGGEDY CLOTHES, MOM!
NO USE GETTING MY GOOD CLOTHES DIRTY WHEN SPRING CLEANING!
Betty in A SPRING DAY'S DREAM
(SIGH!) I DON'T UNDERSTAND WHY SPRING CLEANING AND SPRING FEVER HAPPEN AT THE SAME TIME!
WHAP!

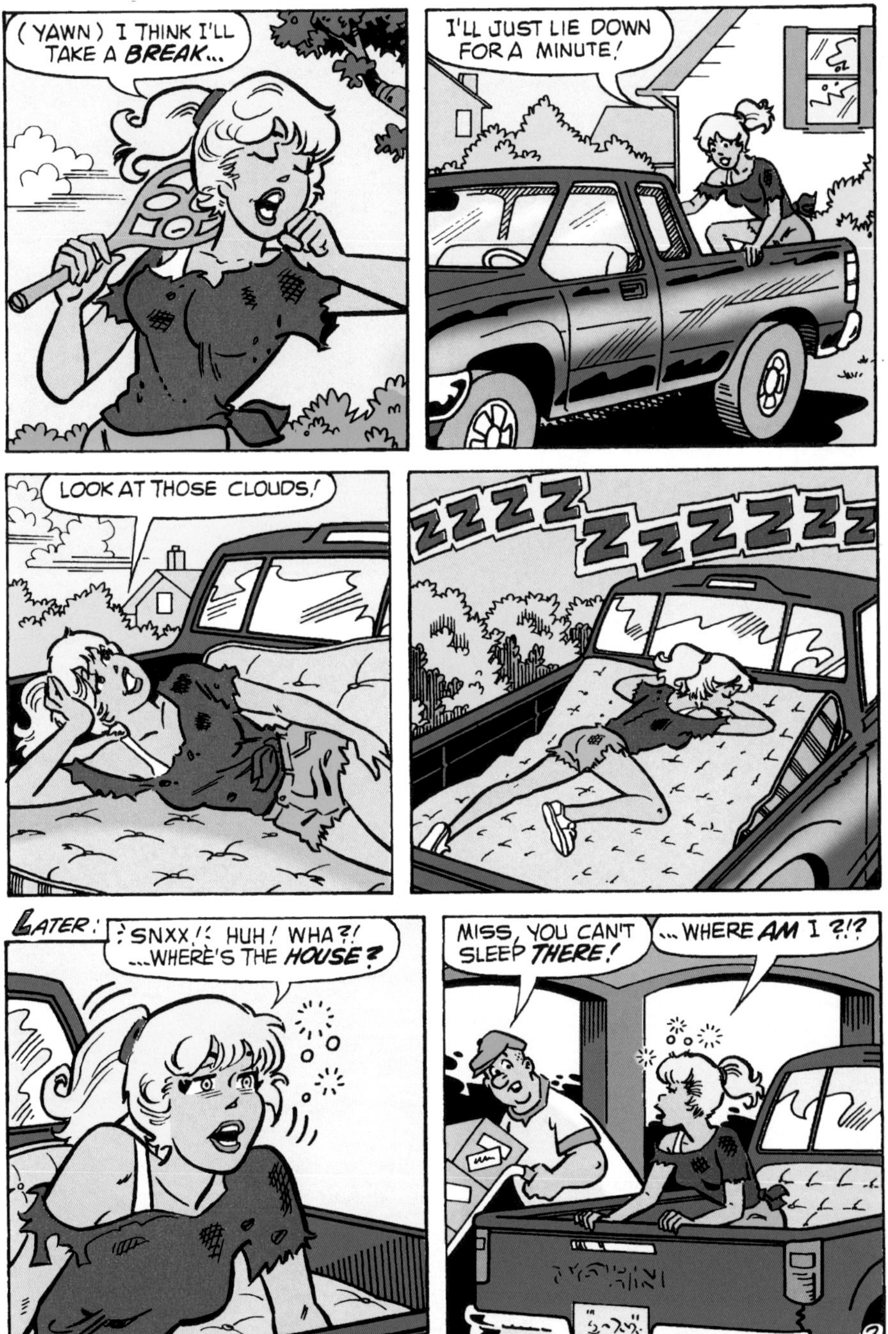
(YAWN) I THINK I'LL TAKE A BREAK...
I'LL JUST LIE DOWN FOR A MINUTE!
LOOK AT THOSE CLOUDS!
ZZZZ ZZZZZZ
LATER:
SNXX! HUH! WHA?! ...WHERE'S THE HOUSE?
MISS, YOU CAN'T SLEEP THERE!
...WHERE AM I ?!?
2

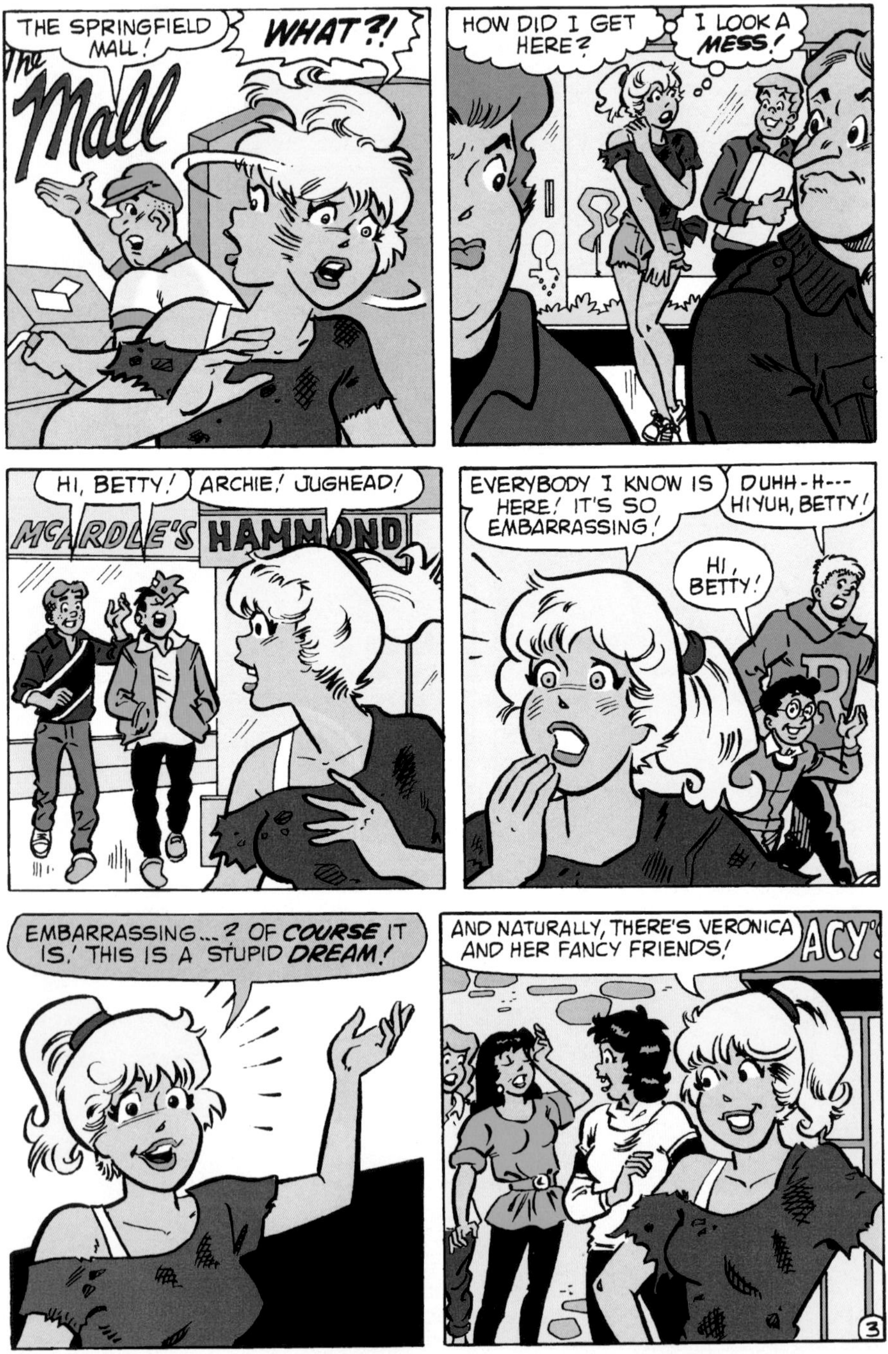
THE SPRINGFIELD MALL!
WHAT?!
The Mall
HOW DID I GET HERE?
I LOOK A MESS!
HI, BETTY!
ARCHIE! JUGHEAD!
McARDLE'S
HAMMOND
EVERYBODY I KNOW IS HERE! IT'S SO EMBARRASSING!
DUHH-H--- HIYUH, BETTY!
HI, BETTY!
EMBARRASSING...? OF COURSE IT IS! THIS IS A STUPID DREAM!
AND NATURALLY, THERE'S VERONICA AND HER FANCY FRIENDS!
ACY'
3

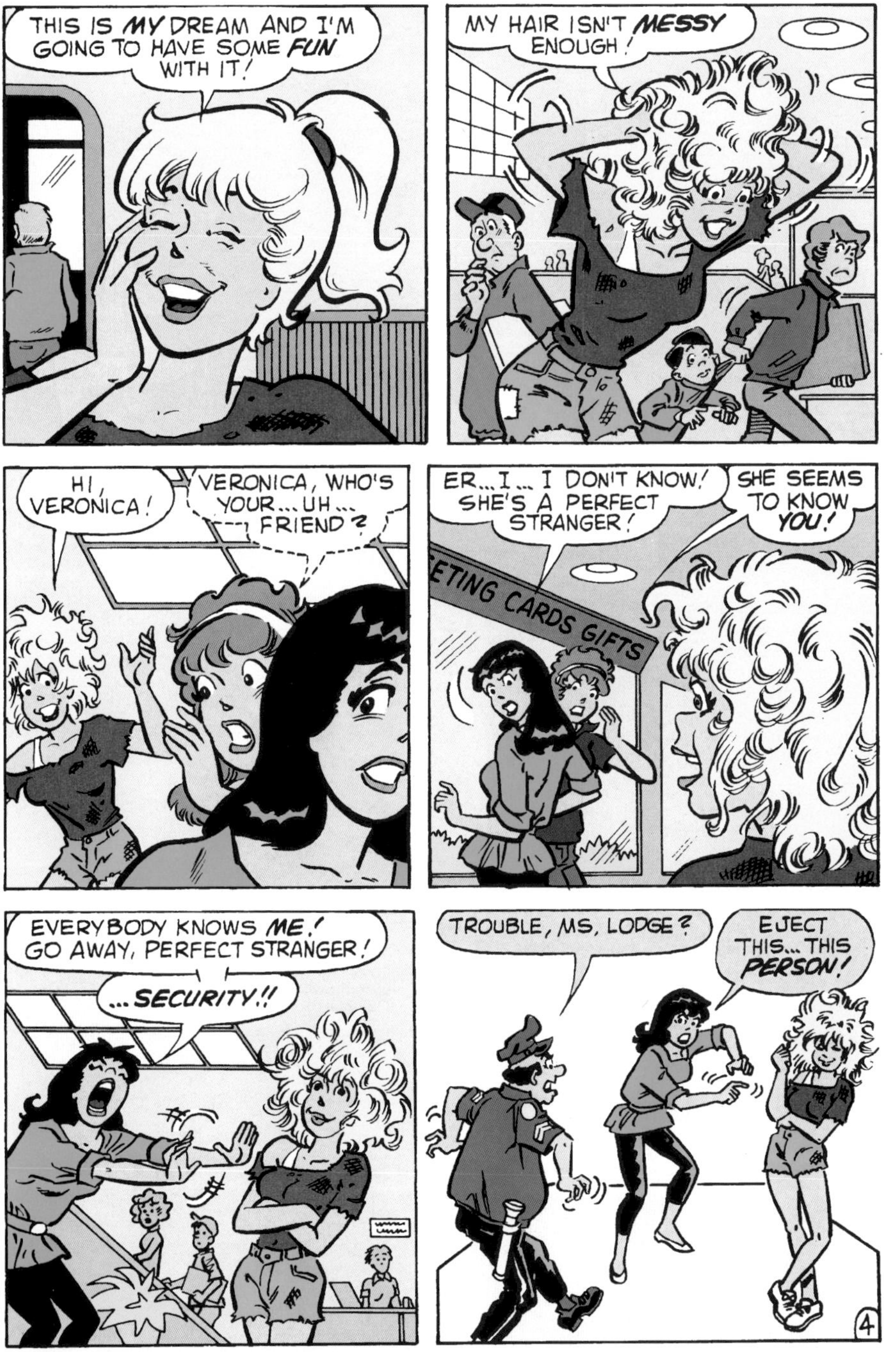
THIS IS MY DREAM AND I'M GOING TO HAVE SOME FUN WITH IT!
MY HAIR ISN'T MESSY ENOUGH!
HI, VERONICA!
VERONICA, WHO'S YOUR... UH ... FRIEND?
ETING CARDS GIFTS
ER... I ... I DON'T KNOW! SHE'S A PERFECT STRANGER!
SHE SEEMS TO KNOW YOU!
EVERYBODY KNOWS ME! GO AWAY, PERFECT STRANGER!
...SECURITY!!
TROUBLE, MS, LODGE?
EJECT THIS... THIS PERSON!
4

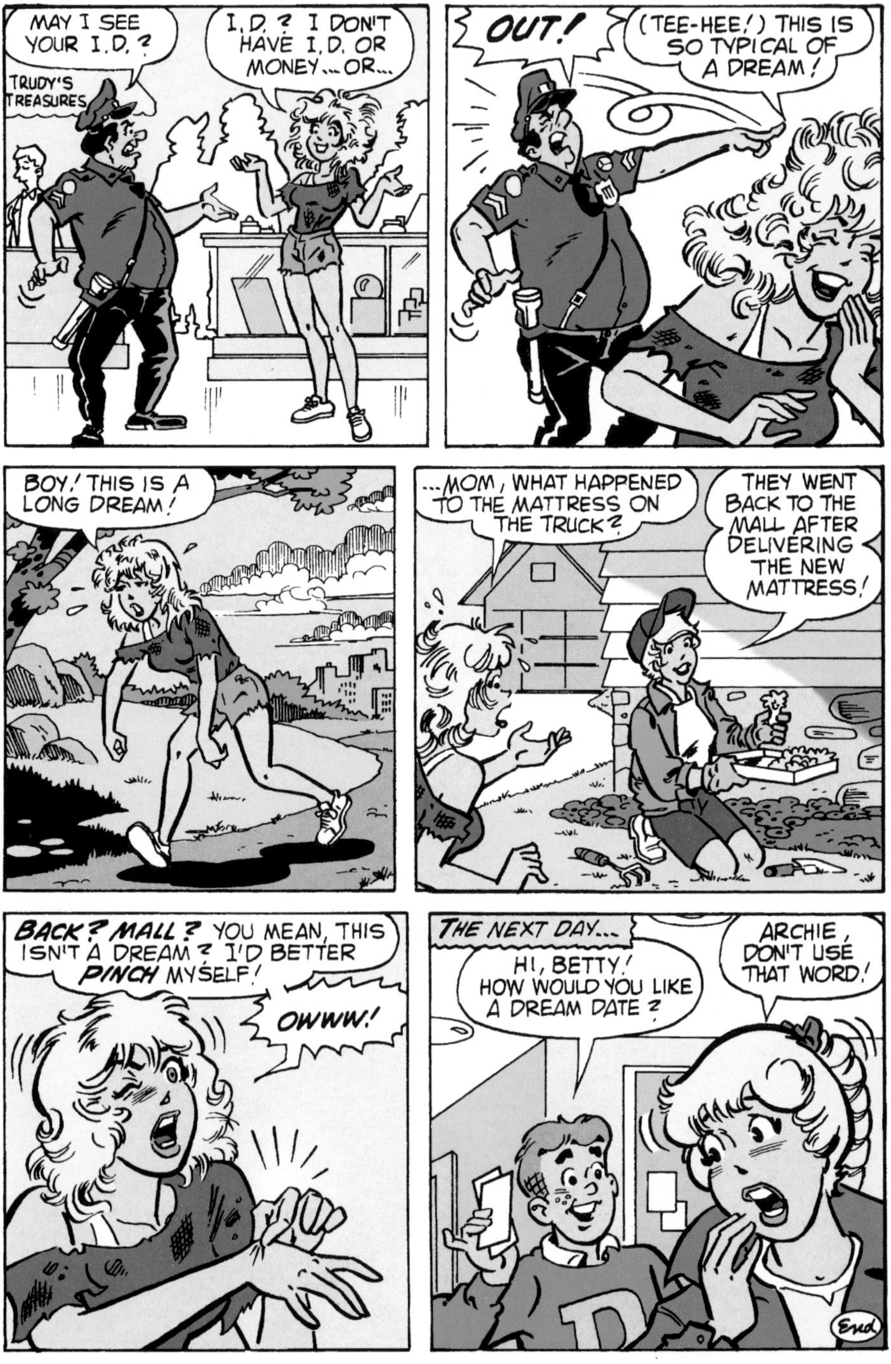
MAY I SEE YOUR I.D.?
TRUDY'S TREASURES
I.D.? I DON'T HAVE I.D. OR MONEY...OR...
OUT!
(TEE-HEE!) THIS IS SO TYPICAL OF A DREAM!
BOY! THIS IS A LONG DREAM!
...MOM, WHAT HAPPENED TO THE MATTRESS ON THE TRUCK?
THEY WENT BACK TO THE MALL AFTER DELIVERING THE NEW MATTRESS!
BACK? MALL? YOU MEAN, THIS ISN'T A DREAM? I'D BETTER PINCH MYSELF!
OWWW!
THE NEXT DAY...
HI, BETTY! HOW WOULD YOU LIKE A DREAM DATE?
ARCHIE, DON'T USE THAT WORD!
End

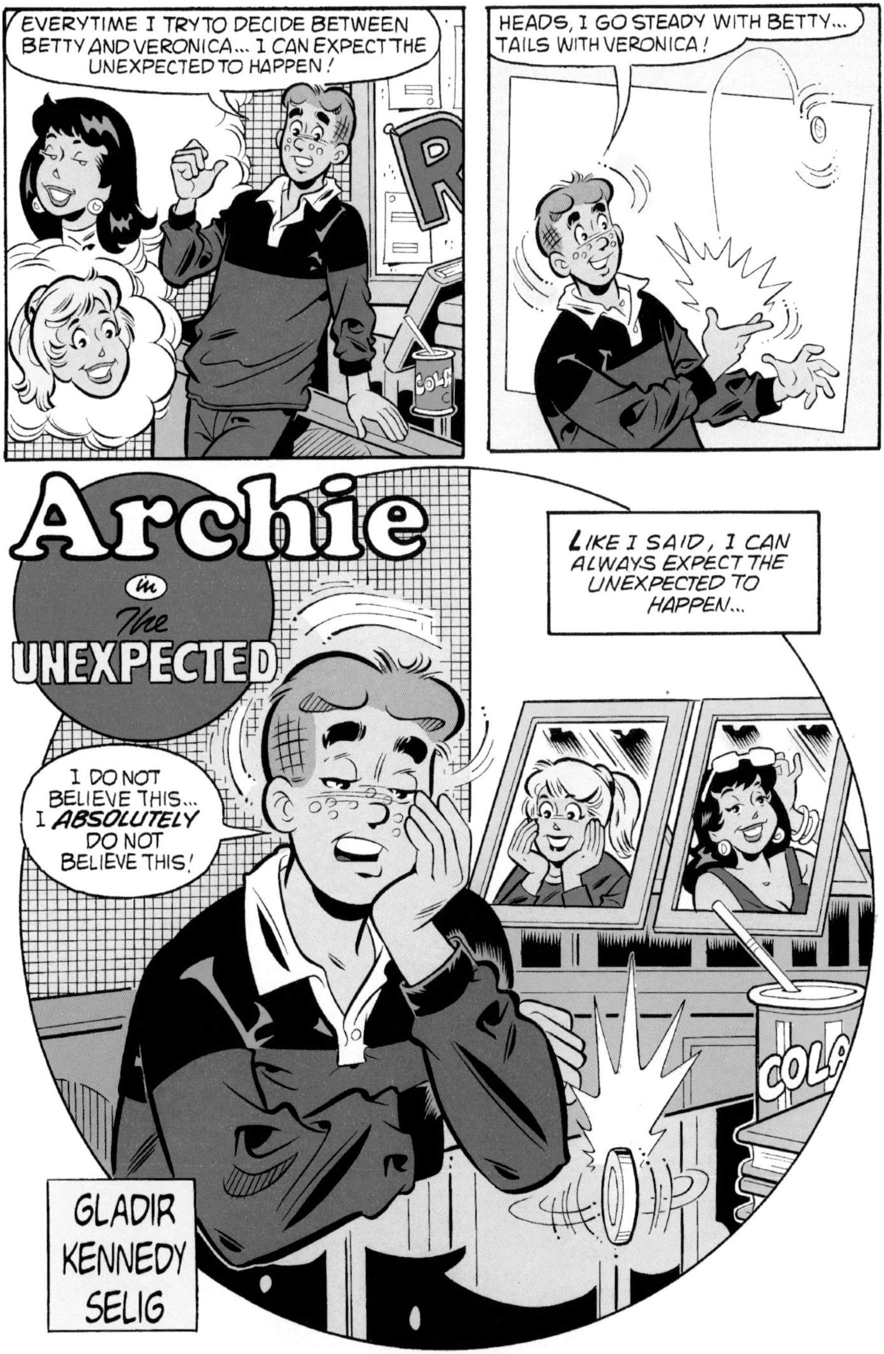
EVERYTIME I TRY TO DECIDE BETWEEN BETTY AND VERONICA... I CAN EXPECT THE UNEXPECTED TO HAPPEN!
HEADS, I GO STEADY WITH BETTY... TAILS WITH VERONICA!
Archie
in
The
UNEXPECTED
LIKE I SAID, I CAN ALWAYS EXPECT THE UNEXPECTED TO HAPPEN...
I DO NOT BELIEVE THIS... I ABSOLUTELY DO NOT BELIEVE THIS!
COLA
GLADIR
KENNEDY
SELIG

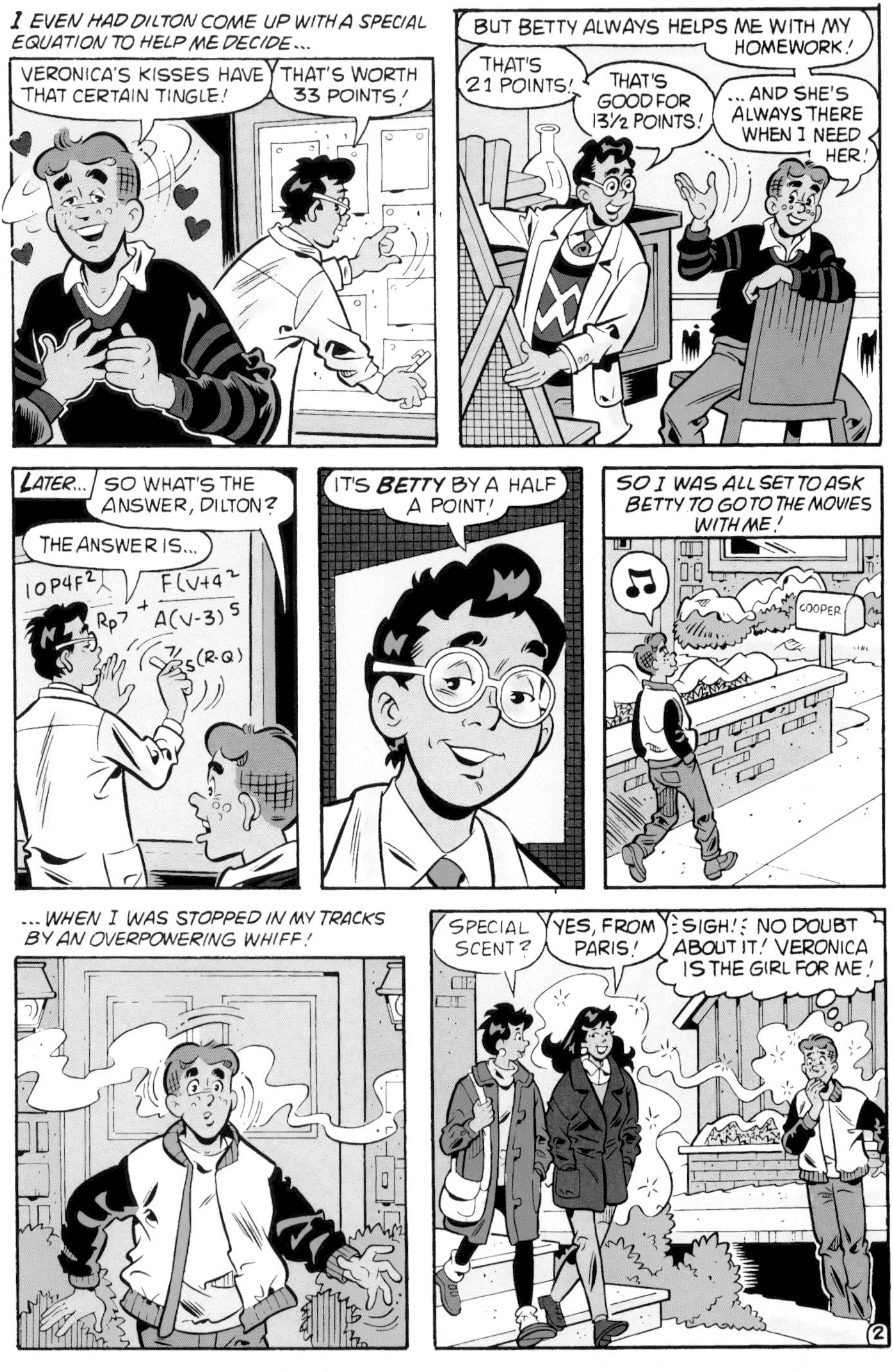
I EVEN HAD DILTON COME UP WITH A SPECIAL EQUATION TO HELP ME DECIDE...
VERONICA'S KISSES HAVE THAT CERTAIN TINGLE!
THAT'S WORTH 33 POINTS!
BUT BETTY ALWAYS HELPS ME WITH MY HOMEWORK!
THAT'S 21 POINTS!
THAT'S GOOD FOR 13½ POINTS!
...AND SHE'S ALWAYS THERE WHEN I NEED HER!
LATER...
SO WHAT'S THE ANSWER, DILTON?
THE ANSWER IS...
IT'S BETTY BY A HALF A POINT!
SO I WAS ALL SET TO ASK BETTY TO GO TO THE MOVIES WITH ME!
COOPER
...WHEN I WAS STOPPED IN MY TRACKS BY AN OVERPOWERING WHIFF!
SPECIAL SCENT?
YES, FROM PARIS!
SIGH! NO DOUBT ABOUT IT! VERONICA IS THE GIRL FOR ME!
2

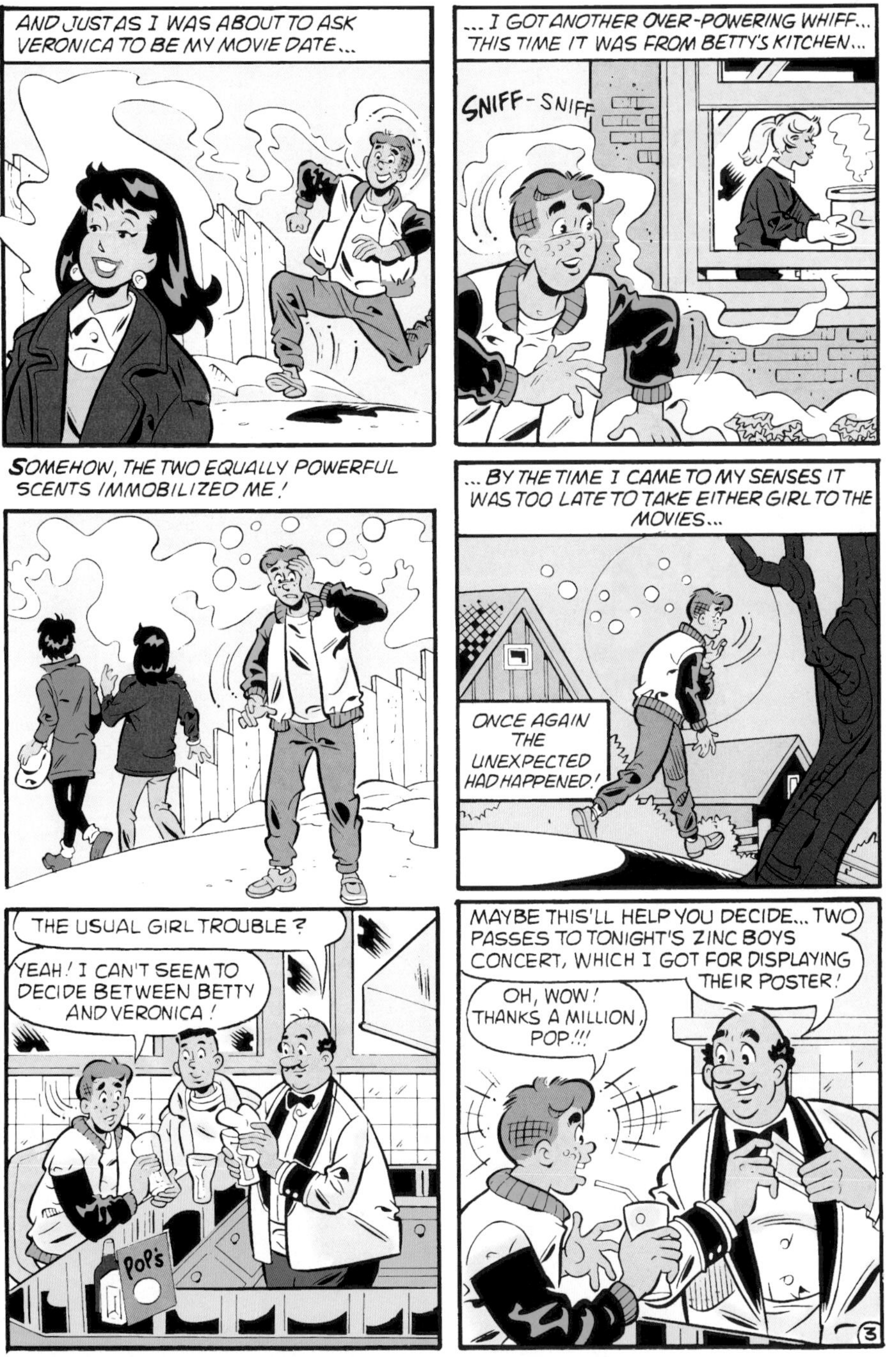
AND JUST AS I WAS ABOUT TO ASK VERONICA TO BE MY MOVIE DATE...
... I GOT ANOTHER OVER-POWERING WHIFF... THIS TIME IT WAS FROM BETTY'S KITCHEN...
SNIFF-SNIFF
SOMEHOW, THE TWO EQUALLY POWERFUL SCENTS IMMOBILIZED ME!
... BY THE TIME I CAME TO MY SENSES IT WAS TOO LATE TO TAKE EITHER GIRL TO THE MOVIES...
ONCE AGAIN THE UNEXPECTED HAD HAPPENED!
THE USUAL GIRL TROUBLE?
YEAH! I CAN'T SEEM TO DECIDE BETWEEN BETTY AND VERONICA!
POP'S
MAYBE THIS'LL HELP YOU DECIDE... TWO PASSES TO TONIGHT'S ZINC BOYS CONCERT, WHICH I GOT FOR DISPLAYING THEIR POSTER!
OH, WOW! THANKS A MILLION, POP!!!
3

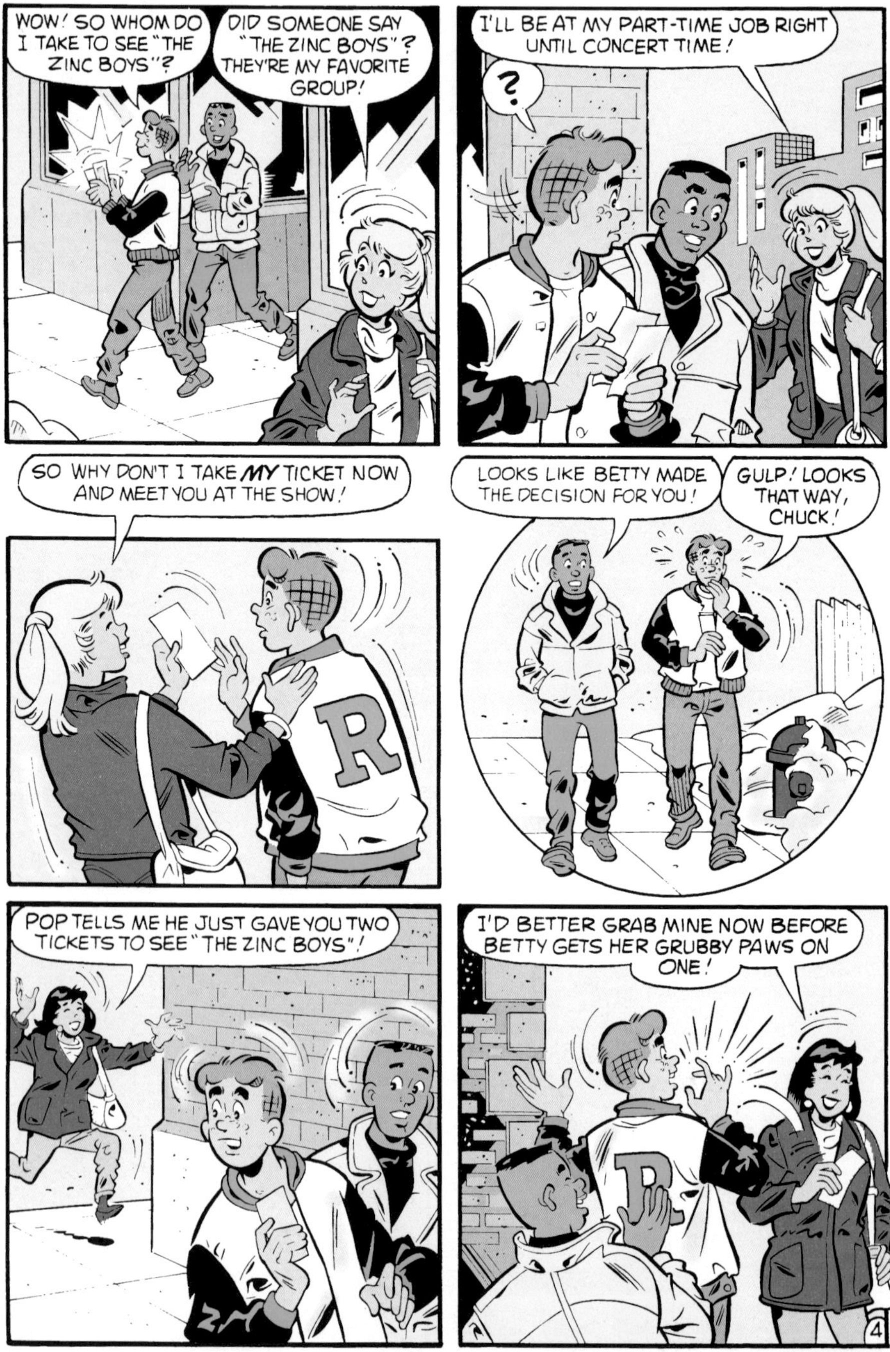
WOW! SO WHOM DO I TAKE TO SEE "THE ZINC BOYS"?
DID SOMEONE SAY "THE ZINC BOYS"? THEY'RE MY FAVORITE GROUP!
I'LL BE AT MY PART-TIME JOB RIGHT UNTIL CONCERT TIME!
?
SO WHY DON'T I TAKE MY TICKET NOW AND MEET YOU AT THE SHOW!
LOOKS LIKE BETTY MADE THE DECISION FOR YOU!
GULP! LOOKS THAT WAY, CHUCK!
POP TELLS ME HE JUST GAVE YOU TWO TICKETS TO SEE "THE ZINC BOYS"!
I'D BETTER GRAB MINE NOW BEFORE BETTY GETS HER GRUBBY PAWS ON ONE!
4

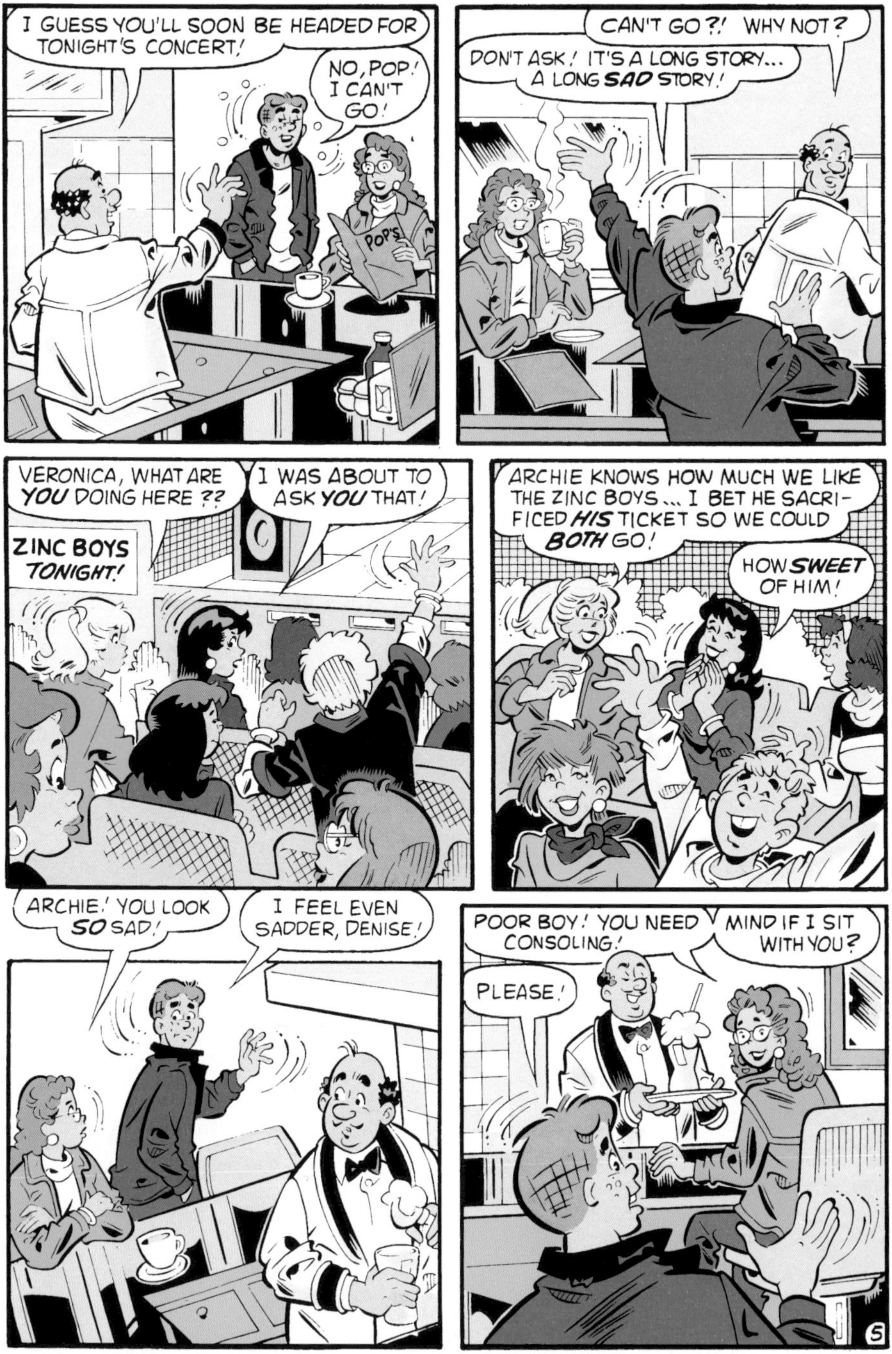
I GUESS YOU'LL SOON BE HEADED FOR TONIGHT'S CONCERT!
NO, POP! I CAN'T GO!
POP'S
CAN'T GO?! WHY NOT?
DON'T ASK! IT'S A LONG STORY... A LONG SAD STORY!
VERONICA, WHAT ARE YOU DOING HERE??
I WAS ABOUT TO ASK YOU THAT!
ZINC BOYS TONIGHT!
ARCHIE KNOWS HOW MUCH WE LIKE THE ZINC BOYS... I BET HE SACRIFICED HIS TICKET SO WE COULD BOTH GO!
HOW SWEET OF HIM!
ARCHIE! YOU LOOK SO SAD!
I FEEL EVEN SADDER, DENISE!
POOR BOY! YOU NEED CONSOLING!
MIND IF I SIT WITH YOU?
PLEASE!
5

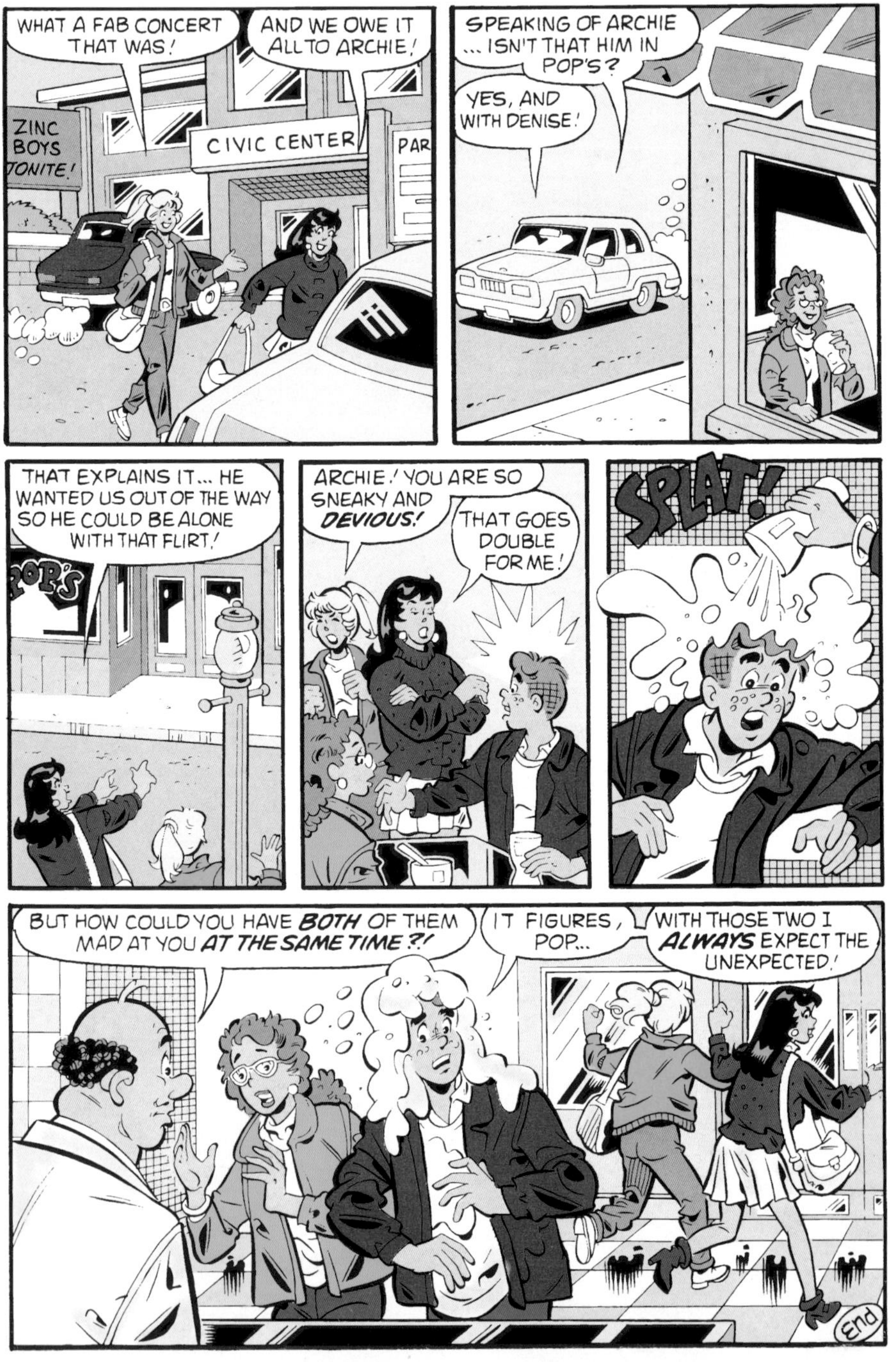
WHAT A FAB CONCERT THAT WAS!
AND WE OWE IT ALL TO ARCHIE!
ZINC BOYS TONITE!
CIVIC CENTER
PAR
SPEAKING OF ARCHIE ... ISN'T THAT HIM IN POP'S?
YES, AND WITH DENISE!
THAT EXPLAINS IT... HE WANTED US OUT OF THE WAY SO HE COULD BE ALONE WITH THAT FLIRT!
POP'S
ARCHIE! YOU ARE SO SNEAKY AND DEVIOUS!
THAT GOES DOUBLE FOR ME!
SPLAT!
BUT HOW COULD YOU HAVE BOTH OF THEM MAD AT YOU AT THE SAME TIME?!
IT FIGURES, POP...
WITH THOSE TWO I ALWAYS EXPECT THE UNEXPECTED!
End